"A wildly original and magical twist on the Robin Hood narrative, Kendra Merritt's *By Wingéd Chair* is packed to the spokes with complex characters, wry humor, and flawless world building."

-Darby Karchut, best-selling author of DEL TORO MOON and FINN FINNEGAN

"With a wonderfully crafted blend of swords and sorcery and characters based on Robin Hood, Merritt tops this story off with the lead character readers need nowadays; a strong, independent, powerful female mage who also happens to be in a wheelchair. Readers will be constantly turning pages to see what happens next to this fun group of characters through the twists and turns they won't see coming."

-The Booklife Prize

"Kendra Merritt's prose is fresh, with one-line descriptions that crack like a whip, and she doesn't miss an opportunity to surprise the reader.  From the first line to the last, I was enchanted with *By Wingéd Chair*."

-Todd Fahnestock, best-selling author of FAIRMIST and THE WISHING WORLD

# ALSO BY KM MERRITT

**<u>Mishap's Heroes Series</u>**

Magic and Misrule

Death and Devotion

Trust and Treason

Illusions and Infamy

Sparks and Scales

Wastelands and War

**<u>Mark of the Least Series</u>**

By Wingéd Chair

Skin Deep

Catching Cinders

Shroud for a Bride

A Matter of Blood

Unmasked

After the Darkness

The King in the Tower Collection

**<u>Daybreak Colony Duology</u>**

Surviving Daybreak

Daybreak Sentinel

**<u>Eldros Legacy</u>**

The Pain Bearer

The Truth Stealer

The Death Bringer

# MISHAP'S HEROES

## Magic and Misrule

# KM MERRITT

BLUE FYRE PRESS

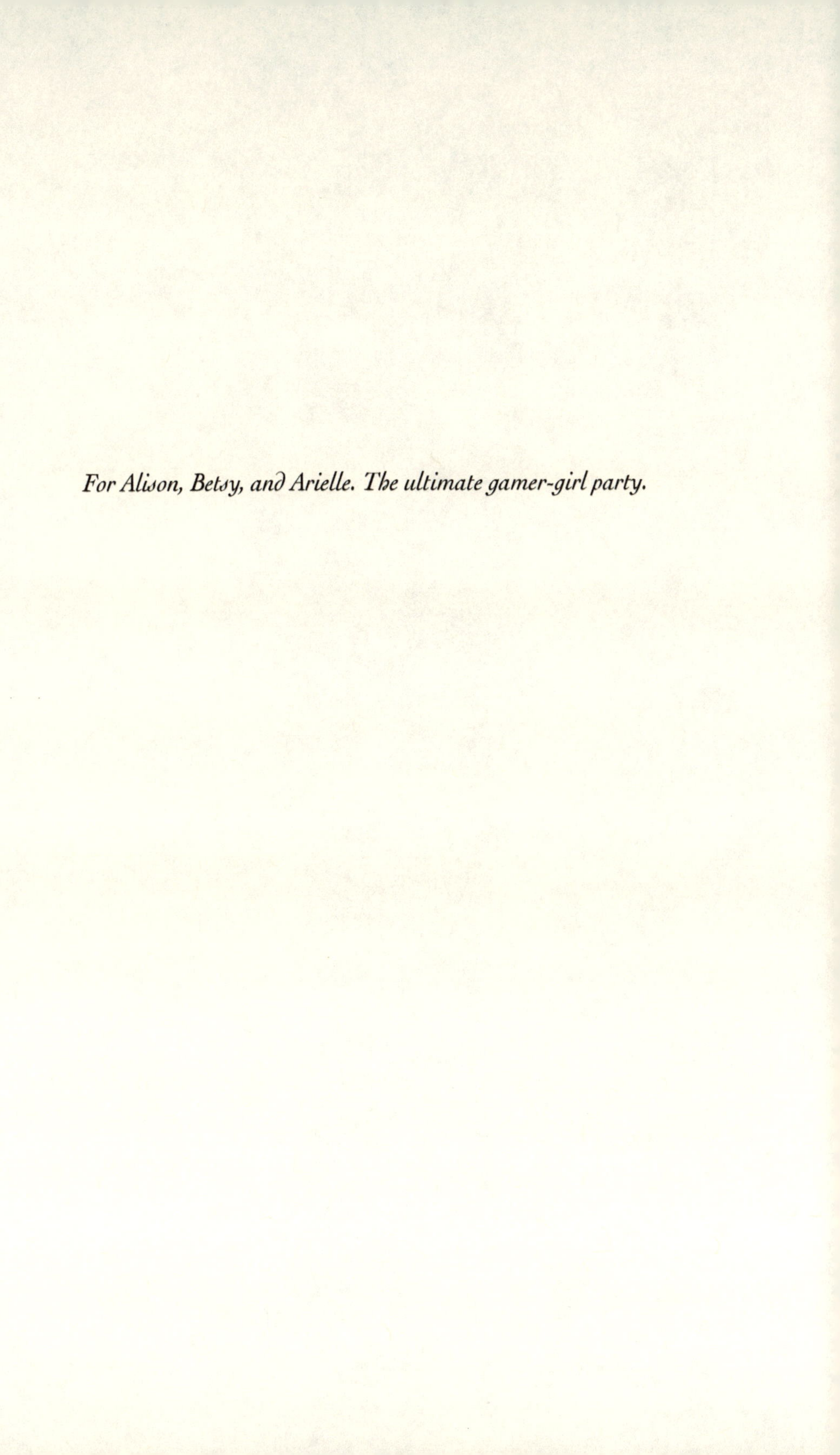

*For Alison, Betsy, and Arielle. The ultimate gamer-girl party.*

# ONE

Volagra Lightbringer, Paladin Candidate of the Whiteshield Academy and wandering adventurer, rode into Water's Edge on a broke-down, bare-backed horse with nothing more than sheer determination, a rusted sword, and a purse that echoed.

Her dusty, dun-colored horse stumbled step by step down Main Street, wheezing all the way, before coming to a crooked stop in front of a brightly painted sign that read:

Becky's Tea and Tap Room. Please wipe your feet.

Her companion reined his horse in beside her without so much as a twitch.

Vola leaned forward to give the nag a sympathetic pat. But the horse's head jerked up, and it shied away from her touch. The ancient beast had one more good buck in it, and it caught Vola by surprise, dumping her in a heap of chain mail on the dirt before it tottered away, making a zig-zaggy break for freedom.

A knight who couldn't even keep her seat on a geriatric horse. This was going so wonderfully already.

There was a shrill neigh and a splash from around the corner of the building.

"I'll go fish it out of the swamp," Henri said with a chuckle. Her companion hid a smile and turned his own horse to go rescue the stupid creature as it floundered.

Vola heaved a sigh and pulled herself out of the dirt. The afternoon sun had made her sweaty under her chain mail, and sweaty and dirty always equaled itchy.

Her mom always said when life gives you lemons, make lemon cake. Of course, that had a slightly different tone when you watched her crushing citrus with her bare hands.

Her Aunt Urag made it simple and just said "Screw life; it's trying to screw you anyway." Which sounded much more poetic in orcish.

Vola wished she had some lemons to crush right about now. At the very least, the feel of pulped fruit between her fingers might make her feel better.

Henri returned, the nag trotting at his side, now wet and muddy. Vola caught its bridle and dragged it back toward the horse trough.

Its nostrils flared.

"All right, all right," Vola muttered. "You've made your point."

She tried to remind herself that it wasn't the horse's fault that its distant ancestors had looked at people like her and thought "monster." At least the poor beast had gotten her here, to the thriving metropolis of Water's Edge.

A couple men sat on a porch across the street, their boots up on the railing and their stained hats pulled low over their eyes. Their wives chattered idly nearby. The only movement within miles.

Henri pulled his mount up beside her, a sleek gelding who'd weathered Vola's presence with the same aplomb as it had weathered heated battles.

Vola eyed the nag. "I think it's time the poor thing was retired," she said. "Maybe find a buyer who'll take it off our hands."

"And if no one wants to pay for it?" Henri said, giving the horse a sideways glance.

"Give it away," Vola said. "To some farmer who will treat it nicely before it dies. I'm not going to subject innocent horses to monsters anymore."

Henri gave her a look like she'd insulted his favorite kind of pastry. "You know I don't like it when you call yourself that."

He pulled the helm from his head and ran a gloved hand through his short silver hair. He smiled at her to take the sting from his words, his expression pulling at the scar that ran from the corner of his eye down his neck.

She rolled her eyes to cover the twinge of shame in her gut.

"The academy was never going to give someone like me a valuable animal right after graduation." She planted her hands on her hips and looked around. "But I can't help but feel they were trying to throw up as many roadblocks as possible. Do you really think I'll find a quest good enough to earn my shield in this…town?"

Henri eyed the main street with its collection of mismatched cottages and storefronts.

Vola could smell the swamp that stretched just on the other side of the buildings, like a million wet feet packed into one little cabin. Water's Edge was a nice way to put it. But if anyone with a nose had been around for the naming of things, the town would have been called something much worse and probably a lot more accurate.

There were a decent number of homes and shops, though, and over the roofs rose a low hill, topped with an impressive manor house.

"A quest is just an official way to help people," Henri said. "And there are people to help—"

"Anywhere you look," Vola finished for him.

Henri grinned, tying his helm to his saddle. He wore an eclectic combination of leather and steel armor, supple enough to keep him mobile, but Vola had seen him absorb hits that would have felled a line of knights.

He cocked his head at the town. "Sometimes you do have to look harder. I've never seen a countryside so amazingly clear of bandits and highwaymen."

"I know. No one tried to rob or murder us at all. It's weird." Vola's eyes widened in realization. "They sent me here on purpose, didn't they? They sent me to the middle of nowhere so they can claim any quest I find isn't good enough to earn my shield."

A face wavered in her mind, vivid enough to feel real even this far from the academy. Knight Commander Imralen's flint gray eyes narrowed at her, his face as hard as granite with the sharp edges to match.

"Good will always prevail over evil, Volagra," he'd told her the last time she'd seen him. "I will not allow you to besmirch this academy with your evil, no matter how hard you try to deny it."

She'd ground her teeth and clenched her fists, but in the end, there had been nothing the master of the academy could do to keep her from riding out with Henri. Thank the goddess.

Henri's fingers gripped her shoulder, pulling her from the memory just as red flickered at the edges of her vision. She blinked back at him.

"They're not the ones in charge of giving you your shield," he said, knowing full well what she was thinking. "I am. If they didn't like that, then the masters shouldn't have put me in charge of training paladins."

Vola's lips twisted. "I know what comes next. Get off my butt and stop moping."

Henri took his reins and Vola's with a shrug. "Your choice. Not mine."

The old trainer disappeared around the corner, urging the nag and the gelding to follow him.

Vola blew out her breath and glanced around the town again, wondering what kind of quest she could find in a place like this. She was already getting strange looks from the housewives on the street and their men had sat up to glare, bushy eyebrows lowered and waiting for an excuse to spring at her. She fought down the urge to bare her teeth and settled for resting her hand on her sword hilt instead. They didn't have to know it was almost rusted through. They only had to know she was willing to wield it.

Vola scowled at the little town. There was no way anyone here would have anything that would help her earn her shield. Paladin academies were pretty particular about what kinds of things were considered heroic. Saving a town from a raging dragon. Heroic. Picking turnips for a crotchety farmer. Not so much.

This place probably didn't even have a job board. She should just call Henri back and keep moving down the road. She'd have better luck riding through the swamp, listening for calls of help.

Just as she was seriously considering turning around, a bell tolled, striking deep in her bones and making her stagger. The townsfolk, who'd been giving her shifty looks, fell to their knees, holding their heads. The resonance shook the buildings and weighed on Vola's chest, making it harder to breathe.

As far as Vola could see, the town didn't have a bell tower.

She caught a glimmer out of the corner of her eye and turned to see a brief, bright aura light up the colorful storefront where her horse had thrown her. Becky's Tea and Tap Room.

The bell didn't toll again, but it didn't have to. Vola could take a hint. She'd heard the blasted thing often enough before.

"Fine," she grumbled under her breath. "I'll check it out. If you could tone down the signs and portents, though, that would be great. Thanks."

A cloud passed over the sun for a second, making it seem like the sky winked at her, and Vola rolled her eyes.

She climbed up the front steps of the building and pushed through the door.

She knew she'd made a mistake the moment she crossed the threshold. She should have announced her presence, called out a warning, or done something—anything—other than walk in the front door like a normal person.

Screams echoed in the cake and beer-scented air as bodies scrambled away from the door, the strong trampling the weak in their haste to escape. The tinkle of crashing glass carried across the room as the mob made a back door where there'd only been a window before.

*Sheesh*, Vola thought. *I haven't even smiled, yet.*

It was clear the place had been a bar once, but evidently, some new management had heard the words "tea room" and tried to replicate the feeling using clippings from lady's magazines.

Frilly lace curtains draped the windows, and the booths had been re-covered with a bright, floral fabric that made Vola's eyes water.

"Here you a—wait. Where'd everybody go?" a bright voice asked. A woman with a mop of gold curls fading to gray and a cheery red face appeared through the door marked 'employees only.'

Vola sized up the short, stout woman and gave her the least intimidating smile she could manage. "They left in a hurry," she said, trying very hard to speak around her tusks without accidentally lisping. Or growling.

The woman blinked, a lone soldier facing an ogre.

"I love your curtains," Vola said with a calculated gesture at the window. "Did you make them? They're lovely."

The words broke the woman's paralysis, and she beamed. "Why, thank you so much. Aren't you the sweetest...thing?"

Vola didn't miss the hesitation. Her eye twitched.

The woman set down the tray she'd been carrying, her gaze traveling from Vola's worn steel-tipped boots all the way to the thick black braid hanging over her shoulder. Her head didn't quite brush the ceiling, but it was a near thing.

"And, er...what sort of thing are you exactly?"

Vola could have bristled, but she'd heard the question often enough. Usually in much less friendly tones.

"I'm a paladin, ma'am," she said, deliberately misconstruing the question. "Trained at the Whiteshield Academy."

"Oh." The woman clapped her hands. "A real paladin. You must be here on a quest. The mother of sharp kitchen implements must have heard my prayers." Faster than Vola thought possible, she hurtled around the end of the counter and threw her arms around Vola's waist, ignoring the green skin and chain mail.

Vola deliberately didn't mention that she wasn't a full paladin. Not yet.

"Who do you serve? A Greater Virtue? A Lesser Virtue? Do they talk to you? Sit, sit." The woman bustled back around the counter. "Let me get you something to drink. Tea? Coffee? Or would you like something a little stronger?" She winked and pulled a flask out from under the counter and sloshed the liquid inside.

Vola held up her hands. "Just tea, thank you. I only drink to celebrate victory. Never before. It angers the gods."

The woman's face fell a little, but she took a swig from the flask and brightened considerably before setting a dainty teacup decorated with pastel roses in front of Vola.

"I'll take another if you're offering, Mistress Becky," a voice said from the air around Vola's waist. "I have no problem drinking before a victory, after a victory, during a victory."

Vola jumped as a hand reached up over the bar and clunked an empty mug onto the counter.

"You've had three already," Mistress Becky said. "How are you still standing?"

"There's a lot less of me to fall over when I get drunk," the voice said.

Vola tilted her head to peer down and down until she finally encountered a pair of hazel eyes in a nut-brown face under a thatch of curly roan colored hair. "Are you even old enough to drink?" she asked the girl, who stood less than three feet tall.

The girl scowled. "Is that a short joke?" She turned to the bar stool beside Vola and scrambled up like a squirrel to sit with her feet swinging in the air. In the second it took her to get to the top, she was grinning again, clearly not one to hold a grudge. "That's all right," she said. "We can't all be as tall as trees."

Vola had seen enough halflings to recognize one, but she'd never had a chance to talk with one before. It was hard to imagine someone that small being competent at anything except maybe catching mice. But then people made a lot of assumptions looking at Vola, too, so who was she to judge?

The halfling leaned forward to cradle the mug Becky handed her and disappeared completely when she raised it to take a swig.

Shuffling noises from the back of the bar indicated the return of the frightened customers.

"Becky," someone hissed. "Becky, there's a monster at your counter."

Vola stiffened.

Becky glared at the man who'd spoken. "You leave my customers alone, Will Cartwright. This one's a paladin, here to help the town. And she likes my curtains," she added as an afterthought.

There was some grumbling, but gradually the bar room filled up again with a crowd.

The halfling glanced at Vola out of the corner of her eye. "I've never seen an orc before."

"Half-orc," Vola growled. Then she braced herself for a rude question. There was always a rude question.

"Is it always like that?" The halfling cocked a thumb over her shoulder, indicating the humans milling like frightened sheep.

"Mostly," she said.

"Hmm. I'm sorry." The halfling stared into the distance. "You know, I've always wanted tusks."

"What?" Vola barked a laugh.

The halfling tapped her own pearly whites, eyes unfocused. "They just seem so...effective."

Vola shook her head and slid off her stool while the halfling quaffed her lager.

"Mistress," Vola said to Becky.

The tavern owner smiled up at her. "I'm so glad you've come to help. I've been praying to my lady, Cleavah, goddess of vengeful housewives. She's only a Lesser Virtue, but she's fierce as anything when you threaten her people."

That explained a lot. "Has someone threatened her people around here?"

"Well," Becky said, leaning across the counter with a furtive look around the room. "A few days ago, my husband, Porter, started acting really strange. Not that the man isn't strange normally, but this was different."

"Different how?" Vola asked.

"Quiet. In twenty years, the man's never had a problem making his opinion known. Now, all of a sudden, he won't speak two words to me. Just leaves the house in the morning, does all his chores without complaint, and lays down at night without a grunt."

Vola kept herself from making a face. This sounded like a domestic dispute, one she didn't want to get in the middle of. She opened her mouth, but Becky went on without noticing.

"Then that tart, Leyla, started doing the same thing. Won't speak to her husband, just goes about her day, minding her own business, and if that's not weird, I don't know what is. She and Porter never had anything in common before."

Vola tilted her head and tried to keep her gravelly tone delicate. "You think they might be having an affair."

Becky shook her head with a laugh. "Not a chance. Leyla would never have Porter, even if he was the last man on earth. That woman has standards." She sniffed. "But now it's not just them. Half the town's gone quiet and strange. Standoffish. Lots of angry wives and husbands, worried daughters and sons. You can see why we've been praying."

"What are we whispering about, huh?" a voice said.

Vola jumped and glanced down. The halfling stood between them with a wide, innocent grin.

"Nothing for the likes of you now," Becky said, making a shooing gesture. "Not unless you serve one of the Virtues."

"Well, actually—"

"Go back to your beer. You've had too much to handle anything serious like this."

"I suppose if you insist." The halfling skipped back to her seat and clunked her empty mug against the bar expectantly.

Becky took Vola's hand, ignoring the calluses across her palms. "You're going to do something about this, right? That's why you're here?"

Vola hid a wince. This wasn't exactly a dragon burning down the town or a swamp creature dragging people away to eat at night. But Becky was right. The tale was strange. And what kind of paladin would she be if she rejected a quest just because it wasn't glamorous?

Besides, it could turn out to be the invasion of a cult or brain-washing. Something even slightly exciting.

Vola drew herself up and angled her chest so the sunlight coming through the window flashed against her chain mail. It might have been cheap and full of holes, but she'd shined it till the right light would blind a charging bandit.

"I will learn what I can about your people, Mistress Becky." Vola placed her hand on her heart. "You have my word."

Half-orc paladins couldn't be choosers after all.

# TWO

Outside, Vola caught sight of Henri rubbing down the horses in the stable beside Becky's Tea and Tap Room. He smiled as his gelding leaned into his strokes, and he gave the horse a loving pat. Even the old nag lipped his sleeve hopefully and rested its head on his shoulder. Henri reached up to rub its nose.

Vola steered clear of the idyllic scene. Henri's horse didn't care much about her, but anytime she got close to the nag she triggered its fight-or-flight response and ended up having to chase it down before she could actually ride it.

One day, she promised herself. One day she would have a real horse. A noble charger who would be as brave as she was, who would carry her into battle with its head high without any of that running away in terror business.

Vola sighed. Time to get to work so maybe one day reality would match up with the fantasy. Her academy wasn't going to be sending her stipends, so her only option was to earn her shield and start working as an adventurer.

She headed for the edge of town where Becky had told her Porter worked as a carpenter.

Main Street hosted most of the shops and one stout temple. Outside its wrought-iron fence, a woman gathered her children against her skirts and hauled them all back a step to avoid Vola's path.

"Mama—"

"Hush now, stay out of her way."

"But why?"

"Orcs worship the Obstacles. And the Obstacles are evil."

There were so many things wrong with that statement, but Vola had long since given up on arguing theology with strangers in the street. It always worked better if she could find someone who was a more acceptable color to do it for her.

Vola smiled at the woman, carefully keeping her lips closed over her teeth. The mother gasped and hurried her children away, leaving Vola alone on the street with a couple of workmen. Their grips tightened on their tools and Vola moved along. She was used to the stares and the not-quite-hidden hostility. As long as she kept her hands away from her weapons and her expression placid, she could usually avoid getting stabbed more than once by accident.

Vola was so busy watching the workmen, she didn't see the one who ran into her. A burly fellow dressed in the long leather apron of a blacksmith bounced off of her chest. He jerked back a few steps to find his balance, his face blank.

"Sorry," Vola said, waiting for the curses and the threats.

The blacksmith rolled his shoulders and walked away.

Vola blinked. Okay, that was new.

A beautiful young woman with long, dark hair and impossible eyelashes sashayed down the street, her blank look completely at odds with her gait. Vola deliberately strayed a little too close, brushing the woman's sleeve. She turned, ready to apologize again.

But the woman just kept walking, her hips swaying while her

gaze drifted from one side of the street to the other, never settling on anything in particular.

Vola stared after her. In her entire life, no one had ever outright ignored her. The Knight Commander had deliberately overlooked her once or twice, but that had been as malicious as the threats and hazing. Was this what it was like to be normal? Or at least human?

She shook her head and made for the workshop with a hammer and an awl nailed to the sign. Inside, someone sawed away with a constant shushing noise.

Vola peeked around the side of the workshop and spied a man working in the gloom. He hadn't lit any of the lanterns around to illuminate his work.

"Mister Porter?" Vola said. She didn't want to startle him. Startled humans with sharp implements tended to stab first and apologize later.

The man didn't look up.

Vola sidled around the doorframe and stepped into the shop. Lank, straw-colored hair fell in the man's eyes and a thin faded shirt strained over his belly. He matched Becky's description of her husband.

"Mister Porter, may I speak with you a moment?"

He didn't respond. He kept sawing away at the plank he'd balanced across two sawhorses.

Vola planted her hands on her hips. "Hey, you!"

Nothing.

She stepped forward to wave a hand in front of his face.

He didn't respond to that either.

What the heck? Bracing herself, Vola took a deep breath, then roared in the man's face. Orc breath, orc tusks—she gave him the full experience.

Porter didn't even flinch.

"Huh." Vola stepped back and crossed her arms.

"I'm a little worried he's going to saw his thumb off and not even notice," a voice said.

Vola spun to the door to see the halfling lounging against the frame.

"Sorry, didn't mean to scare you." The halfling grinned at the irony. "Are you going to roar at him again? I don't think it did what you wanted it to, but it was highly entertaining."

Vola joined her at the door. "If that didn't shake him, nothing will. What are you doing here?"

The halfling examined her nails. "I was bored. Mysterious personality changes seemed like fun. Do you think it's a cult? Or some kind of brainwashing?"

"I'm…not sure yet." She could have said she had absolutely no idea but she was supposed to be a paladin. Almost. And it wouldn't do to go around admitting just how little she knew.

Vola rubbed her mouth as she leaned against the other side of the door.

A market square stood on this edge of town. Several farmers waited behind stands of produce in the open space. From here, Vola could see a couple of townspeople with blank stares meandering from one stall to the next. One housewife laid down her coins, put her selections in her basket, and moved on without acknowledging the farmer at all.

Vola's eyes narrowed as an older woman with a blank stare approached another man with the same wooden movements. The two stopped.

"How are you today?" the woman asked, voice flat and toneless.

Vola straightened.

"Yes. Lovely weather we're having," the man said, matching her inflection.

"I'm fine. Thank you for asking."

"Be seeing you."

The two went their separate ways, leaving Vola watching with lips pursed.

"They talk," the halfling said, voice rising in surprise.

"Yes, but did that sound like a real conversation to you?" Vola said.

"Hardly. More like a kid playing dolls. A lonely kid who's never had any friends."

"Exactly." Vola glanced back at Porter, who had sawed through his board and picked up another one to start over again. "It's like they're going through the motions of life. Going through the routine, but it doesn't mean anything."

A slow smile spread across the halfling's face. "So disrupt their routine."

Vola glanced at her, then waved a hand, telling her to go on.

"Let's see what happens when we knock one off their predestined path."

"We?" Vola had sized up the halfling in the bar as short and friendly. Now she took a closer look, her eyebrows went up. The halfling wore a gray linen tunic crossed and belted at her waist. Loose pants were bound around her calves like the monks from Maxim's monasteries. She carried herself tall and straight, even if she only stood three feet tall, and balanced on the balls of her feet. Like someone used to fighting.

The halfling shrugged. "Yeah. I want to see what happens, too. And no one else is lining up to help you." She extended her hand. "Sorrel Thornbough."

Vola grinned, not bothering to hide her tusks. The halfling seemed like she could handle them. "Volagra Lightbringer."

"Lightbringer, cool name."

Vola shuffled her feet. "Thanks, I—uh, chose it myself."

"Aw, jealous. Mine was picked for me. Bunch of old humans trying to decide what a halfling's name should sound like." She waved her hands in the air. "Woo, nature blah blah."

Behind them, the sawing stopped. Porter lay down his saw and grabbed a covered basket. Then he walked out his door without a word to either of them.

"After him!" Sorrel said.

Vola raised an eyebrow. "It's not like he's trying to get away."

Sorrel rolled her eyes. "Fine, pursue him slowly. Is that better?"

# THREE

Sorrel scampered after Porter while Vola followed, her long legs eating up the ground between them.

"What are you going to do?" Vola said.

"Knock him out of the routine, remember? Hey, you."

Sorrel jogged to catch up to the carpenter, then darted around and planted herself right in front of him. She held up her hands, palm out. "Stop."

Porter didn't hesitate or blink. He kept walking.

The halfling bounced off his legs, stumbled, and went down. She curled into a ball as Porter walked over the top of her.

"Ouch."

Vola gave her a hand up out of the dirt. "You all right?"

"He didn't even flinch."

"Maybe I should try next time."

"Be my guest." Sorrel dusted off her rear end.

Porter turned abruptly between a house and a feed store.

"Follow him," Vola said. Then she took off around the store, racing Porter to the other side. She arrived in the opening ahead of Porter, who hadn't adjusted his steady pace.

"Brace yourself," Vola said to Sorrel, lurking behind him. Then she turned her shoulder and planted her feet.

Porter walked into a wall of Vola. And stopped.

He jerked, his foot raised. Then he shuddered and tried to walk forward once again. Vola leaned into it this time, and Porter stumbled back. He spun into the wall and fell over in the dirt.

"Mister—" Vola started, then choked on the word.

Porter seemed to flicker for a moment, then his form disappeared entirely, leaving a man-shaped mud monster lying in the narrow alley.

The mud shuddered and then collapsed, sinking into the ground as Sorrel and Vola stared.

"Shit," Vola said.

A miniature lightning bolt zapped the ground at her feet, and she glanced guiltily at the sky. "Sorry."

Sorrel didn't even notice. She gaped at the splotch of muddy alleyway. "Sooo, that just happened."

"What just happened?" Vola threw up her arms. "A man turned into a pile of goo? Did you see it, too? Or am I going crazy?"

Sorrel knelt and used two fingers to poke at the spreading mud.

"Ew, stop. That used to be a person," Vola said.

"I don't think it was," Sorrel said. "If we'd killed a person, this would be a pile of much redder goo."

Vola's brow furrowed as she thought back over all her classes on the various magical enemies she might encounter in her travels. She did not remember anything about goo monsters dressed as people.

"I guess it could be a simulacrum. Or maybe a golem." She wasn't too sure about the difference. She'd always paid more attention in the lessons about pointy things. Magic was her connection to her goddess. But anything beyond that was just a pretty light show.

"Some sort of construct with an illusion over top?" Sorrel said. "At least it's what I imagine an illusion would look like. I never paid much attention to things I couldn't hit with my fists." She looked at her hands with her lips twisted.

"Do you think they're all like this?" Vola peered around the corner of the building and spied another blank-eyed townsperson sweeping the front step of the house next to them. A boy sat on the railing beside him, staring up at the sky, unblinking.

"Only one way to find out." Sorrel stood and dusted off her hands. Then she strode purposefully out into the street, heading for the two on the porch.

"No, wait." Too many other townsfolk were watching, and they didn't have the blank-eyed stare. They were more on the suspiciously horrified side.

Either Sorrel didn't hear her or didn't care. She stepped up on the stoop, and without ceremony, shoved the boy off the railing.

"Ah!" he cried, falling into the street. "What did you do that for?" He blinked up at Sorrel, definitely not disappearing or turning into a mud monster.

"Sorry," Sorrel said, popping her head up over the railing like a tunnel drake. "Just testing a theory."

The other man still swept the porch, eyes not quite on his work. Sorrel dropped to one knee and her other leg shot out to hook the sweeper behind his ankle, dumping him on the ground.

He immediately flickered, just like Porter, and his image disappeared, leaving behind a pile of mud splattered across the porch. It oozed between the cracks.

The boy on the ground gasped and scrambled backward.

There was a thump behind Vola. "What did you do?"

A man with red hair and broad shoulders stood at the corner

of the house, a sack of grain at his feet. He stared at Sorrel and her victim. The others crept forward, craning to see.

Vola stepped between them while Sorrel examined the mud. "Official business, sir," she said in her best paladin voice. "Just investigating a disturbance."

"She killed him."

"Well, no," Vola said and hesitated. How did she explain when she wasn't even sure what she was seeing herself?

"Can't kill something that was never alive," Sorrel called from the stoop.

The guy's breath hitched, and he stumbled back a couple steps. Vola buried her head in her palm.

"That's not what she meant. Just give us a second to figure out what's going on." She deliberately turned her back on him and his cry of outrage.

"So, they're all illusions?" she asked Sorrel quietly.

"Covering something solid, yes. Which means these people aren't brainwashed or anything like that."

"They're missing," Vola said. "And they've been replaced."

Sorrel glanced up at her. "You sure?"

"Well, the real people aren't here, are they? Unless Becky has Porter stashed in a closet somewhere. But then why would she draw attention to his replacement?"

"No, not Becky. But you're probably right. Someone took these people. But why bother replacing them?"

They stared at the seeping mud.

Vola glanced over her shoulder at the crowd led by the big redhead. "It kept people from guessing the truth for a while," she said. "If these folks have been abducted or kidnapped, no one noticed because it seemed like they were still around."

"So now we're dealing with a kidnapper." Sorrel stood, eyes still on the mud, her mouth pressed into a thin hard line. "Damn. I think I would have preferred cultists. Those at least I can hit."

Vola knew how she felt. At least the next step seemed obvious, even if it was a little terrifying. "I have to tell Becky. The town needs to know what's going on. And she should know her husband's missing."

Sorrel nodded, mind still obviously elsewhere. "Uh huh. Definitely."

"You all right?"

"Yeah," Sorrel said. "I'll uh…I'll meet up with you back at the Tap Room, all right?"

The halfling jumped off the stoop and trotted off without a backward glance.

Vola almost reached out to stop her. But it wasn't like they were friends or anything. If Sorrel didn't want to help her face Becky, then there wasn't anything Vola could do to convince her. That was her responsibility alone.

*You volunteered*, Vola told herself. *She didn't. And it's not like you don't know how to deal with abandonment.*

She turned, and her eyes fell on the redhead, who stood with his arms crossed. She stepped up to him. The others around him fell back a step.

"What did you do to them, you monster?" he said.

Vola rubbed her forehead. It shouldn't get under her skin. It wasn't even original. She rolled her shoulders as if letting the words slide off. "Has anyone gone missing in Water's Edge?" she asked. "Anyone disappeared recently?"

His eyes narrowed like he was about to spit in her face, but then his gaze flicked to a building across the street.

Interesting.

The structure loomed over everything else in the town, big, but dilapidated. It hadn't seen a new coat of paint in years, and the roof sagged from water damage.

"What's that?" she said.

"Orphanage," the man said. "Chock full of kids from all around the countryside."

"But?"

He glared at her but still answered. "I haven't noticed any of them underfoot in the last few days. Didn't think anything of it 'cause it's a relief not to have them in the way."

Vola was moving before he'd finished speaking.

The door hung ajar, too warped to close properly, and she stuck her head in to examine the long hall.

"Hello?" she called.

No one answered.

She stepped inside and a puff of dust and dirt rose around her boot. The air of emptiness made her nose itch, and she rubbed it absently.

Empty rooms lined the hallway, leading to a set of stairs at the back of the orphanage. A school room with a wide chalk board at one end, "Annie's a poop head" scrawled in one corner. A play room with toys scattered across the threadbare carpet as if abandoned in the middle of a mock battle, and in the corner one lone picture book lying open on a painting of a princess. A bathing room with a rubber duck, long dry, waiting on the rack. And a room full of bunks, some made neatly and others with the blankets pulled half off the bed.

All silent. All empty.

At the back of the hall, another door stood open and Vola found the only occupant in the house.

A young woman sat at a desk, her hands flat on its surface and her eyes fixed on the wall ahead. The headmistress or caretaker. Except there was no one for her to take care of.

Vola waved a hand in front of her face. "Miss?"

She didn't have to knock the girl from her chair to know she was an illusion, too.

Vola's lips pressed tight enough to hurt, and she left the girl sitting at the desk in an empty orphanage. On her way out, she stopped and bent to pick up a toy lying in the shadows beside the front door. A stuffed rabbit, worn around the neck and arms. Like it had been dragged everywhere.

Vola weighed it in her hand.

Someone was stealing people from this little town on the edge of a swamp. Stealing them and then replacing the ones who would be missed.

They hadn't bothered with the kids. Because no one cared about orphans.

Vola's fingers stroked the stuffed rabbit before she tucked it into her belt.

That wasn't true anymore. Someone cared about them now.

She stepped out of the orphanage. The townspeople still crowded the street, whispering to each other, but the redheaded man was gone.

Vola squared her shoulders and started down the street, facing the arduous task of informing a woman that her husband was literally a pile of mud.

The crowd parted around her, women drawing back their skirts and men avoiding her gaze. They moved stiffly as if she'd chase them down if they showed their fear and ran. Prey before a predator.

Vola let her lip lift just a little and the rest of the crowd cleared out of the way, scattering down alleys and into houses. A couple of doors slammed.

Vola grunted. Humans were such sheep.

# FOUR

She shouldn't have worried about breaking the news to Becky. Someone got there before her.

The crowd had migrated until it stood outside the Tea and Tap Room, blocking Vola's way forward. The dull roar echoed off the buildings, emphasizing her heartbeat.

She reached the edge of the crowd, but the two women in front of her didn't even notice the armed and armored half-orc sneaking up on them from behind. They waved their hands in the air and called out things like "oh, what is this world coming to?" and "who can we trust?"

Vola shouldered her way through. When someone stepped in her way, she picked them up and set them off to the side. She moved through the crowd, leaving a wake of gasps and horrified looks.

On the porch of the tea room, Becky stood with her arms crossed. Her foot tapped as she listened to the red-haired man who'd called Vola a monster.

Becky caught sight of Vola and raised her hand to the man. "Stop." Then she held out her palm to Vola. "Tell me."

When Becky spoke, the crowd quieted and Vola cleared her throat.

"Porter wasn't real," Vola said shortly. Becky didn't need her to sugar coat it and professionalism would get her farther than prevarication. "He was an illusion. They're all illusions. Your people are missing."

Becky's shoulders sagged. "I was hoping it was something simpler than that. Fungus in the well or a new cult. But I guess missing is a damn sight better than dead."

Vola did her best not to wince. She actually had no idea if the victims were still alive, although a fierce hope burned in her chest. It was more likely that the kidnapper had left the replacements to keep the townsfolk from pursuing their missing people, rather than setting up this elaborate hoax just to cover up murder.

Becky stood straight and…well, not tall. She only came up to Vola's elbow, but she carried all five feet of her height with dignity. And she stared straight at Vola.

"We can't afford a real paladin contract. I know that requires paying you half up front and posting the job to the council and everything. But…" Becky raised her chin. "Will you help us find them?"

Vola sucked in a gasp.

Becky held her gaze. She knew exactly what she was asking.

Paladins often answered contracts, yes. There were plenty of fat, lazy knights who lounged in their quarters at the academy, waiting for lucrative paychecks.

But fifty years or so ago, it had been well known that a paladin knight had to answer any call for help. It was in their oaths, even if the council tried to downplay it now.

Vola had never expected anyone to ask *her* for help.

She placed her fist over her heart and inclined her head. "I will find them." Her other hand touched the stuffed rabbit in her belt. *All of them. Even the ones who have no one to ask for them.*

Never mind the fact that she'd only taken novice and candidate oaths. That hardly mattered when someone was standing there looking at her like that and down the street, there was an empty orphanage.

The red-haired man glared at her from over Becky's shoulder.

"We're supposed to trust an orc—"

"Half-orc," Vola said.

"With our wives and daughters?"

Vola tilted her head. "What do you think I'm going to do to your wives and daughters?"

His mouth worked, but he didn't come up with an answer.

"Find them?" Vola raised an eyebrow. "Yes, I promise to find them."

"That's not what I meant," he said with a glower.

"Then what did you mean?" Vola lowered her voice and casually lifted her hand to touch the hilt of her sword. She'd never actually draw it against an innocent—even one like him—but he didn't need to know that.

"I'm not trusting my family to an unproven orc who's just as likely to murder us all in our beds."

Vola's teeth creaked as she clenched them. "Not sure why I'd wait till you're in bed," she said. "I could murder you right here. Notice the fact that I'm not."

Becky rolled her eyes and planted her hands on her hips. "Enough, Braydon. She's a paladin. You don't get to be a paladin unless you're chosen by one of the Virtues. You want to anger one of the gods?"

Braydon scoffed. "I haven't seen any evidence of a god, yet. Have you?"

Vola glanced at the sky. Nothing but a couple of clouds scudding along. No divine fire bolts. *You want to talk to this guy?* she asked in her head.

"Nope," a voice like the whisper of a breeze spoke beside her ear. No one else reacted.

*Sure, now you get all modest.*

"My goddess is pretty picky about who she talks to." Vola crossed her arms. "You're not on her list." She turned back to Becky. "I promise I'll find them. Luckily, I don't need everyone's approval to do so."

Braydon spun on his heel and pushed through the crowd.

Vola frowned when half the townspeople left with him. She may not have needed their approval, but it sure would have been nice to have it. This was going to be a lot harder if she had to fight Braydon and half the town every step of the way.

Across the street, Vola caught sight of a figure in leather and plate armor leaning against the clapboard side of a building. Henri watched the whole scene with his arms crossed.

When Vola stood like that it was a deliberate gesture to prove how nonchalant she was. And if she was being honest, it covered a host of insecurities that lurked under her skin. But when Henri lounged, it was as natural and thoughtless as breathing, as was the air of competence that exuded from every pore.

*One day,* Vola thought. *One day, I'll be able to lounge like that and it'll mean something.*

"I might not be able to pay," Becky said as she headed for the door of the Tea and Tap Room. "But I can feed you. Come see me before you leave."

Vola gave her a nod then stepped down off the porch to approach her trainer.

Henri had never graduated from the academy; he had never been selected by one of the Virtues. He carried a shield, but it did not signify his rank. More often, he used it to bash the heads of his thicker students. There was no rank that could describe a teacher the way Henri was a teacher. Because there was only one Henri.

Henri was not a full knight. Henri created knights.

Becky might have been impressed that Vola had been chosen by a Virtue, even a Lesser one. But she should have been more impressed by the fact that Vola had been chosen by Henri.

Even the paladin council didn't dare tell Henri who he could and couldn't teach. And every student he'd ever taken had gone on to become renowned knights, champions of justice, and defenders of the innocent.

Vola wondered if every other student of his had realized they were the last in a long line of success that could fail at any moment. With them.

"That could have gone better," Vola said as she came up beside Henri.

"Could have gone a lot worse." He shrugged, his pauldrons moving smoothly with the motion. Henri's armor would never do anything so uncouth as clank. "I especially liked the 'notice the way I'm not murdering you' bit."

Vola sighed. "I'm a little tired of having a reputation that I didn't earn just because of the way I was born."

Henri snorted. "So does half the world, kid. And the other half doesn't give a wargle's ass. Get used to it. 'Cause you'll spend the rest of your life earning their trust."

"How? By not murdering people?" she said with a huff. "I tried that. People don't seem to notice when you deliberately don't murder them."

"Even when you point it out to them so nicely?" He gave her a sidelong look that made her flush. He gripped her shoulder so she could feel the comforting pressure through her chain mail. "Keep moving forward, Lightbringer. You want your shield? Find those people."

Vola straightened. "Really?"

"You think you volunteer for that and I'm just going to ignore it? A paladin *has* to answer a call for help. But a real paladin *wants* to answer a call for help."

Vola touched the stuffed rabbit again. "There's no one else," she said. "I can't just walk away if there's something I can do about it."

"Then find them. And you'll have earned your shield and your title. If I knight you, there's nothing the academy can do to say you didn't earn it."

Warmth swelled in Vola's belly and a tingle went down her arms, making her fingers itch for the hilt of her sword. This was what she'd been working toward for years. A chance to prove to everyone back at the academy that she was as good as them. A chance to prove that Henri hadn't made a huge mistake picking her.

She let her hand rest on her hilt, calming the itch just a little.

Henri had knelt to rub a stray dog under its chin while its tail thumped in the dirt, raising little clouds. "Where are you going to start?"

How many times had he asked her something similar, getting her to think through her training? "What's the next step, Vola?"

A part of her wanted to go charging into the swamp ready to bash anything that moved. But Henri never charged anywhere. Not without knowing exactly what he was charging into.

Vola rubbed her neck, thinking of the illusions and the mud sinking into the ground. Magic. She was good at a lot of things, but magic was not one of them. And with so many people gone, this plot was probably part of something bigger than one person or bandit.

She was going to need help.

"I need a team."

# FIVE

Becky let Vola and Henri spend the night in front of the fire in the common room since she didn't have any rooms to rent. In the morning, Vola set herself up at one of the tables at the back of the Tea and Tap Room, and Becky kept her tea cup full throughout the day. Vola had set up a billboard right outside the door of the bar and another in front of her table which read:

Looking for Adventurers!
Experienced explorers apply inside.
Vanquish evil and earn both money and fame!

Henri's lessons had not included compelling sign writing.

By mid-afternoon, Vola was ready to beat her head against the table.

A knobbly youth dressed in dirty trousers and a faded shirt stepped up to her table.

"Name?" Vola said. Then made the mistake of smiling at him.

He staggered back a step. "R-Ricky," he said. He tried to hide his hands, but it didn't do him any good when his entire body shook. Apparently, the promise of gold outweighed the terror of conversing politely with a half-orc.

"Well, Ricky, do you have any previous combat experience?" Vola asked.

"Not—not yet."

Over his shoulder, she noticed Braydon. The redhead was setting up a table at the opposite end of the room. The sign propped next to him read:

HONOR! GLORY! AND FAME!
FIND THESE AND MORE WHEN YOU JOIN YOUR FELLOW
NEIGHBORS TO FIGHT EVIL AND WIN BACK YOUR FAMILY
MEMBERS!

Vola scowled. He'd stolen her idea. And he was better at writing signs than she was.

Already, a line was forming at his table, full of strapping young men and promising-looking women.

And here she sat with…Ricky.

"Have you handled a weapon?" she said.

"My da says a pitchfork is a weapon if you hold it right."

"Hmm," Vola made a show of shuffling through a stack of papers. "Well, thank you, Ricky. I'll keep your application on file and get back to you with a decision."

Ricky's head bobbed, and a smile flitted across his face as if he was a little relieved she hadn't thrown some gear at him and marched him out of town. The youth hunched away. Over to join Braydon's line.

Vola let the papers fall and buried her face in her hands.

She might have been desperate, but she wasn't in the business of recruiting farm boys with delusions of not dying.

She rubbed her eyes. Henri was fair and gracious to a fault and he wouldn't blame her if she couldn't find anyone to help in a town like this, but leaving this table empty-handed would feel like she'd failed one of the first lessons he'd ever taught her. How to make friends.

Someone sat with a thump on the seat in front of Vola's table, making her jump.

"So, when do we leave?" Sorrel asked.

The halfling had slung a quarterstaff across her back, and she'd managed to sit with it even though the thing was twice as tall as she was.

Well, Vola had been looking for competent adventurers.

She pulled the stack of paper closer and smoothed the edges self-consciously. If the halfling leaned forward, she'd see there wasn't actually anything written on any of them, but Vola felt more official with the paper serving as a barrier between herself and the rest of the world.

"I didn't think you were coming back," Vola said.

Sorrel's brow drew down with hurt. "I just had to go get my things. I figured we'd be going after the kidnappers. That's what we're doing, right?"

Vola glanced around the table but the only thing the halfling had brought with her was the quarterstaff and a tiny pack.

She shrugged. So far, Sorrel was the closest thing to an adventurer she'd seen in this town.

"You can fight," she said without a hint of question.

The halfling nodded succinctly. "Since I was four."

Vola dropped the pages with surprise. Four? She beat Vola by at least two years. And she'd thought *her* parents were insane to take a six-year-old on a camping trip in goblin territory.

"I was raised by the monks in one of Maxim's monasteries and trained in martial arts since I was old enough to force the issue," Sorrel said.

Vola blinked, wondering what exactly that meant. She cleared her throat. "Aren't monks supposed to be peaceful? All that medi-tation and self-reflection stuff."

"Just because we know how to hold our tempers doesn't mean we don't know when someone needs a kick in the shins, too. The abbot always preached non-violence, but he still let Master Bao teach everyone how to throw a punch."

"You're not a spell caster, too, are you?"

"Nope."

"Drat. I'd really like one of those."

"Because of the illusions? Smart," the halfling said and reached for one of the papers. She held the blank sheet in front of her, then frowned. She laid it back down on the table and smoothed it with broad, capable fingers.

"About the pay," Vola said, clearing her throat. "It's not set in stone yet." She actually had no idea where they were going to get the money to outfit themselves, since this wasn't a full contract. But her sign had looked so incomplete without those squiggly little gold coins she'd drawn in the corners.

Sorrel waved a hand. "I don't care about the money. You can keep my share."

Vola blinked. "What?" All adventurers cared about was gold.

"I've been sleeping on a stone slab since I was a baby. I eat gruel and drink cheap beer. I fight with a glorified stick." She touched the quarterstaff on her shoulder and shrugged. "What use do I have for gold?"

"Then why are you so eager to come along?" Volagra said, eyes narrowing. Becky bustled by with a steaming teapot, leaving the sweet scent of wake blossom in the air.

Sorrel shrugged again. "I won't make any secret of it. It's the illusions. The golems. I'm trying to find Maxim's Warhammer. And the last time it was seen in the mortal world, it was capable of that sort of magic."

Sorrel was looking for the weapon of a god. Not just any god either. A Greater Virtue. Maxim was the god of strength and loyalty. Vola had lost count of the number of paladins who followed him.

"So, you think the kidnappers might be using a god's weapon to replace townspeople?" Vola said, tilting her head.

Sorrel sighed gustily. "It's the only clue I have. And I'm not a spell caster so I don't have a lot to go on to begin with." She shifted her chair with a bright screech against the floor to survey the room. "Do you think any of these guys have magic?"

The assorted blond and brown humans who sat at their tables and waited in Braydon's line scowled at them. Vola scowled back. Sorrel was getting some equally strange and hostile looks, but the halfling just swung her feet and returned the looks with a bright, open grin.

Sorrel took a swig from her mug, and Vola struggled to remember if she'd had the drink with her the whole time.

Over Sorrel's shoulder, the door of the Tea and Tap Room opened and a young woman poked her head in. Red-gold hair fell down her back in silky waves and she pushed it over her shoulder with a practiced gesture. She glanced around the room with a pair of vivid blue-green eyes before her gaze latched on Vola's table and the sign.

The girl shuffled inside and made her way across the floor. Halfway through the room, she tripped over the leg of a chair, stumbled a few steps, and then righted herself, her cheeks stained red. She skipped the last few steps to the table and said breath-lessly, "Are you the one offering gold for a rescue mission?"

Her voice was sweet and melodic. Vola could imagine her with a lute and a filmy gauze dress strumming for the pleasure of some noble lord.

Vola leaned back in her chair and crossed her arms, then swept her gaze up and down the young woman's figure. She wore a blue vest over a white blouse and a pair of pants that showed off a set of curves that would make an hourglass jealous. A book bound in blue leather hung from her wide hip. The girl flushed even harder under Vola's scrutiny.

Vola tried not to roll her eyes. This young woman was the mirror image of the perfect pale village girls Vola had longed to look like when she was a little younger and less settled in her own skin. From the perfect hair to the wide beautiful eyes. Sure, she was shorter and thicker than the stick figures Vola's village had revered ten years ago, but that didn't hide the clear pink skin and delicate features she undoubtedly took for granted.

There was no way this soft beauty would be worth anything out in the field save as bait.

Vola tapped her sign. "I'm looking for warriors. Are you trained in combat?"

"Er, no, but I..."

Vola met Sorrel's eyes, and the halfling monk gave her a sympathetic shrug.

"Have you had any experience fighting?"

The young woman's face went sickly pale, losing all of its healthy glow, and she dropped her incredible gaze.

"Yes. A little. Once." She raised her eyes again to catch Vola's unguarded expression. She swallowed. "I'm sorry I'm so...so..." She gestured to herself." But I need the money."

Vola tried to soften her expression. If nothing else, this woman had enough courage to look a half-orc in the eye and ask for a job with no skills or recommendations. "What for?" she asked.

"I'm traveling," she said simply. "And that requires gold. More than I thought. Even just a place to sleep costs money."

Vola's eyebrows went up. She said that as if it had never occurred to her before. And now that she was looking, Vola could see bits of straw sticking out of her near-perfect hair as if she'd spent the night in a hay rick.

Vola sighed. Paladins were called to help all those in need, and it would break her heart to turn away this lovely hobo, but she couldn't afford to have someone on her team who couldn't defend herself. Sorrel and Vola would spend all their time trying to keep her alive.

"I'm sorry," Vola said. "But—"

A beefy farmer from the next table over stood up, letting his chair screech back. In the back of her mind, Vola had noticed him ogling.

The farmer stepped up behind the young woman and put a hand on her shoulder. He leaned close to breathe on her neck. "If you need a place to stay the night, half of my bed is empty," he said. "And I can think of lots of things you can do to earn some gold from me."

Vola's hand closed over the hilt of her sword which hung in its sheath behind her. But before her fingers could even find their grip, the young woman's gaze flashed up, all uncertainty gone.

"I suggest you remove your hand from my shoulder before I remove it from your person," she said.

The farmer guffawed.

The young woman placed her fingers on the back of his hand and a spark zipped between them.

His laughter turned into screams, and he snatched his hand back to cradle it against his chest.

The girl turned, her fingers twisting in a complicated spell before a ball of fire formed between her palms. "Would you like to continue this conversation?"

Vola met Sorrel's eyes, and the halfling mouthed "spell caster," then wiggled her fingers like she was casting a spell.

The farmer took one look at the young woman's hands and her implacable expression, then ran.

Her mouth thinned into something that wasn't quite a smirk. "I didn't think so."

She turned back to the table. Then tripped on her boot lace, fell backward, and sent a fireball directly into the ceiling.

Vola leaped around the table and extended a hand to the young woman, Sorrel beside her.

"Wow, that was something," Sorrel said.

Vola eyed the scorch mark suspiciously to make sure it hadn't set the whole building on fire. "You didn't say you were a spell caster."

"You didn't ask," the young woman said. "And it wasn't on your...sign."

"Can you cast anything else?"

She drew herself up indignantly. "I am a graduate of the University of Arcana."

The book hanging on her hip must have been her spell book.

"Witch then?"

The girl cleared her throat. "Witches work with magic in the natural world. I am a wizard."

Which didn't do anything to clear up the difference for Vola, but it sounded promising.

"Do you know anything about illusions?"

"A lot of theory. I have more practice with things like fire. But I have several useful spells in my repertoire."

Most people Vola knew would have said repertoire with a laugh or a slightly ironic tilt, indicating they knew how silly they sounded. This girl said it with all seriousness like it was the type of word she used every day.

"And you're all right using said spells against people?" Vola thought it was prudent to make sure.

"As long as they deserve it," the girl said.

Vola smothered a snort. "Fair enough. Don't worry about the ceiling. We'll take the cost for repairs out of Sorrel's share."

Sorrel shrugged. "I was planning on giving it to charity. But I feel obliged to point out that a third of zero is still zero."

Vola cleared her throat. "We'll figure something out."

The girl brushed her hair back behind her ears with an unconscious gesture, revealing the gently pointed tips.

The detail didn't go unnoticed by the men in the room. A disgruntled murmur swept through them.

It was good to know it was all non-humans they didn't like, Vola thought. Not just orcs and halflings. Vola always thought of elves as tall and willowy rather than short and stout but maybe this girl wasn't a full elf the way Vola wasn't a full orc.

"Does that mean I have a job?" the girl said.

Vola hesitated a moment. She could just imagine getting into combat and having this klutzy spell caster accidentally shoot her in the back. But she didn't see anyone else lining up to join them and a university-trained mage was a godsend she wouldn't turn away in this backwater village.

"It does. We're cash strapped right now, but I promise I'll find a way to pay everyone by the end." Vola held out her hand, and the woman didn't hesitate to shake it. "I'm Volagra Lightbringer and this is Sorrel Thornbough."

"Lillie," the girl said.

Vola waited for the rest but nothing more seemed forthcoming. Her brows drew down. "That's it? Just Lillie?"

"Just Lillie," the young woman said firmly.

As long as she could cast straight and she didn't turn out to be some sort of murderer, Vola didn't care what was up with the missing last name.

"Welcome to the club, Lillie," Sorrel said with a bright smile and a fanciful little bow.

"Thank you, Miss Sorrel."

Sorrel screwed up her face. "Miss?"

Vola surveyed her little party, her lips twitching between a smile and a frown. This was possibly the worst idea she'd ever had.

The scuffle of a shifting crowd made her glance to Braydon's side of the room. The man was packing up his table with a broad smile. As the rest of the crowd dispersed with disappointed looks, Vola picked out three other figures standing near the man: a tall black man with a long, green cloak slung back to reveal a quiver, a middle-aged woman with a pair of hand axes hanging from her hips, and another man wearing a set of expensive embroidered robes. The last one smirked at Lillie.

Vola fought down a growl. Then she scanned the room. She would have loved to find at least one more member for their eclectic little party, but the saloon was clearing out fast. At least they didn't need to find a healer as well. Vola had some help covering that gap.

Braydon led his people through the door, casting a superior look over his shoulder at Vola.

She stood abruptly, making the table jump sideways.

"You two want to come pick out some gear?" she said, making her decision. "We head out in two hours."

"I don't wear armor," Sorrel said with a sniff. "It slows me down."

"A-and I wouldn't know what to do with any kind of weapon," Lillie said, her eyes darting from Vola's face to Sorrel's.

Vola rolled her eyes. "I meant like bedrolls and cookpots."

# SIX

VOLA GLARED at the gear spread out on the shop floor and huffed.

"I know it's not much," the shopkeeper said. "But Braydon came through before you got here. Cleared out my whole collection of basic armor and equipment. This is what's left unless you want to look at my higher end stock." The shopkeeper wiggled his eyebrows hopefully and swept his hand toward a display wall featuring a full set of plate armor and a dazzling variety of polearms and edged weapons.

Vola's eye caught on the center of the display. A silver shield polished to a bright sheen, edged with gold. A screaming eagle was embossed in the very center, wings spread in defiance or protection.

Vola had always been a sucker for wing motifs. She stepped toward it and raised her fingers to brush the edges.

There was zero chance she could afford it but she still had to ask, "How much?"

The shopkeeper's expression didn't change. "36,000."

Lillie's eyebrows went up as Sorrel choked.

Vola let her hand drop back to her side. "Never mind."

They wouldn't be able to afford anything on this wall. Heck, they probably wouldn't be able to afford the equipment on the floor and that wasn't even the basic level she'd been expecting. Braydon had taken everything that was both serviceable and affordable.

Well, then it was probably a good thing Sorrel didn't wear armor and Lillie wouldn't know what to do with it if she did. The only one who would suffer was Vola in her very old, very cheap chain mail.

"We'll just take the equipment then."

The shopkeeper held out his hand. "That'll be thirty-six gold."

"Er," Vola said, the noise escaping her involuntarily. She unfastened her belt pouch and peered inside. Two coins clinked together at the bottom.

"Is that a lot?" Sorrel asked.

"It is when you don't even have an employer." She was starting to see why those paladins sat around waiting for jobs that actually paid.

"I have two silver," Lillie said, rummaging in her own purse. "But that's all I have left after…I mean, that's all."

Lillie was round in a way that told Vola she'd never been hungry growing up, and her clothes were well made. But clearly, it had been a little while since the wizard had benefited from that wealth.

Sorrel just shrugged. "I think I gave Becky the last of mine."

"Could we prevail upon your good nature, sir, to give us a discount?" Lillie said. "We are, after all, trying to save your people."

"None of my family are the ones missing," the shopkeeper said, deadpan. "And Braydon will find the others."

"Would you be willing to let us have it for credit?" Lillie said.

"With the promise that once we are paid for our services, we will then pay you for your goods?"

"I only offer credit to friends I trust."

Lillie threw up her hands.

Sorrel tapped her chin. "Do you trust Mistress Becky?"

The shopkeeper's eyes narrowed, probably wondering if this was a trick question. "Yes."

Sorrel stepped over and put her hand on Vola's hip. It was as high as she could reach. "Well, Mistress Becky vouches for the paladin. She said so in front of all your neighbors. I can't imagine what would happen if it got around that you didn't trust Mistress Becky's word. No more drinks for you. That would be a shame." Sorrel shook her head sadly.

"It would be," the shopkeeper said. "If I drank."

Sorrel stared up at Vola. "I give up."

They glanced at each other and then looked down at the pile of gear.

"I guess we probably don't need all of this stuff," Vola said after a brief hesitation.

It didn't look like much already: a tent, and all the accompanying tent pegs and rope, some bedrolls, some cookware, a crowbar. It was basic adventuring gear.

Sorrel crouched beside the gear, her brows drawn down in concentration. "I don't even know what some of these things do." She held up a couple of metal spikes. "What are these?"

Vola checked the list the shopkeeper had given her. "Uh, pitons."

"But what do they do?"

"I think they're spikes that you put down into water?" Vola said. "For…some…purpose."

"You're thinking of pylons," Lillie said. "Pitons are for climbing."

Vola raised her eyebrows. She doubted Lillie had ever been climbing in her life, not with those soft hands.

Lillie flushed as if she could read thoughts. "I read a lot," she said by way of explanation.

Sorrel snorted and dropped the pitons with a clank. "The day I need some metal spikes to help me up a wall is the day I call it quits."

"What if it was a very, very smooth wall?" Lillie said curiously.

"I bet I could still get up it," Sorrel said.

Vola chewed her lip, rolling the flesh between her tusks as she thought.

"Do you think we'll be doing lots of climbing, Miss Volagra?" Lillie said apprehensively.

Vola wanted to be the kind of paladin that could afford shiny shields and great camping equipment, but the truth was she was the kind of paladin that could barely scrape together a party. She was going to have to work up from there.

"All right, let's put the pitons back, and the crowbars. We're going into a swamp, not a dungeon so I can't imagine we'll be prying anything open."

"How much does that make it?" Lillie asked the shopkeeper.

He surveyed the arrayed equipment. "Thirty-five."

"Oh, come on. You're not even trying," Sorrel said.

Vola rubbed her forehead. "Do you have any chores you need done? Errands or tasks that you'd be willing to trade for the equipment?"

"Hey, that's true," Sorrel said. "She's a paladin. If you ask for help, she has to give it to you."

Vola sent Sorrel a glare and a little shake of her head. She really wanted to get paid this time. Preferably in equipment.

The shopkeeper stroked his chin. "Well, actually. You mentioned going into the swamp."

"I did," Vola said, cautiously.

"I'm trying to start up an apothecary business on the side. I need petals from the crimson swamp blossom. You bring me ten of those, and we'll call it even. You can even take the gear now, in advance."

That…seemed a little too good to be true. "Only ten?" Vola asked.

"Just ten. They're very valuable."

What other choice did she have? "Deal," she said and extended her hand.

In his defense, the shopkeeper didn't hesitate to shake.

"Thank you, sir," Lillie said.

The shopkeeper waved a hand as he stalked into his stock room. "Ten petals by next week, or I send collection agents to repossess my goods."

"Quick, grab it all before he changes his mind," Sorrel said.

Lillie and Sorrel each grabbed a handful, leaving Vola with the bulk of the pile. She hefted it in her arms and followed them out into the bright sunshine. Of course, the stingy shopkeep hadn't offered to throw in a bag to hold it all.

"What now?" Sorrel asked while Vola juggled the tent and all its stakes and ropes.

She had a brief burst of a daydream where she packed all the equipment onto a horse. Something tall and noble, perhaps in a sleek midnight black, or maybe a blue roan, with all the latest features like a glossy mane and flowing tail. And while she was imagining impossible things, she added herself riding to the rescue of the townsfolk. Striding down the main street on her horse while Braydon cried along the edges and everyone else clapped and cheered.

Vola shook her head, reminding herself she wasn't a fourteen-year-old girl anymore.

Across the street, she caught sight of Braydon. He wore full plate armor. Nothing too fancy, but a great deal more impressive than Vola's chain mail. Beside him stood the competent looking woman with the hand axes and the dark man with the bow, both of whom sported new leather armor. The wizard trailing behind them still wore the same robes, but he carried a pristine book in his hands, caressing its pages.

Then Braydon shifted to the side, and Vola recognized the squirrely little man with buck teeth he was talking to. He looked out of place here without Knight Commander Imralen's shadow to stand it.

The Paladin Council must have sent him to check up on her progress. This day was just getting worse and worse.

Braydon caught sight of Vola, standing in the dusty street with an armful of eclectic camping gear, and raised his chin with a smirk. He gave her a jaunty little wave then gave his party the signal to head out. They moved toward the edge of town while the squirrely man straightened his notes.

Vola groaned. "We have to get moving."

Between the shop and the Tea and Tap Room stood the orphanage where Vola had picked up the stuffed rabbit. She tried not to feel like the boarded windows were judging her.

Sorrel paused and stared up at it.

"It's empty," Vola said quietly. "No one left. They were all kidnapped. The only one in there is the golem of the caretaker."

"Creepy," Sorrel said.

"You mentioned illusions," Lillie said, staring at the cracked paint and sagging stoop.

"Yeah," Sorrel said. "The missing townspeople were replaced with illusions."

"Is this one still active?"

"I guess so," Vola said. "Unless someone messed with it after I was in there."

"Here," Lillie said, dumping her load into Sorrel's arms. "I'll be right back."

"We don't have time—"

"It won't take long. I need to see the spell if I'm going to be able to identify it again."

Since that was exactly why she'd wanted to bring a spell caster in the first place, Vola couldn't exactly argue. She glanced over her shoulder, but the man Braydon had been talking to still stood on the corner. "All right, but hurry."

Lillie disappeared into the empty building.

In the corner of the overgrown lot stood a little altar to one of the Lesser Virtues. It didn't even have a statue. Just a fish knife nailed above the flattish offering bowl. A couple of boys knelt beside it, giggling as they chalked rude words on the side.

"Hey," Vola said and dumped the equipment in the road. "Stop that."

She didn't even have to growl. She stepped forward, and the boys shrieked and ran away, knocking the bowl from its stand with a clang.

Vola knelt and picked it up. She cast a surreptitious look down the street before she shined it with her sleeve and placed it carefully back on the pedestal.

Sorrel stepped up and rubbed at the graffiti. "Why is there an altar to the goddess of vengeful housewives outside an orphanage?"

"She has a soft spot for widows and orphans." Vola ducked her head. "Or so I've heard. She takes care of the ones no one else does."

"Are we praying?" Lillie asked from behind the fence.

Vola jumped.

"That was fast," Sorrel said.

"I told you it wouldn't take long."

"Did you learn anything?" Vola stood and brushed off her knees.

"I know what the spell looks like. Which means I might be able to pick it apart next time."

Lillie held a book under her arm. A different one from the one that hung from her hip.

"What's that?" Vola said.

"Oh." Lillie flushed and glanced at the cover. "Botany. I found it inside in the schoolroom. I thought it would be a good idea if we could identify that flower the shopkeeper wanted."

Prescient of her. Vola wished she'd thought of it first.

Someone cleared their throat and then coughed like they'd choked on their own phlegm. Vola glared at the man across the street. He grinned, revealing a set of teeth that would look better on a gopher, and pushed a pair of spotted spectacles up his nose.

She'd only seen one man wipe that smarmy grin off the representative's face and that had been Henri the day he'd told the council he would be training Vola despite their protests.

"Who is that?" Lillie asked as the man set his pencil to his paper and started taking notes.

Vola blew out her breath. "A representative from the Paladin Council," she said. "He's…keeping an eye on me while I earn my shield."

"Oh, would you like to say hello?" Lillie raised her hand, but Vola dragged it down.

"No. No, I just want to get on with it." She scanned the street, looking for the flash of silver-gray hair and was rewarded when she saw Henri playing with a group of kids two buildings down. He wore his old, battered shield across his back even in the hot sun, and still managed to dance around, kicking a ball back and forth. The kids squealed with glee as he slipped his toe under the ball, flipped it into the air, and kept it in the air with his feet.

Vola whistled.

Henri caught the ball one-handed and glanced her way. He gave a brief nod, tossed the ball to the tallest kid, ruffled his hair, and then trotted over to Vola and the party.

"Did you see him?" Vola asked quietly.

Henri didn't even glance at the representative. "I did. I'm not worried."

"Henri—"

"All he can do is watch. He can't interfere. Which means you have everything under control."

Vola didn't feel under control. She felt like this whole thing could unravel at any moment, leaving her standing on nothing. If Braydon came back with the townspeople before her...

"Right, sure," she said. Then she raised her voice enough to include the others. "Henri, this is Sorrel and Lillie. Lillie, Sorrel, this is Henri."

"Pleased to meet you, Mr. Henri," Lillie said.

Henri doffed his round helm like it was feathered cap. "Ladies."

"Could you get this packed away?" Vola asked, nudging the tent still lying in the road. "We're leaving as soon as I'm done talking to Becky."

The mistress of the Tea and Tap Room was waiting for them just inside with a sack. "I tried to pack things that would keep," she said. "Even in the damp of the swamp. Bread, meat, cheese, that sort of thing. It's everything I could spare. I hope it lasts for however long it takes you to find them."

"Thanks, Becky," Sorrel said with a broad grin.

"Yes, thank you," Vola said.

"Where will you start?" Becky asked.

Vola hesitated. "Uh."

Lillie cleared her throat. "Perhaps we should start by asking questions. The local lord might know more."

Vola made a face. She'd noticed the manor on the hill when

they'd first rode in but she hadn't thought about it since. "I'm not sure lords really know what's going on in their towns, usually. Aren't they busy being all, I don't know…noble?"

Lillie's mouth dropped open in affront but it was Becky who answered. "Actually, Lord Arthorel isn't that bad as far as nobles go. He leaves us to our own devices, mostly. But he keeps the roads free of bandits and highwaymen."

"I did notice that on the way in," Vola said, reluctantly.

"As your liege lord, he should be doing far more than that," Lillie said. "He should not be ignoring you."

Becky shrugged. "That's the way of the world, Miss Lillie."

"Well it shouldn't be," Lillie grumbled.

Sorrel flicked a glance between Lillie and Vola. "We could at least ask if he's noticed anything suspicious while he takes care of all those bandits," she said. "And who knows? Maybe he'll want to make it official and hire us to solve the problem."

That made Vola brighten considerably. "I suppose it's worth a shot." She'd wanted to set off right away and try catching up to Braydon and his party, and she definitely didn't like the idea of leaving the council's representative here to poke about asking questions. But if they didn't have a firm direction, they'd just end up stumbling around the swamp blind. That wouldn't get them any closer to finding the townsfolk or the orphans.

Did Braydon have some kind of direction already?

Sorrel grinned and held the door open. "Yes. Let's get this show on the road." She thrust her fist in the air. "As Jodin Battle-called always said, 'Let our blood be strong and their asses whomped.'"

Lillie tilted her head. "Is that a direct quotation?" She seemed to be genuinely asking.

Sorrel's grin turned sheepish. "Well, maybe a paraphrase," she said. "But the sentiment is the same. Let's go kick some kidnapper booty."

"Hurrah?" Lillie added half-heartedly before she tripped over the edge of a paving stone and hit the ground palms first.

# SEVEN

Vola led her motley party up the hill, carrying their tent and all its pieces in a bulky pack. Henri had found a farmer to take the nag, and Vola didn't ask any questions, just waved goodbye to the poor creature. The gelding was enjoying life in Becky's stable since Henri had said a swamp was no place for a horse. More likely it was because Henri felt bad riding when everyone else was walking.

Vola wished they'd brought it just as a pack animal. Their one and only pack outweighed Sorrel by at least fifteen pounds, and the first time Lillie had tried to carry it, she'd fallen on her face outside the Tea and Tap Room. And there was no way Vola was asking Henri for help. She was supposed to be earning her shield, not wrestling with the gear.

And Henri wasn't really there to be helping. He was there to observe and judge her progress, and really he was the only one Vola trusted to do so fairly.

The idea hung unspoken between them that he was also her safety net, there to catch her if she really screwed up.

Not that she was planning on it. She'd die of mortification on the spot and Henri would have to bury her remains in the swamp.

Sorrel followed Vola, swinging her quarterstaff in a complicated pattern, and Lillie came after, her nose in the botany book. Occasionally, the spell caster tripped and righted herself without even looking up from the page. Henri brought up the rear, reaching out now and then to keep Lillie on the road.

Scraggly trees lined their path, and about halfway up the hill toward the manor, Vola stopped. Something rustled in the scant undergrowth, sending a prickle down her neck.

She held up her hand, but Sorrel clearly wasn't watching or didn't understand the sign for "stop." The halfling ran into the backs of her legs, and Lillie crowded into them both a moment later.

"What—"

"Shh," Vola said.

"Ouch." Sorrel rubbed the back of her heels which Lillie had stepped on.

"I heard someth—"

A long, slithery, scaly body burst from the undergrowth and hissed. Vola had just enough time to register rows of slick, sharp teeth and short legs tipped with claws before the thing sprang at them.

She yanked her sword from its sheath and brought it up to block.

But the creature slammed to a stop just short of swallowing Vola and slid back a foot. A big, black wolf had its jaws clamped around the scaly tail, and it hauled the thing backwards.

Vines shot out of the ground and wrapped the creature while it thrashed, pinning it to the road.

Vola raised her sword, but before she could lunge, an arrow sprouted from the monster's eye. It jerked once, twice, and then lay still.

Vola stared at the long, scaly corpse, sword still raised. Lillie and Sorrel crowded around her to see. Henri hadn't even moved.

"What the heck just happened?" Sorrel said.

The wolf spat out the creature's tail and trotted over to the tree line where a cloaked figure slung a bow onto their back. They waved a gloved hand and the vines snapped away from the long corpse, getting sucked back underground.

The figure stood a good four inches taller than Lillie, who was fairly short for a half-elf, and the deep hood hid the figure's face along with any other identifying features. So much so that Vola couldn't even be sure if she was looking at a man or a woman.

"Thanks," Vola called.

The figure didn't move, but Vola got the impression all their attention was fixed on her now.

"Are you the ones going after the missing people from town?" The voice emanated from the hood, low and grating as if unused for decades.

Vola glanced at the others, but they didn't seem inclined to speak up. "Yeah," she said. "That's us." She sheathed her sword and took a couple steps closer to the figure so she didn't have to shout.

Their rescuer flinched, and Vola stopped moving. She got some mixed messages from the pair: menace from the wolf, competence from the hooded figure, but also a level of uncertainty and discomfort in the way they both held themselves.

Vola didn't try to press closer.

"What's your name?" Vola said. She couldn't keep thinking of them as "the figure."

There was a hesitation. "Claw," the figure said, in a growl Vola would have expected from the wolf.

The three women looked at each other.

"Claw," Sorrel said. "You sure you want to go with that?"

The hood shifted, and Vola got the impression the…person's

eyes moved between them uncertainly. Not that she could actually see eyes in the deep shadow of the hood.

"Talon?" the voice said again, a plaintive note threading their voice.

"Talon is better," Lillie said, looking at Sorrel and Vola for confirmation. "Talon is a lovely name. Very fierce."

"You're a fighter?" Vola said.

Talon grunted what Vola assumed to be an affirmative.

"Ranger, I'm assuming." She jerked her head at the longbow slung across their back and the wolf.

"The blood of my enemies speaks for itself," Talon grated out, jerking their chin at the dead monster.

"Er," Vola said.

"Well, not really," Sorrel said.

"What?" Talon said.

"Well, I mean it's dead. Can't really speak, can it? No tongue." She touched the tip of her own tongue thoughtfully. "And I feel like blood isn't particularly articulate most of the time."

"Sometimes it can be very articulate," Lillie said diplomatically.

"And that's not really the point," Vola said with a pointed look at Sorrel.

"You are looking for fighters?" Talon said. "I will come."

There was no doubting the ranger's competence. Vola liked to think she would have done just fine herself, but the reality was, Talon had killed the giant crocodile faster.

"Why do you want to help? We…can't really pay anyone, yet." Vola held out her hands and glanced at Lillie. "Though we are working on it."

"You look for missing family," Talon said. "I know what it's like to lose people and never find them. If I can stop it from happening to others, I will."

Vola glanced backward, and when no one immediately

objected, she gave Talon a smile. "Welcome aboard. We're on our way to ask the local lord some questions."

As melodramatic as the hood was, Talon seemed like they'd round out the party nicely. Two fighters, a spell caster, and a ranger. So long as everyone could actually do what they said they could do, they might have a chance at this.

And it really didn't matter if Vola couldn't figure out whether Talon was a he or a she. The voice seemed male but there was something about the mixed air of menace and uncertainty that felt young and female. Nothing that Vola could put her finger on, just a feeling.

"And what's the name of the wolf?" Vola asked, glancing down at the rugged animal panting behind Talon's legs. Although now she wasn't quite sure she should bother with names. It had sounded like Talon had made theirs up on the spot.

Talon made a noise somewhere between a growl and a bark. Their tone was much firmer this time and Vola blinked.

"Uh, say that again," Sorrel said.

Talon repeated it. The wolf's ears pricked forward. The two wild animals looked at each other, then slid away from the crocodile's corpse and up the hill.

Sorrel planted her hands on her hips and then shrugged. "I'm going with Gruff."

"What?" Lillie said, her perfect golden brows arched in question.

"For the wolf." Sorrel waved her hands in the air for emphasis. "You know, 'grrr-ruff.'"

Vola rolled her eyes and started after Talon. Lillie lurched to follow.

Sorrel scrambled after them. "Get it?" she said. "Did you get it? Grr-ruff."

"Yes," Lillie said. "We all did. We just didn't think it was funny."

Talon waited at the point where the road widened and the manor rose, looking back at them.

When Vola glanced back, Henri was hiding a smile. She rubbed her forehead and sent up a short prayer to her goddess that she'd be good enough to keep an overenthusiastic pummeler, a klutzy spell caster, and a monosyllabic mystery all in one piece.

## EIGHT

THE ROAD SNAKED up the low hill, leading directly to the wide wrought-iron gate set in a thick wall. Vola's eyebrows went up. It must have cost a fortune to haul all that cut stone through the swamp. Either that or there was a quarry hidden somewhere in the wetlands, which she doubted.

As they approached the gate, Sorrel spun her staff, then secured it to her back again, the majority of it sticking up over her head to keep it from dragging in the dirt. Lillie put her book away and stared about with interest.

Talon's hood scanned back and forth, alert.

"What do you see?" Vola asked.

"Only two guards along the walls, but if we have to flee the place, we'll have to take them out before we can escape."

Vola pursed her lips. "I...did not notice that. Good catch."

"Flee?" Lillie said. "Why would we have to flee? This seems like a lovely summer home."

Vola frowned dubiously at the gate. She'd be the first to admit she knew nothing about summer homes, but did you normally have to lock people out? She shifted her weight and tried not to clank.

A large lock kept the gate barred across the first paved road Vola had seen in days. Through the wrought-iron, she could make out an empty courtyard and the manor itself beyond.

"Um, hello?" Vola called.

A startled clattering sounded from the gatehouse and a young man in full plate armor stumbled out of the little building set into the wall.

"Hi," Sorrel said as the young man stood blinking at them from the other side of the gate. "Can we come in?"

The gate guard's mouth opened once or twice as if he couldn't decide what to say or to whom. His eyes flickered nervously over Vola's large frame and landed on the hilt of her sword. His throat bobbed.

"Er, no?" he said.

Sorrel tilted her head. "No, we can't come in? But we're here to see Lord Arthorel. This is his house, isn't it?" Sorrel stepped back to eye the imposing facade one more time. "Unless there's more than one filthy rich guy in the area. Is there?"

The guard's spotty forehead furrowed in response to Sorrel's chatter. "What? No. This is his manor, but I can't let you in." He shook his head, then drew himself up, knuckles going white around the haft of his spear. "Lord Arthorel isn't seeing anyone today."

Sorrel scowled, but Lillie stepped forward and placed one long-fingered hand on the gate. All traces of her unease had left her posture, leaving her straight and confident.

She smiled brilliantly at the guard.

"We're not here on a social visit, sir. We are here to discuss a problem that relates to Lord Arthorel's duties as the liege lord of this area. Not only is he obligated to respond, but he will be greatly displeased with anyone who gets in his way. I would hate to be the one who failed him like that. If you don't have the authority to let us in, I would like you to go find someone who does. Now. Before I lose my patience."

Lille's head tilted sweetly, and she gave the gate one more caress with her fingertips.

Vola heard the guard gulp as he stumbled forward and fumbled with the lock.

"Yes, my lady. Right away, my lady. I will tell the lord you're here."

The lock clanged, and the gate swung open as the guard bobbed his head and let them through.

Vola raised her eyebrows at Lillie as the guard gestured them through, but Lillie had her chin in the air and wouldn't meet her eyes.

The guard counted them with his eyes as they filed in, and his gaze went glassy as the wolf stepped up.

"Er, I'm sorry, my lady. I can let you in but not a wild animal."

Vola expected Talon to object or to refuse to come in if Gruff wasn't allowed. But the ranger barked an order at the wolf and Gruff melted into the trees around the manor.

Talon turned back and caught Vola's expression. "We're used to splitting up. If I need him, he will find me."

"Even in here?" Vola asked.

Talon snorted. "Walls could not keep him out."

The guard led them across the courtyard to a set of big double doors leading into the manor itself. But as they drew close, an armored body stepped between them and the door.

"Captain Wiselyn," the guard squeaked. He threw up a belated salute.

Vola's eyes narrowed as she surveyed over six feet of tall, dark, and deadly. Full plate armor gleamed in the sunshine and dark eyes glared at Vola and her party. Few humans actually matched her height, but this one got close and he managed to look down his hooked nose at her.

"What are you doing?" the captain growled at the guard who had let them in.

"I—I was just taking them to see Lord Arthorel," the guard stammered. "They said—she said something about his noble duties."

"Duties?" The corners of the captain's mouth pulled down sharply as his gaze settled on Lillie.

Lillie's eyes widened just a fraction before she threw back her shoulders and raised her chin to meet his hostile glare. "Is it your habit to question your betters, *guardsman*? The last person who did so ended up hanging from a spike along my wall."

Vola tried not to snort. She couldn't imagine Lillie hanging anything from a spike except maybe some lingerie. Even then it would have to be a very dainty spike.

Still, she could respect the woman for standing up straight under the captain's glare. Vola moved into position behind Lillie's left shoulder, where a real bodyguard would stand. Sorrel glanced at them once, then followed suit on the other side.

The captain surveyed them for a split second longer than was polite before he jerked his head at the guard. "Get back to your post," he growled. "I'll take them the rest of the way."

The guard jumped, then scurried back to the gatehouse, his armor clanking along the way.

The captain opened the door with one smooth motion and gestured them inside.

Lillie sniffed as if she found his manner impertinent but not rude enough to bother with, then stepped inside. The rest of them trotted to keep up with her.

Behind them, the captain snapped his fingers at a passing serving girl, then swiftly stepped around them to lead the party through a sumptuous hall draped with burgundy curtains. Bright mirrors flashed their reflections back at them while their boots sank into a plush carpet.

"What are you here to discuss with my lord?" the captain said as he stalked beside Lillie.

She sneered. "I do not make a habit of discussing personal matters with the help."

Vola and Sorrel exchanged an incredulous look. But whatever Lillie was doing was working.

"Very well," the captain said, however, Vola couldn't help noticing that he left off the "my lady."

At the end of the hall, the captain opened a door and gestured them inside. "You may wait here," he said. Vola and the others filed through the door. "Don't touch anything," he added as he shut the door behind them.

"That just makes me want to break something," Sorrel said and glanced around at their surroundings. "Anyone else have the sudden urge to knock into a few china cabinets?"

"Let's not," Vola said.

The room seemed like a small living room. A parlor? Is that what rich people called them? A couple of oil paintings hung on the walls and a patterned carpet covered the floor.

As soon as the door clicked shut, Lillie's shoulders slumped, and she covered her cheeks with her hands.

"So, am I the only one wondering what the hell that was?" Sorrel asked.

Henri planted himself beside the door with his arms crossed while Talon picked a corner to lurk in.

Lillie took a shuddering breath, and when she lowered her hands, her cheeks were bright pink. "What was what?"

Sorrel waved her hands in the air. "Whatever that was. You talked all different and…and they just let you in."

Vola glanced at the furniture, but it looked too spindly to actually use with intricately carved legs and embroidered cushions.

She ran a blunt fingertip along the edge of a table, and her fingernail left a scratch on the gleaming surface. She snatched her hand back.

"It…it wasn't that different. I always try to be polite."

"There's a difference between polite and commanding."

Lillie bit her lip and looked away. "It's a facade. It's all a facade. You just have to look the part and no one will ever dig deeper."

Vola opened her mouth to ask if she'd grown up in the theater since her facade was as good as any noble, but the door opened, interrupting her thought.

A man with stark black hair and straight brows walked in. He wore a long tunic that fell to his knees and opened like a robe over an embroidered shirt and loose trousers.

Captain Wiselyn stalked into the room behind him. The guard captain moved as if to station himself beside the door and found Henri there instead.

Henri gave him a winning smile and twiddled his fingers in hello before settling himself more comfortably against the wall.

Captain Wiselyn scowled and chose to stand at attention on the other side of the door.

The man, who Vola assumed was Lord Arthorel, gave them all a once over glance and then an uncertain smile. "Hello," he said. "I was led to understand that you wanted to speak to me about a matter of some urgency."

"Yes, my lord," Vola said, throwing back her shoulders. The room and the company were making her hyper-aware of herself. "The folk of Water's Edge sent us. There have been kidnappings in town and they've, er, asked us to investigate."

The lord opened his mouth then closed it again as he stared at Vola. "They…what?" He seemed to be fascinated by Vola's tusks.

Vola raised her eyes to the ceiling to calm herself. She wasn't a stranger to distracted humans, but goddess, it was annoying as hell to have to spoon-feed them.

She managed not to growl, but she pulled her lips back and bared her teeth. Just a little. "Kidnappings," she repeated. "Some of the townsfolk have gone missing. I counted about twenty. Surely that concerns you since you have some responsibility toward them."

Lord Arthorel drew himself up and gave his head a little shake. His eyes found Sorrel and then settled on Lillie as a more palatable spokesperson.

"Missing, you say? I wasn't aware anyone was missing. Why wouldn't they come to me with this information?"

Vola bristled. Did he think they were lying?

Lillie gave him a sad smile. "Perhaps they were worried you wouldn't listen to them."

She put enough gentle censure in her tone to make the lord flush to the roots of his perfectly combed hair. He half-turned his body away from them and raised two fingers toward Captain Wiselyn, then jerked his thumb at Vola.

The captain flung the door open. He stepped out to whisper to someone on the other side before closing it behind him.

Vola's eyes narrowed. What was that?

"Very well, ladies," Lord Arthorel said.

Talon flinched, though Vola was sure she was the only one who noticed.

"You have my full attention. What's been happening down there that the townspeople have sent you to me?"

Again, he looked directly at Lillie. Lillie gave Vola an uncertain half-smile.

Vola grimaced and stepped forward to place herself clearly in the man's field of view. "They noticed some people acting strange. And when we looked into it, we learned they weren't people at all but complicated illusions covering up simulacra."

The lord blanched, and Vola couldn't tell if it was because of what she was saying or if it was because it was a half-orc saying it.

"So you've decided that someone is kidnapping these people," Lord Arthorel said. "And then…replacing them?"

Vola took a deep breath. It was like he was being deliberately slow, running them around in circles.

"Yes. With illusions."

*If he says, "with illusions, you say"…*

"To what purpose?"

*Oh, thank goddess.*

"We don't know yet. That's what we intend to find out."

"How?"

Lillie stepped forward as if to speak or reassure the lord, but her leg stopped halfway up and she pitched forward like she'd tripped over something low and long.

For a split second, Vola thought it was just Lillie's normal clumsiness.

But that was before the air said "Oof!" and Lord Arthorel staggered as if something had run into him. He caught himself against a spindly end table which rocked alarmingly.

Before Vola could do more than narrow her eyes, Sorrel dropped into a crouch and swept her leg around. There was a solid thunk and another cry.

Vola stepped forward, pinpointed the sound, and wound up to hit the invisible attacker. Her fist shot out, connecting with something solid and slightly giving about knee height to the lord.

Colors flickered and Vola stepped back to rub her eyes. When she looked again, a man in black clothing and a fitted mask collapsed to the floor, knocked out cold.

The group stared down at their now visible assailant.

Lord Arthorel found his balance again and straightened up from the end table.

Vola glanced between the assailant and the lord, her heart pounding. "An assassin."

"You—you saved my life," Lord Arthorel said, face pale.

Lillie knelt beside the attacker. "It looks like the same magic that masked the simulacra in town. Except this spell disguised a real person."

"We should make sure there aren't any others hiding out in here." Sorrel pulled her quarterstaff from her back.

"Right," Vola said. "Yes. How do we do that?"

"I have a spell…" Lillie said hesitantly. She twisted her hands in a complicated gesture and whispered a few words.

A wave of gold light rushed from Lillie, washing the room in sunrise hues. Everything glowed.

"So, what does that mean?" Vola said.

Lillie frowned at the room. "The spell is supposed to detect magic."

"And everything that glows is magic?" Literally everything was glowing. How useful.

Sorrel spun, her staff trained on a candelabra which glinted from the mantle. "Ha!" she said. "Show yourself, villain. We're wise to your tricks now."

"Er, that's a family heirloom," Lord Arthorel said. "I'm not sure what magic it might possess, but I doubt it's holding another assassin."

Vola reached out to push Sorrel's staff down with two fingers.

"I'm sorry," Lord Arthorel said. "There are layers of protection spells all over the manor. They'll make everything light up."

A crease formed between Lillie's eyebrows. "My spell should be able to differentiate between them."

"Oh, these are special. Put them up myself."

Lillie brightened. "Really? Could you teach me? I'm always looking for new ones."

Lord Arthorel shifted his feet.

"Maybe when we're not being attacked," Vola said and surveyed the glowing room again. There was nothing man-shaped.

"I think we're alone once more," Lillie said.

"That was the same type of illusion that was used on the false townsfolk." Vola glanced at Lord Arthorel. "Whoever is kidnapping your people, is trying to get rid of you, too."

Sorrel's gaze shifted from Vola to Lillie to Talon. "Do you think they followed us?"

"But...why?" Lord Arthorel asked.

Vola fought not to roll her eyes. This guy really couldn't come up with a single reason a bad guy would want to get rid of the local guy in charge?

Lillie stepped forward to place her hand on Lord Arthorel's arm. "There are plenty of reasons they might want you out of the way," she said, echoing Vola's thoughts. "They probably don't want you to notice anything is wrong or come after them if you do." She bit her lip with dainty white teeth, and Lord Arthorel swallowed.

Gah, did Lillie even know how much she was flirting with the lord?

Vola sighed. Of course she knew. The girls in Vola's village had been able to spot a handsome face or physique from a mile away and planned accordingly.

"I know this is frightening, my lord," Lillie said. "But we're here to help you."

"We'll find your people," Talon said from the corner, making Lord Arthorel jump.

Sorrel made some quick shushing noises drawing their attention. She leaned against her staff, knee cocked forward, the very image of nonchalance. "A classic adventuring party like ours is perfectly suited for hunting down your attackers. But of course, a quest like this comes with its own share of costs and startup margin."

Vola raised her eyebrows. Did they teach adventurer's accounting in Maxim's monasteries now?

"We'll be a lot more effective at keeping you safe if we didn't have to worry about finding odd jobs along the way to cover our expenses."

Lord Arthorel relaxed. "Ah. I may not know much about adventuring, but I am very familiar with the idea of hiring experts. You shall be my specialists and I will pay you handsomely for your time."

"You will?" Vola said and then bit her tongue. Never question the person offering to pay you.

"Of course. You can't put a price on safety," he said. Then he took Lillie's hand and kissed her knuckles. "And I know I'll be safe with guardian angels like you."

Vola made a face, expecting Lillie to bat her eyelashes, just like the girls back home.

Instead, Lillie gulped and blanched before red flooded her face, and she backed up stuttering "I-I-I-" She tripped over the prone body of the assassin and stumbled to right herself against the wall, keeping her eyes on the plush carpet.

The wizard practically radiated discomfort, and Vola reacted without a second thought, putting her arm around Lord Arthorel's shoulders and steering him toward the door.

"We should discuss our terms," she said. "As guardian angels go, we don't require much. Just enough to cover our day-to-day costs. Things like meals and equipment maintenance. We already have a tent so we don't need to worry about lodging."

Lord Arthorel twitched under Vola's arm, but she ignored it and he allowed her to steer him toward the door.

"A-all right," he said. "We'll put it in writing, and you will officially be my employees for the purposes of finding my people and keeping them and myself safe from this kidnapper."

"Wonderful. Do you have any suggestions for where to start?" she said smoothly, glossing over the fact that they'd come up here without much of a plan. "Have you seen anything suspicious recently while you've been looking after Water's Edge?"

Henri raised his eyes to the ceiling.

"Now that you mention it, I have noticed some strange lights. Magical obviously. Perhaps they are the same magic." He gestured to the fallen assassin. Captain Wiselyn took that opportunity to step forward and bind the man's hands and feet.

Sorrel perked up. "Where is this?"

"Out toward the center of the swamp, there is a tor. A big rocky hill sticking up above the bog with a ruin on top. Strange place. My people avoid it because they think their ancestors lived there. I avoid it because I don't like getting my feet wet. But there have been colored lights shining from the summit for a little while now." He frowned as Wiselyn slung the assassin over his shoulder. "That's all I have. We shall interrogate this one and let you know if he reveals any further clues."

Vola glanced at Sorrel, who rubbed her hands together, but the halfling didn't say anything more. Lillie stared at the floor, and Talon's eyes narrowed on the unconscious assassin.

Magical lights and a strange tor. The connection was nebulous at best but it wasn't like they had much else to go on. At least now they had a direction, and Vola was good at charging straight forward.

## NINE

The next morning, they stood at the top of the hill, and Vola wished they'd picked any other direction. The sun illuminated a thick blanket of fog hanging over the swamp which stretched wide and green and a little fuzzy.

"Bleh, I itch already," Sorrel said.

"Well, at least we got a good night's rest in a nice bed before we have to head into that," Lillie said though her voice lifted at the end as if she wasn't exactly sure she agreed with what she was saying.

"I'm glad you could sleep in that mausoleum." Vola rubbed her neck. "I couldn't get comfortable."

"Yeah, it's hard to sleep on a mattress after years of sleeping on a stone floor," Sorrel said, and stretched her back, hands on her hips.

"Couldn't you just sleep on the floor?" Lillie asked.

"Well, yeah. But the bed was sitting right there, and it seemed a shame to waste my first chance to try one."

Vola gave Sorrel a doubtful look, but she had to agree that the beds had been weirdly soft. And the sumptuous surroundings had just made her too frightened to touch anything. She kept thinking she'd sit on a chair and break the damn thing.

Talon didn't appear to feel the need to comment on their night. They stood slightly apart, staring out across the wetlands. The big black wolf coalesced out of the surrounding trees and padded up to the ranger. Talon didn't even look to see him coming. They just held out their hand and suddenly the wolf was butting it with his head.

In the distance, standing up through the fog, Vola could make out a tall, narrow hill, almost a mountain in the middle of the flat swamps. The tor Lord Arthorel had mentioned.

It actually wasn't that far. Maybe a day's brisk hike. Vola's spirits lifted. They could easily get there and back before Braydon's party found the missing townsfolk. Unless, as a local, he already knew about the lights and was on his way there now.

Not that it was a competition. It was just that the council representative knew there was another group on the way. She really, really needed to get to them before Braydon.

Really, really.

"Let's move out," Vola said. "If we don't dawdle, we can spend the night on the tor. It's probably a lot less damp."

Sorrel snorted as Vola set off, taking the lead. "Did you really just use the word dawdle?"

Vola cast a glare over her shoulder. "Yes, why?"

"It just doesn't seem like a very Orcish word."

"Half-orc," Vola said quickly.

"Is there such a language as half-orcish?" Lillie said, falling in behind Sorrel and Vola.

"No, I just…Look, you'd rather I didn't say it in Orcish. It involves lots of swearing. Besides, it makes my throat hurt."

"But isn't it your native language? Or at least, half-native language?" Sorrel gasped. "Oh! Is that why orcs are always in such a bad mood?"

"Because they're always in a little bit of pain?" Vola said. "Yeah. Or well, that's part of it."

"Fascinating." Lillie pulled a book from her pack and a charcoal pencil. "Poor things. But still fascinating. Do you mind if I take notes?"

"On me? Or my people?"

"Don't you mean half of your people?" Sorrel said.

"Yes, half," Vola snapped.

"The top or the bottom?"

"What?" Vola said.

"The top half or the bottom half of your people?" Sorrel said before breaking into chortles.

"That's not how it works," Vola said. She started down the hill, leaving the rest to scramble after her.

"I agree," Lillie said. "Although I will be the first to admit I know very little about the biology of orcs. Or half-orcs."

There was an aborted bark of laughter from behind them, and Vola cast a glare at Henri who brought up the rear of their party.

At the bottom of the hill, the land under their feet turned gooshy, making their feet squelch and splash. The trees closed in, dark and hanging with strands of soggy moss.

Vola led the way into the swamp, testing each step carefully. She didn't want anyone to fall into a puddle and not come out again. Especially not someone wearing armor who would sink faster than a stone.

Sorrel followed her, using her staff to poke the surrounding ground, feeling for soft spots.

Next came Lillie, who walked with her nose stuck in a book. Vola sighed and resigned herself to pulling the beauty out if she managed to disappear into a puddle.

Henri brought up the rear, walking as nonchalantly as he would down a street in town but still managing to keep an attentive eye out behind them.

Talon and the wolf ranged behind them all, keeping an eye on their flanks. Vola only saw them half the time. The other half she assumed they were hidden to better protect the group.

It was a broad assumption.

Vola's calves ached and sweat dripped down the length of her spine underneath the pack, and she squinted up at the sky. How long had they been walking?

The fog had burned off, finally, and when she ducked under a branch, she could glimpse a clear patch of sky.

Her heart plummeted. If her placement was correct, it was past noon. She spun in a circle. Yup. They'd been traipsing through this swamp for hours.

She'd tried to keep them on a fairly straight course but it was nearly impossible to see anything through the moss and the drooping tree branches, and they often had to detour around big puddles and swathes of swampy ground.

A splash and a yelp rang out behind her.

She turned to catch Sorrel dragging a dripping Lillie from a patch of seemingly solid muck. Vola was starting to regret not hiring a local guide. With her luck, Braydon was probably an expert in swamp navigation.

Lillie slipped and skidded back onto the path, holding a much soggier book, and shifted her feet sheepishly. She pulled a soaked handkerchief out of her pocket and used it to mop the worst of the algae from her arms. Then she grimaced and used it to wipe her running nose.

"Sorrel," Vola barked. "Think you can shimmy up one of these trees and tell us how far we are from the tor?"

Sorrel straightened with a snap and gave Vola a mock salute. "Yes, ma'am. Hold this for me." She handed Vola her staff and scrambled up the trunk of a nearby tree. Her sandals slipped against the bark once or twice, but she never lost her grip entirely and soon her rear end disappeared between the branches.

"Ugh," they heard Sorrel say. "It's sticky. Why is the tree sticky?"

"Probably just sap," Vola said.

"It's slimy, too. How can it be slimy and sticky at the same time? I always thought those were two separate things."

"Just—can you see the tor from there?"

"Well…no."

Vola's heart thumped. "What do you mean 'no?'"

"What do you think I mean? I mean, no, I can't see it. Oh, wait, it's back that way."

"If you're pointing, we can't see it," Lillie called.

"Hang on," Sorrel said. "I've got it now. I'm coming back down."

Vola groaned. "Shit, how long have we been going in the wrong direction?"

A little tongue of forked lightning struck the ground beside Vola.

Lillie jumped and spun around, nearly losing her balance again. "What was that?"

"Nothing," Vola muttered.

The wizard frowned and leaned down to study the blackened moss at their feet.

Dammit, Vola had no idea what she was doing. She glanced back at Henri, who waited, eyes trained on the path and the surrounding trees. She opened her mouth to ask if there was anything she should know about pathfinding in a swamp, then thought better of it and snapped her jaw shut with a click. Of course there was. She knew nothing right now, which meant everything was left over. But she was supposed to be ready for this. Asking for help would only prove to him she didn't know what she was doing.

Lillie sneezed violently.

"What's wrong with you?" Vola asked.

"I think I am allergic to algae," she answered, sounding stuffed up.

"Great."

"Ouch," came a call from above them.

"Sorrel?" Vola said.

"The tree just bit me."

"Trees don't bite," Lillie said.

"Well, this one did. Ah!" There was a crack and a rustle, and suddenly, Sorrel was on the ground between them.

"Oof," she said faintly.

Vola and Lillie sprang to help her up.

"Are you all right, Miss Sorrel?"

"Slipped my grip," she mumbled.

Sorrel regained her feet and rubbed her palms across her pants, leaving streaks of brownish-green. A large gash glared at Vola from Sorrel's elbow.

"You're bleeding," Vola said.

"I told you, the tree bit me." Sorrel rubbed her elbow, examined the blood smeared on her hand, then added it to the stains on her pants.

Vola made a face over Sorrel's head. She'd never heard of trees biting, but maybe that was one of the many, many things she didn't know about the swamp. Maybe Sorrel was going to turn into a rampaging tree monster now.

"Here." Vola took Sorrel's arm and laid her palm across the bloody mark. She reached deep inside herself to the well of yellow light and the feeling of acceptance. "Lady bless," she muttered under her breath.

A dull light flashed between their skin, so brief it was easy to miss, but when Vola took her hand away, the blood was gone, leaving nothing but an angry red welt on Sorrel's elbow.

"Hey, that's handy," Sorrel said, twisting and crossing her eyes to see her elbow.

"Are you a healer, Miss Volagra?" Lillie said.

"More like a field medic. It's…it's a paladin thing."

"So you ask your god for help and they just heal whoever you want?" Sorrel flexed her arm. "Mine doesn't do that. Maxim only rewards big things like loyalty and justice."

"It's a little more complicated than that. There are rules and… and consequences to all power. She chose me and I made my oaths to her. But if I ever break those oaths, I'll be cut off, my connection to her lost."

"You don't seem like an oathbreaker to me," Lillie said with a little smile.

"And you get to heal wounds in exchange," Sorrel said, rubbing her elbow.

"I haven't learned everything yet. I've barely covered the basics. Right now, I can heal minor wounds, but it's not as easy as it looks."

She raised her own arm to show them her elbow which stung. The edge of her chain mail fell back to reveal a long gash, mirroring Sorrel's wound. As they watched, the ragged flesh began to knit and close.

"Any wound I heal, I have to take for myself and my goddess heals it that way."

Lillie's eyes went wide, and she reached out to touch Vola's arm. Vola jerked away.

"So, say someone was dead…" Sorrel said.

Vola rubbed her healing arm as Lillie pulled out her soggy notebook and jotted something down.

"Yeah, that's one of the things I don't know yet. Theoretically, I'd have to die, and I don't know if C—if my goddess would fix that. There are some paladins who have managed it before, but they're all connected to greater gods. Mine's one of the Lesser Virtues."

Lillie cocked her head, pencil poised over her page, and Vola cleared her throat before she could ask more questions. "Sorrel, did you see the way to go while you were up there?"

"Yeah, we were heading north. The tor is more east."

"How far east?"

Sorrel bit her lip. "It actually doesn't look any close than it was this morning."

Vola groaned and put her head in her hands.

"And I'm not sure how to get there." Sorrel gestured at the swamp to the east. "'Cause that looks very wet."

The briefest rustle made Vola jump.

Henri spun, weapon unsheathed. But it was only Talon stepping onto the path.

"This way," they said. "I have found a dry route."

"That's convenient," Lillie said.

Talon turned to head back into the swamp, and Vola lurched to follow. "A dry route to the tor?"

Talon's hood moved like they were glancing over their shoulder. "Yes, we were listening."

"We didn't even know you were there," Sorrel said.

"Gruff and I can move unseen when we wish to. I can speak to the land and it listens." They cocked their head. "Sometimes."

Vola tried to decide if that irked her or not. She felt like a battering ram, clanking and smashing through the underbrush.

"Walk where I walk," Talon said. "Do not stray from my footprints."

Vola nodded, then she half-turned to check that the rest of her party was following. Sorrel trotted to keep up, idly scratching the back of her hand.

Lillie had finally put her book away and was concentrating on her feet. Henri moved like a deer, sword drawn, eyes vigilant, feet sure and steady.

Vola turned to follow Talon's back, doing her best to move as smoothly as Henri.

Even with Talon leading the way around the biggest pools, they crawled through the swamp, slower than the snails that crawled along the branches above them. Every few feet they had to stop as Talon searched out the firm ground. They had to fish Lillie out of dank algae-filled pools three more times and Sorrel once. Every time Vola strayed a little too far right or left, the wolf, Gruff, appeared out of the gloom to herd her back to the path.

Vola checked her companions frequently, wincing when she found Lillie mopping her streaming nose or Sorrel scratching at her sides and shoulders.

The light filtering through the trees hadn't changed at all—everything still looked murky—but Vola's muscles burned like she'd just finished a training run in full armor.

Lillie sneezed, tripped, and splashed into the water along the edge of the path.

Vola closed her eyes, trying to ignore the nagging feeling that this was not how things were supposed to be going.

"Talon, we need a minute, I think," she said.

The ranger stopped and looked back at Sorrel, who was trying to lift Lillie out of the water with one hand and scratching herself violently with the other.

"Looks like it," Talon said.

Vola still couldn't see the figure's eyes, but she got the distinct impression that they had just exchanged an empathetic glance.

Lillie bent over in a sneezing fit, barely able to breathe in between, and Vola nudged her over a step or two so she wouldn't fall in the water. Then she reached for Sorrel.

"Stop scratching," she said. "You're making it worse."

"I can't help it," Sorrel said with a low growl. "I itch. Does that goddess of yours do anything about itching?"

"Not that I know of," Vola said, holding Sorrel's arm gingerly between her hands. Sorrel used her other hand to scratch at her side.

Vola turned the arm over to glance at the elbow, but the "tree bite" had subsided to a small red mark barely visible against Sorrel's tanned skin. The mirrored wound on Vola's elbow still ached but it would be gone soon.

"I think you've got a rash," Vola said.

"You think?" Sorrel said, trying to yank her arm back.

Vola didn't let go. "Henri," she said. As much as she didn't want to ask her mentor for help, Henri knew a lot more about everything than she did. And he had taught her to use all her resources. Right now, he was a resource.

Henri sheathed his weapon and stepped up from the back of the group. He turned Sorrel's arm over, examining it clinically. "Contact poison," he said. "Probably a defense mechanism for the tree. Anywhere the sap touched you, you're going to itch."

"Wonderful," Vola said, glancing sidelong at Sorrel's stained clothes. "Do you have anything for itching?" Vola asked, knowing Henri traveled prepared for everything.

He was already sifting through the satchel at his waist, lines forming at the corners of his mouth as he smiled. "I can whip something up."

Shadows flickered across their faces and Vola glanced up at the light filtering through the foliage. The sun was falling rapidly, leaving big orange streaks she could see even through the tree branches. Lillie blew her nose loudly.

Vola sighed and let go of the idea that they would be spending the night on the tor. "Talon," she said. "I think we're going to need a place to camp."

# TEN

By the time the orange streaks across the sky had turned purple, Talon had led them to a firm patch of ground. Sagging trees surrounded clumps and tufts of brownish grass. Vola always thought brown meant dead, but this was thick and thriving. Big, brown flower buds almost as tall as Vola's waist were spaced in an oddly even pattern between the trees.

Through a big gap in the trunks, Vola could see the tor, standing tall, stained with the deep red and gold of sunset. Her shoulders slumped. The hill stood almost as far away as it had that morning. She did some quick calculations to determine how far they'd come and then gave up when she realized the answer would only depress her. At this rate, it would take them a week just to get to the tor. And a week to get back.

Surely Braydon's party would have beaten them by then.

Vola reached for the stuffed rabbit in her belt and stroked her thumb down its fuzzy head. What was happening to the missing people? What were the kidnappers using them for? A week could make all the difference in their survival.

This wasn't going to work. They had to move faster.

Vola turned to her group, ready with a few choice words, but her censure died unspoken. Henri was smearing a green paste up and down Sorrel's arms. He'd concocted the remedy as they'd trudged through the last mile of swamp. Sorrel wasn't wincing anymore, and Lillie was leaning close with her book and pencil out.

"Can you teach me?" she asked Henri even though her nose was still streaming and her eyes were red.

"I'll show you what I can," Henri said with a quirk of his lips. "It's not much. Just enough to keep a soldier alive until they can be moved to a healer."

"It's still more than I know," Lillie said quietly, scribbling in her book.

"You'll want to change into something clean," Henri told Sorrel. "This will have to be washed. Or burned." He held the hem of her tunic between two fingers.

"Washed, please," she said. "It's the only one I have."

"You don't have a change of clothes?" Vola said.

Sorrel shrugged. "I'm a monk. We don't really go in for worldly possessions. I can run around naked while they dry as long as no one else cares about an undressed halfling."

"I would let you borrow one of mine," Lillie said with a flush. "But I also only have one set of clothes."

Vola rubbed her forehead. Who'd have thought she would be the best outfitted of the group? Unless Talon was hiding a wardrobe underneath their cloak.

Vola dropped her pack to the ground with a squelch and dug around for a spare shirt which she tossed to Sorrel.

"Here. It…might be a bit big."

Sorrel held it up. The cuffs dragged on the soggy ground. "At least no one will accuse me of being immodest," she said with a smirk.

Vola huffed a laugh and dug out the tent. Then she disappeared behind some trees to take care of some necessary business.

When she got back, she found that her party members had started setting up camp.

The sight of Sorrel dressed in a shirt-gown trying to hammer a tent peg with another tent peg and Lillie tangled in the support cords nearly made her sigh and roll her eyes for the hundredth time since the day before. Couldn't her lady have sent her anyone who was at least a little competent?

Then she saw Henri walking back into the clearing with a pile of wood dry enough for a fire and an amused expression.

In a couple of swift movements, he handed Sorrel the mallet with a laugh and a brief explanation on how to use it without crushing her fingers, and then he turned to untangle Lillie.

Talon strode back into the clearing and tossed a couple of rabbits and a grouse next to Vola. Vola hadn't even noticed they were gone.

"Dinner," Talon said simply.

"How did you—Where did you—Do rabbits even live in swamps?" Vola said.

Talon's hood just stared. The wolf padded up beside them, and Talon reached out to rest a calloused hand on his fur.

"Never mind. Thank you," she added after a pause. And she meant it. She'd fully intended to pass out the dried meat and nuts Becky had given them. Instead, she set about skinning and gutting the animals.

A gagging noise made her look up. Sorrel looked a little green and leaned as far away as she could.

"What's wrong?" Vola said.

"What's wrong is your rabbit's inside out."

Vola raised an eyebrow. "Didn't you ever help out in the monastery kitchen?"

"I tried not to, most of the time. For the same reason."

Vola paused in her task. "You're squeamish?"

"Why do you think I fight with my fists and blunt instruments? Less bloody that way."

"Unless you crush a man's skull," Lillie said. "I was always under the impression that that was particularly messy."

Sorrel gagged again. "Don't remind me."

Lillie knelt beside Vola. "I don't know much, but I'm willing to learn if you'll teach me."

Vola's mouth fell open. She blinked and for a moment all she could see was a gaggle of blonde beauties laughing as she knelt in the middle of a dirt road and snatched handfuls of bruised fruit off the ground. The memory superimposed itself over top of Lillie's face, and Vola swallowed, the dichotomy making her gut clench.

Apparently, she hesitated too long because Henri knelt on Vola's other side and took up the other rabbit. He leveled a quirked eyebrow in Vola's direction before showing Lillie how to slit the hide before ripping it from the animal.

Sorrel nearly lost her lunch and scurried to the far side of the tent. Talon made room, and the two sat together in silence.

Vola finished skinning her rabbit with her head down and her fingers tight on the hilt of her belt knife. Beside her, Lillie murmured questions and Henri answered each one thoughtfully.

By the time the sun had fully set, they had a crackling fire and a halfway decent meal of rabbit stew and stuffed grouse. Talon had brought them enough that Vola had tossed half a rabbit to the wolf. The offering didn't appear to change how he felt about her. He took it with an indifferent sniff and gnawed on his dinner with better table manners than a lot of the knights back at the academy.

Sorrel popped back over to them as soon as the food actually looked like food.

Within the circle of firelight, Vola looked up to find the night sky streaked with little sparks. She blinked and stood, picking out several that didn't belong to their fire.

"Look," she said quietly.

She couldn't see the tor anymore in the dark, but flicks of light danced across the sky to a tall shadow in the distance, converging at a point above it.

"The lights Lord Arthorel mentioned," Lillie murmured.

"They're divine," Sorrel said.

Vola glanced down. The halfling stood with her eyes on the sky, the sparks reflecting in their depths.

"They are?"

Sorrel nodded, lips tight. "Maxim's Warhammer. It might actually be there."

Vola blew out her breath. If they were up against a divine weapon, they had more to worry about than just being late.

She sat back down to cram her dinner in her mouth. "We need to move faster tomorrow."

It didn't actually matter if she scarfed her food and went to bed early. That wouldn't get them going in the morning, but it felt better to be doing something.

Henri sat on a moss-covered log with a pail full of murky water and Sorrel's clothes, rinsing the fabric over and over. Vola could see it was still stained, but hopefully it wouldn't be the bearer of bad itch anymore.

"Do you think we can make it by tomorrow?" Lillie asked.

"Maybe. If we don't have any more delays."

She heard the rumble in her own voice and hid a wince. She didn't mean to sound so aggressive. It's just this wasn't how she imagined her first quest going at all. Everything seemed to rub her the wrong way, and an irritated orc was an aggressive orc.

Half-orc, she reminded herself. Vola struggled to find the human half of herself as Sorrel and Lillie took her hint and cleaned up their plates before heading into the tent. Henri bent to bank the fire without being asked, and Vola tried not to read disappointment in the angle of his neck.

Vola stepped toward the tree line to check the perimeter. The black wolf lay across the narrow opening between the trees, and he raised his head as Vola went by. His eyebrows twitched as Vola gave him a wide berth. When she'd circled the whole way around, Henri was laying his bedroll out on the other side of the fire. For as long as Vola had known him, Henri had never slept in a tent. When they were on the road, he preferred to lay so he could see the stars as he fell asleep.

Talon squatted by the fire.

"There's room in the tent," Vola said.

The hood turned and Vola got the impression Talon's eyes examined her from under it.

"No. First watch," they said. "I'll wake you when I need sleep."

Then they disappeared into the trees. Vola flushed, the heat of her blood beating in her cheeks. She couldn't believe she'd forgotten something as basic as setting a watch.

If Henri had noticed, he said nothing, laying back with his head on his crooked arm.

Vola climbed into the tent and yanked her chain mail over her head. The leather straps creaked, and she forced herself to slow down. She was stuck with the old armor, and if it broke now just because she was angry, she'd have to fix it herself.

Lillie had created a little ball of magical light and was trying to come up with a way to hang it from the ceiling, making shadows bounce around the canvas walls.

Finally, Vola took it from her, wrapped a leather thong around the thing, and strapped it through a loop so it swung free and cast fewer shadows across the occupants.

Lillie smiled, and Vola was taken aback by the genuine pleasure in her expression. "Thank you," she said. She shuffled around on her knees, shifting the bedroll around. "I've never actually slept on the ground."

"Never? That's odd," Sorrel said. "Where are you from?

Lillie busied herself with the blankets. "Nowhere."

"No one's from nowhere."

"I just meant it doesn't really matter anymore. This is my life, and I'm going to live it."

Sorrel shrugged, accepting that at face value. "You get used to it. And this is way better than my stone slab in the monastery."

Vola shook her head. "Is that actually a thing? Or is it just something monks say to make everyone think they're lofty and austere?"

Sorrel played with the rolled-up sleeves of her borrowed shirt. "Well, all right, it was a thin pallet on a stone floor. But that's a lot like sleeping on a stone slab."

And probably a lot closer to what they were about to do than the feather bed Lillie was apparently used to.

"I like this," Lillie said with an airy gesture. "It's cozy. Just like a slumber party, isn't it?"

"Uh," Vola said, completely at a loss for words. Lillie was the kind of girl who normally ran screaming from green skin and tusks, but there she sat, beaming at Vola like they were little girls in frilly pajamas waiting for bedtime.

"Just like," Sorrel said. "Er, I think. I mean, our dormitory housed all the other monks and most of them snored. So that's sort of like a slumber party, right?"

Lillie's mouth dropped open. "Not even remotely." She looked at Vola, wide eyes beseeching, as if she expected the half-orc to back her up about the whole slumber party thing.

"Uh," Vola said again and shifted uncomfortably.

"You've never had a slumber party, either?" she asked.

"Of course not." What kind of childhood did Lillie think she'd had? Village girls didn't invite the local monster over for tea parties and sleepovers.

Lillie bit her lip and sank back on her heels. Vola had never kicked a puppy before, but she could imagine this was what it felt like.

Lillie just kept saying the wrong things, and then Vola kept saying the wrong things back to her. Like two actors reading from different scripts.

Resisting the surge of irritation, Vola reached up and returned the light to Lillie who doused it with a word.

Vola lay in the dark listening to the rustles of Sorrel and Lillie. It would be so easy to let the worry roll over her. And drown under the overwhelming idea that she'd picked the wrong partners, the wrong quest, maybe even the wrong profession.

She squeezed her eyes shut and tried to think of something that had gone right today.

Talon knew what they were doing, obviously. And Sorrel had already demonstrated she could fight. And Lillie…Lillie was trying.

Henri had spent so much time slathering Sorrel in cream and teaching Lillie to skin a rabbit and watching their backs while they'd walked.

An image stirred in her mind's eye. A lonely half-orc all elbows and knees, folded awkwardly at a desk in the academy library, sniffling over a book of troop movements. A grizzled trainer had came over to point out the enemy line's weaknesses.

"Deep breaths, Vola," Henri said in her memory. "How do you expect to be good at something you haven't learned yet?"

Vola's stomach clenched in remembered relief. Henri had always taught her so patiently. The least she could do was extend the same courtesy to the others.

This wasn't a disaster. At least, it didn't have to be a disaster. She just had to be more patient. Like Henri.

Vola sighed. Orcs weren't known for their patience.

But then, neither were they known for being paladins.

# ELEVEN

Vola took the last watch which meant she was awake when someone started thrashing about in their bedroll near dawn. The whole tent nearly shook with it, and Vola ducked inside. Lillie shivered under her covers, legs kicking out. Vola nudged her shoulder, trying to wake her without scaring her.

"Bad dream?" she said low enough not to wake Sorrel, who still snored.

Lillie lay on her side with her face in her hands. "Running," she said, slurring like she was still half asleep. "Always running. Except my feet are glued to the floor and I can't escape."

"Yeah, I've had that one, too."

Lillie rubbed her face and blinked up at Vola in the dim predawn light. "What?"

"The dream about running. I think everyone has that one sometimes."

"Right," Lillie said, sitting up. "Yes. Everyone has it. Of course." She wrapped her arms around her knees and rested her cheek on them.

Vola chewed her lip. "Do you…want to talk about it?"

*Please say no. Please say no.*

"It was just a dream," Lillie said to the tent wall.

Sure it was. Vola surveyed her but didn't say anything more. If Lillie didn't want to talk about it, great. Vola wasn't good with all that emotional stuff.

"How does one become a paladin?" Lillie asked suddenly. "Is it like being a monk?" She gestured to Sorrel's sleeping form. "Were you brought up to it?"

"Not really." Vola settled back on her heels. "I knew how to fight but you have to graduate from a paladin academy to be able to call yourself a paladin."

"So, you chose to serve the gods."

"It's a little more complicated than that. Anyone can choose to become a novice, but a god has to choose you in order to become a full candidate. There's this whole ceremony." Which Imralen had tried his best to bar her from. He'd only relented finally because of who chose her. He'd thought it fitting that an orc would serve a laughingstock.

"So you were chosen by one of the Virtues."

Vola shifted uncomfortably, ready to steer the conversation away if Lillie asked which one.

"Is that unusual?"

"How so?" Vola said. "Gods choose paladins all the time." Ona, the Greater Virtue of Honor and Maxim, the Greater Virtue of Strength and Loyalty being the most prolific.

"I just thought that orcs revered the Obstacles," Lillie said, her cheeks going red in the dim light. "That's why…"

"That's why everyone hates us," Vola finished for her.

"They don't hate you," Lillie said quietly. "They're afraid of you."

"It's the same thing sometimes." Vola stared up at the canvas ceiling. "Orcs revere strength above everything else. Strength of body, yes. But also strength of mind and heart. And they're always looking for ways to make themselves stronger."

Lillie cocked her head, finally meeting Vola's gaze again.

"And the one thing that reliably makes you stronger is overcoming hardship," Vola said.

Lillie's mouth parted in recognition. "And since the Obstacles represent the hardships of mortal existence…"

"Adversity, shame, guilt. They welcome them all as a chance to grow. They even have a very special relationship with rage."

"You say 'they' like you're not one of them," Lillie said quietly.

Vola picked at the edge of a blanket. "I chose something else."

"A chance to become a paladin and serve one of the Virtues. Why?"

"Because I was fourteen and wanted to prove something." She still wanted to prove something. She would always want to prove something for as long as the world looked at orcs and saw aggression and violence instead of strength and a deep honor.

"Who is it you serve, then?" Lillie asked. "Which Virtue?"

Vola cleared her throat and lifted the tent flap to indicate the lightening sky. "We should get moving."

Lillie's face fell, but she leaned over to wake Sorrel without asking any more questions Vola didn't feel like answering.

She stooped to leave the tent, ignoring the little stab of guilt that made her stomach hurt. She forced herself to remember the way Lillie had avoided answering questions about her past. And when Sorrel spoke of the monastery, she never mentioned any people, no relationships or friends or mentors. And Talon was a complete mystery.

Seemed like they all had things to hide.

"Talon," Vola called to the ranger, who squatted at the edge of the clearing feeding bits of jerky to the wolf. The ranger had slept outside with Henri. "Could you scout the best path to the tor from here? Something high and dry." She just barely kept herself from glancing at Lillie, who was tumbling out of the tent. "I'd rather we didn't fall into any more puddles today."

Talon stood and brushed their rear end off before disappearing into the trees. Vola didn't like the idea of splitting up, but it made perfect sense to send the scout out to, you know, actually scout.

When Vola turned back to break down the tent, she found Sorrel rubbing the back of her neck and Lillie glancing at the forest where Talon had disappeared.

"What is it?" Vola asked.

"It's just..." Lillie said. "Do you think Talon is male? Or female?"

"That's pretty rude," Sorrel said.

Lillie flushed scarlet. "I'm sorry. I must have missed some clue then. Maybe this is common where you come from, but I've never met...anyone like Talon before."

Vola sighed. "Don't worry. We don't know either."

Lillie's shoulders relaxed. "Oh good. I thought it was just me."

"And you didn't know how to be polite about it," Vola said. She hadn't missed the way Lillie had carefully addressed each of them.

"That's why I am asking. I don't know what to call...them. Miss? Mister? Sir Talon? Madame Talon?"

"Yeah, but you can't just ask," Sorrel said.

"Why not?" Lillie asked. "Isn't that more polite than guessing and getting it wrong —"

Without a sound or even a hint of movement, Talon appeared at the edge of the clearing in front of them.

Lillie gulped down whatever she was about to say. "Hi!" she said instead.

Talon's hood turned toward her and Vola could almost imagine the look that would be on the invisible face. "Head east," Talon growled. "When you're ready. I've marked the trail."

Then the figure was off. Lillie leaned toward Sorrel. "I don't even know if they're human," she whispered.

"I think that's species-ist," Sorrel said.

"That's not a word."

"Well, it should be."

Vola finished folding up the tent and shoved it as far into the pack as it would go.

Henri stood beside the tree where he'd hung Sorrel's clothes, gazing at them with his mouth twisted into a grimace.

"What's wrong?" Vola asked.

"They're still wet," he said. Then his shoulders drooped with a big sigh. "It's this humid air. And look at these stains." He pulled them from the branch. "If anything, they got bigger." He tsked between his teeth like a disgruntled housewife.

"It's probably mold," Vola said under her breath. Then she called out, "Sorrel, you'll have to wait another day for your clothes. Unless you want to wear them damp."

"That's all right," Sorrel said. "I'm liking my new outfit. It's roomy." She flapped her arms so the loose fabric around her middle waved like a banner. She looked even more child-like than usual.

Vola tried not to laugh.

As Henri gathered the clothes and folded them, the light from the sun finally made it over the distant tor, and streams of gold speared toward their clearing.

"Time to move," Vola said.

One of the beams of light hit the big ugly flower bud directly beside her, and with an audible creak, the plant shivered.

"Uh," Vola said.

The bud snapped open, revealing crimson petals. Orange veins sprinkled with black plunged toward the center of the blossom where they converged into a thick spiral. The thing clicked and surged upward until it stood face to face with Vola.

"Whoa." She stumbled back a few paces.

Henri had already drawn his sword.

Was she really running from a plant? Vola shook her head. The thing had startled her. That's all. It was a flower, right? How bad could it be?

All around the clearing, blossoms opened in response to the sun's beams, some of them hissing and stretching like they were waking up from a good night's sleep.

"I think we should get out of here," Sorrel whispered.

"I agree with Miss Sorrel," Lillie said.

The pit in Vola's gut was the deciding vote.

"East," she said. "Make your way east. Talon marked a dry path." She shifted her feet and backed toward the others.

The movement made the nearest blossom rear back, and with a menacing hiss, it spat a stream of liquid.

Vola's instincts took over, and she dove to the side, rolling and coming up with her sword drawn and on guard. The liquid, a foul, orange viscous solution, hit the grass and sizzled. The brown blades shrank and turned black.

"Well...poop on a stick," Sorrel said.

Vola had been thinking of something decidedly stronger.

"Pro tip," she called. "Don't let them spit at you."

"You think?" Sorrel said.

Vola darted for an opening on the east side of the clearing but two blossoms leaned toward each other, effectively closing the gap. They were trapped. At least until they could do some weed whacking.

Vola growled and rushed the nearest plant, drawing back her sword. Then with two fists, she swung down as hard as she could.

The plant...dodged. That's the only way she could think to describe it, except that plants didn't dodge.

"You're not supposed to be sentient, dammit," she said as the blossom jerked back and spit. Vola ducked and spun, swinging again. This time, she managed to take off the tip of a petal.

"Talon," Vola called. "Talon, we need you."

The plant reared back and the spiral at its center unwound and opened onto a chasm, looking horribly like a mouth. It screamed at her.

Vola grimaced. Then she opened her mouth and roared back.

The plant jerked and straightened as if surprised. Then whipped around and knocked Vola off her feet.

Suddenly flat on her back, Vola had a great view of the rest of her party.

Sorrel spun wildly, her staff a blur above her head. Unfortunately, her shirt-gown billowed just as wildly. As Sorrel planted her feet and struck out toward the blossom nearest her, she caught the hem of her shirt under her foot. Her eyes went wide, and she face planted into the soggy ground.

Beside her, Lillie flipped through her spell book muttering to herself.

"Just pick something," Sorrel yelled.

"Yes, but what?" Lillie went back to muttering. "What is the most efficient? Do they have any weaknesses? Any resiliencies?"

A second blossom reared back and aimed a spit stream at Lillie.

She ducked, covering her head with a scream.

Suddenly, a blur of brown and silver darted in front of her, becoming Henri. His raised shield took the brunt of the spit attack, the rest falling to singe and sear the grass at his feet.

"What are they?" Sorrel called.

Lillie's mouth fell open, and she reached for the botany book she'd taken from the orphanage. The nearest blossom shot another stream of spit at her, and she yanked her hand back.

"The crimson swamp blossom," Lillie said.

"What?"

"These are the crimson swamp blossoms the shopkeeper wanted."

"I don't care about the name," Vola yelled. "How do we get rid of them?"

"I don't know!" Lillie clutched the sides of her head. "The book didn't say anything about that."

"Why would it leave that out?" Sorrel asked, whacking at a nearby flower with her stem.

"Because the author was stupid! That seems like very important information right now!"

"Cut them off at the roots," Henri said.

A menacing click made Vola roll back over to find her own personal blossom hanging over her, its orange spiral mouth wide open. Like it was about to eat her. Did carnivorous plants like orc? Liquid dripped from its petals, making her armor hiss and spark where it hit.

Vola winced. That was going to leave a mark.

She reached for her sword, but her fingers closed on empty air. It had fallen too far.

The blossom reared back to deal the final death blow, and she threw up her hand to protect her face.

An arrow whistled and thunked into the center of the flower. A rumbling growl told Vola that Talon and Gruff had entered the fray.

Vola rolled, and this time, her fingers clenched around the hilt of her sword. As the blossom jerked and flinched, she rose to her knees and swung her sword in a wide arc, catching the plant at the base.

It screamed again, a high shriek that made the hair along her arms stand up, before it fell over and thrashed across the ground, severed from its stem.

Vola stumbled back a few steps to avoid its death throes. After an unnecessary amount of drama, it finally lay still, its petals limp against the grass.

Vola turned, lips pulled back, to find Sorrel pummeling one of the blossoms with her staff. Every time it lunged for her, she danced out of the way.

Lillie cast little bolts of fire at another blossom from behind Henri's back as he fought against another plant, his sword darting like he was fencing the damn thing. His shield smoked from his other arm.

Sorrel darted away from her plant yet again. But this time, the thing shuddered as if frustrated. Then all its petals curled inward for a split second before snapping back out again. And when the petals snapped out, so did a rope-like vine that wrapped around Sorrel's leg before dragging her inexorably toward the gaping spiral mouth.

Sorrel cried out.

Vola started forward, sword raised.

Lillie heard her scream and spun. "Miss Sorrel!" she called. Then she brought her hands together and murmured a spell.

Fire burst from Lillie's palms in a wide arc, catching Sorrel's plant but also singing Sorrel and Vola in the process.

"Whoa!" Vola dove for the ground.

"Lillie!" Sorrel cried. The plant hadn't even twitched at the fire and still dragged Sorrel toward its mouth. "I'd rather you didn't cook me before it eats me."

"Keep the pyrotechnics down," Vola said.

"I'm sorry," Lillie called, hands covering her cheeks. "You were in my way."

"Of course I'm in the way. I'm fighting the damn thing." A little lightning bolt struck the ground at her feet.

Another arrow shot from the foliage and buried itself about a foot to the left of the vine wrapped around Sorrel's leg. Which happened to be two inches from Sorrel's hand.

"Talon!" Sorrel yelled.

Vola's teeth clenched on a growl but before the frustration could do more than sting, Henri's voice spoke in her memory.

"One, two, duck and swing."

She knew that. She'd followed his instruction for years. How could a little panic have made her forget so quickly?

Vola lunged forward and brought her blade down on the vine dragging Sorrel across the ground. Then as if all her training finally showed up, she cut the plant off at the stem with a graceful upswing. It thrashed around on the ground while Sorrel untangled herself and crawled away.

Across the clearing, Gruff growled and shook his head, an entire severed blossom hanging from his jaws. Another one lay hacked to pieces where Henri had defended Lillie and one more lay with half a dozen arrows sticking out of it, looking like the florid pin cushion of an overzealous quilter.

Vola braced her hands on her knees and panted, sending up a quick thanks to her goddess that everyone had made it through in one piece.

With her nose inches from her chest, she noticed the little blackened pockmarks decorating her chain mail. Her nostrils stung with the acrid scent, and she lifted the edge to peek underneath to make sure none of the plant poison had seeped through.

Her shirt was a little singed, but her skin looked okay. It was the same shade of gray-green it always was.

Talon stepped into the clearing, looking as unruffled as they had when they'd left, and placed a calming hand on Gruff's shoulder. The wolf immediately stopped shaking the dead plant and dropped it with a wet thud.

"Glad you got here when you did, Talon," Vola said, straightening.

"It's been too long since I've gotten to murder something trying to eat me."

Vola blinked. Was that a joke? From the hooded mystery? Or were they serious?

"Well, you can always murder the thing trying to eat us," Vola said. "I don't think you'll hear anyone complain."

Lillie knelt beside one of the decapitated blossoms and viciously pulled the thing apart with her hands, stuffing petals into her belt pouch. She seemed to take way more pleasure in it than the collection really warranted.

Talon jerked their head. "The other party from town is nearby. They need help."

Vola's shoulders sagged. "Ugh, Braydon?" The last person in the world she wanted to see right now was Braydon. Their narrow escape was written in the damage to Vola's armor, the twigs in Sorrel's hair, and the half-empty quiver on Talon's back.

"Yes," Talon said.

Vola glanced at her party. Sorrel brushed green slime from her shirt-gown while Lillie flipped through her spell book. Second-guessing her decisions?

Henri stood, wiping down his sword with a damp cloth. He'd slung his shield back over his shoulder where it still smoked. The poison spit had left a blackened scar across the metal. Henri didn't glance up, but Vola knew the sort of look he'd be giving her if he had.

She sighed, her shoulders drooping. "Let's go help them, then," she said. *Help them off a cliff*, she didn't add.

# TWELVE

TALON TROTTED ALONG, sure-footed on the boggy ground. Vola lumbered after them, boots squelching and slipping on the slick grass. There was a splash behind her, but Vola didn't turn to look.

A couple of screams in the distance made them pick up their pace. Geez, had they encountered some sort of predator? Maybe like that giant crocodile Talon had been chasing.

Talon led them to another clearing that looked remarkably like the one they'd spent the night in. Complete with a circle of blood-red blossoms.

Ah. That made sense.

The clearing had to be some sort of trap set by the carnivorous plants. Lure in travelers like them with the prospect of a safe, comfortable-looking campsite. Then bam. Hit them with poison the moment the sun rose.

Vola skidded to a stop at the clearing's edge, her boots leaving furrows in the moss and grass underfoot. It looked like Braydon's party hadn't been quite awake yet when the blossoms attacked.

Braydon's spell caster swung by his ankles where a bright orange vine had caught him, his hands busy casting bright sprays of fire and lightning. Somehow, he'd got the vine wrapped around a branch above their campsite and every time the blossom on the other end of the vine yanked, he bobbed up and down.

The woman with the hand axes had one leg down the gullet of another blossom while she hacked its petals apart, screaming at the top of her lungs.

The other party's ranger stood off to the side next to a dead blossom. "The stems!" he cried, his hands buried in his short black curls. "Cut them off at the stems!"

Braydon himself was half-dressed in his plate armor and wrapped in a choke hold by an orange vine. His sword lay three feet away from his grasping hand.

Vola glanced back at her party, who had just caught up. They looked on the scene with varying expressions of horror and amusement. Except for Talon. Their hood hid their expression as always.

"Um, charge?" Vola said.

"Very inspiring," Talon said.

Sorrel shrugged, grinned, and took Vola at face value, charging into the fray with a wild cry of, "For Maxim!"

This time she'd hiked her shirt-gown up and tucked it under a belt made from one of Lillie's stockings so she could run freely, swinging her staff over her head. Halfway across the clearing, she took a flying leap at the blossom holding the wizard up. She clung to the flower making it jerk and bob.

The wizard swung wildly, spraying the ground with a blast of flame.

"Hey, watch it," Sorrel called. "That's the second time today someone's tried to set me on fire." She ducked and swung her staff at the vine where it attached to the flower.

Vola charged across the clearing to the woman being eaten by a blossom.

"Leave her alone, you monster!" Braydon cried, voice stran-
gled by the vine around his neck.

"That's not very nice, sir," Lillie called.

Vola just rolled her eyes, then she slid the rest of the way on
her knees, swung her sword, and cut the blossom off above the
root. She rose to her feet, slipped her toe under Braydon's sword,
and kicked it to him.

"You're welcome," she said as he caught it.

He scowled but reached back and cut himself free of the vine.
Lillie stepped up beside him as he struggled free from its coils and
raised her hands. Flames burst from her fingers, concentrated on
the stem.

The blossom shrieked that high-pitched scream, but Lillie held
her ground just beyond its thrashing petals. Finally, it shuddered
and keeled over, its stem blackened and smoking.

Henri, Talon, and Braydon's ranger circled the clearing,
taking care of any other blossoms that had escaped the carnage.

Vola glanced around to find Sorrel yelling, "Ha, ha, hiyah,"
while punching the blossom's stem, her tiny fists making the
whole plant shudder with each hit. Since the vine wrapped over
the branch, pinning the plant in place, it couldn't dodge out of the
way far enough.

The upside-down wizard closed one eye and pointed at the
blossom. Fire streamed toward Sorrel and the pinned plant.

"Sorrel!" Vola called.

But the fire split and arced around the halfling, hitting the
plant without hurting her.

Both Sorrel and the flower froze.

"Oh my gosh, can you teach me that?" Lillie cried.

Sorrel recovered first and brought both fists down on top of
the plant with a smack that echoed across the clearing.

It moaned and slumped forward, yanking on the vine, making
the wizard at the other end bob.

He made a noise in the back of his throat. "Oh my," he said, and his robe fell down over his face.

"Ah!" Sorrel said, covering her eyes.

Lillie winced. "And that's why robes went out of fashion years ago."

Vola ignored the spectacle on display above her and helped the sobbing woman free her leg from the dead plant beside them. Her leather armor smelled like overcooked meat, and it peeled back revealing raw pink skin.

Vola tilted her head. It didn't look any worse than a bad sunburn, but just to be safe, she laid her hands along the skin and whispered, "Lady bless."

Light flashed under her fingers and the woman breathed a sigh. Vola's leg flared with pain, then subsided to a dull ache.

"Is anyone else hurt?" Vola asked as she climbed to her feet.

"Er," the wizard in the tree said.

"No." Braydon stooped to pick up the rest of his plate armor which was scattered across the seared grass. "What are you doing here?"

Vola's eyes narrowed at his tone. "The same thing you're doing here. Looking for the missing townsfolk."

"Go home, monster," Braydon said. "Come on, people. We'll try west this time."

"Er," the wizard said.

Talon came up beside Vola. "I know monsters," they said. "Funny how most of them look like you."

Braydon's face went red, then white.

Vola ground her teeth. West, he'd said. They had no idea where they were going either. And Vola had been afraid they'd beat her party to the tor. A savage spike of satisfaction lit her insides, and she almost bid them good luck and walked away.

Almost.

But the stuffed rabbit still hung from her belt, looking shabby and limp without its owner. In the end, what mattered was finding the townspeople. That was her mission. Not beating Braydon to it. If he got to them first, the council representative would keep her from getting her shield for sure. But at least the missing people would be safe.

Her hands clenched, nails leaving divots in her palms, before she forced them to relax.

"Head east," she said with a growl. "To the tor. We had a tip that there have been some strange lights appearing there at night. We think they might be related to the kidnappings."

"Hey, that was our lead," Sorrel said.

Vola leveled a glare at her. "Our goal is to rescue the townspeople. It doesn't matter who does it." She didn't mention that half her anger was because she had the horrible feeling this was the wrong decision.

Braydon sneered. "And why should I believe you? You're probably just sending us in the wrong direction. That representative from the paladin council said you weren't to be trusted. That you would do anything to earn your shield. Even cheat."

Red beat at the edges of her vision, threatening to swamp her, and her palm itched on the hilt of her sword.

She took a couple of deep breaths and sheathed her sword deliberately. She couldn't be tempted to cut his head off if she didn't have a blade, could she?

"You don't know me, so I'll let that slide," Vola said carefully. Calm, calm and eventually the rage would go away. "But we just pulled your asses out of the fire. If I cared that much about beating you, I would have ignored all your screaming."

A miniature lightning bolt snaked down and struck one of the dead blossoms.

"Seriously, what is with that?" Sorrel said, glaring at the sky. "Are freak thunderstorms normal here?"

"Er," the wizard said again, clutching his robe around his fiddly bits. "I'm not hurt but…"

Vola tossed her belt knife to Sorrel, who caught it deftly. The halfling scampered up the tree, swung from one arm, and chopped the vine holding the wizard.

He plummeted to the earth with a squelch.

Vola turned to her party and jerked her head toward the east. "Let's go. We still have an entire day to get to the tor."

"Wait," Braydon said. When she turned back, she caught a calculating look on his face before he plastered on a pleasant smile.

"What?" she snapped.

He held up his hands. "I can see you really do just want to help people. There was someone who needed some help. That way." He waved to the south. "Some sort of merchant who got lost in the swamp. Huron saw him this morning just before the plants attacked. We don't have time to help him, but…"

He held out a palm as if to let her finish the thought for him. He grinned wide and sickening. "Would you do it for us?"

Vola tried to decide if this was some sort of trick, then realized *of course* it was a trick. He knew she had to help anyone who asked. He knew it would slow her down.

But just because she knew he was doing it deliberately didn't mean she could ignore him.

Braydon must have seen something in her eyes because his smile grew wider and he barked an order at his party. They packed up and left, the wizard tugging his robe straight again and the woman limping.

At the edge of the clearing, the other ranger glanced back at them and nodded, either as thanks or good luck Vola couldn't tell and didn't care.

"We don't actually believe him," Lillie said. "Do we?"

Vola paced from one end of the clearing to the other, kicking a dead blossom out of her way. The part that stung the worst was the way he'd smiled. He had her pegged, and he knew it. Vola knew it, too.

"I still don't know why we helped him," Sorrel said with a sullen frown that did not sit well on her cheerful face. "He's just going to think he can keep walking all over us."

"Like feeding a troll," Talon said. "They just get bigger and meaner."

"Would everyone just stop." Vola paused in the middle of the clearing, breathing hard. She couldn't make her decision with all the outside voices muddying up her mind.

Henri waited, leaning against a tree, arms crossed, scarred shield laying at his feet.

Vola didn't mean to stare. But watching Henri always steadied her.

"We helped him because we had to," she said. "The way we have to help this merchant."

"What?" Sorrel said.

"We're believing him?" Lillie asked.

Talon just watched.

"Look, a paladin can't take the time to choose between good for one person and good for another. If Braydon is going up the tor to find the missing townsfolk, then we can take the time to help someone else."

Sorrel glanced at Lillie. "Yeah, but—"

"Look, do we want to be people like them?" Vola gestured west after Braydon's party. "Or do we want to be people that do the right thing?" Vola drew herself up and met Sorrel's eyes, then Lillie's. Then she looked in Talon's direction, hoping the ranger was paying attention.

Sorrel sighed. "Well, when you put it that way…"

"Lead on, Miss Volagra," Lillie said. "We will follow."

Talon's hood nodded.

Vola's breath blew out. "Good. Great. Let's get this over with then."

"Hmm, sounds a lot less heroic now," Sorrel said.

# THIRTEEN

IT TURNED out Braydon hadn't been lying. Not far south of the clearing where they'd saved the other party, a cry for help threaded through the trees.

Between two large trees, a man in a ragged hat treaded water in a murky puddle. Vola could easily see how he'd fallen in. The green scum across the surface would look just like moss when the water was still. Right now, it was heaped in little wavelets while the man thrashed and clutched at the roots of the trees. Nearby on firm ground, a vaguely horse-like shape grazed, but Vola didn't have the attention to spare for the animal.

She stopped beside the tree, testing each footstep to be sure she wouldn't go for a swim, too, and poked her head around the trunk.

"Need some help?" she said.

"Ah!" the man cried, then he lost his grip and slid under the surface of the water. He came up spluttering several feet away. "Ack, pluh. Um, hello! Why yes, help would be lovely."

"Talon, hold my belt." Vola stepped to the biggest root she

could see and leaned over the water. Talon hooked a hand through the back of her waistband.

The man lunged and went underwater again before his fingers clutched Vola's. He slipped twice before she managed to grasp him around the wrist and pull.

With one yank, she hauled him out of the water and up onto the roots.

The breath left his lungs with an audible whoosh as he landed. He slipped and scrabbled across the roots to firm land.

There he collapsed into a wet heap against the limp grass. "Thank you," he said. "From the bottom of my heart." He pressed both palms to his chest.

"Er, right," Vola said. "You're welcome."

Henri stepped up, leading the horse-like creature by the reins.

The man lunged backward. "Ah!"

"You're kind of a jumpy fellow, aren't you?" Sorrel planted her hands on her hips.

"Yes, sorry." The man lurched to his feet and brushed off his knees. It didn't really help. His clothes were soaked through and stained with green. "Thank you again."

"What are you doing out here, Mister…?" Lillie trailed off.

He doffed his cap and bowed. "Redderick Ranser, at your service. I sell the finest horses west of the Firewall Mountains."

The four of them turned to look at the "horse" Henri had grabbed. They all tilted their heads in unison.

The beast looked like a sway-backed cross between a donkey and a swamp lizard with a head cold. Dull gray-green scales covered its body, and a viscous liquid dripped from its severe under-bite. Instead of a mane, it had a stiff crest of filmy skin that stood up a couple of inches from its neck and head. Claws instead of hooves flexed in the mud. It wheezed, then its tongue slithered out from between scaly lips to taste the air.

They all leaned back.

"Horses, huh?" Sorrel asked the salesman.

"Well, most of them got eaten by the swamp."

"Did the swamp spit this one back out?" Vola said.

Henri made kissy faces at the monster. "Aw, he's a big sweetheart."

The creature butted Henri with its broad head and made wet snuffling noises against his shirt. Henri chuckled and scratched it under the chin.

Redderick tapped his lip, and Vola noticed little scars criss-crossing his hands, some of them brand new. "I'll tell you what," he said. "I was headed back to town. How about I give you my last specimen? As a thank you for saving me."

"No, that's okay," Vola blurted.

"No, no. I insist. It's the least I can do. And if you're going to be traveling through the swamp, this newest breed is actually the perfect companion. Resilient to damage, easy to feed and water, it forages on its own, especially in its natural habitat. And..." He paused for dramatic effect. "It carries twice its own weight in gear. I'm practically giving it away."

"You *are* giving it away," Lillie said.

"All the better for you, then." He took Vola's hand and shook it vigorously. "Wonderful. I'm sure it will be very happy with you."

Vola frowned heavily. "I didn't say yes."

"But you didn't say no either."

"Yes, I did."

"What?" He held up a hand to his ears. "Sorry, can't hear you. I've got water in my ear." The creature swayed toward him, and he leaped out of the way. "Pleasure doing business with you," he said, an octave higher. "Thanks again for the help. I'll just be on my way then."

He trotted off in the opposite direction of Water's Edge and ran into a tree that spun him around. He righted himself, glancing up at the branches in surprise, then disappeared between the trunks, still dripping.

They heard a splash and a yelp.

Henri sighed. "I'd better go guide him back to town," he said and passed Vola the reins.

"What?" she said. "You're leaving?" Her safety net! After the last two days it was looking less hypothetical and more inevitable that she would need him.

"It's either that or you're just going to have to backtrack to pull him out of the swamp again," Henri said. "This way you can keep heading toward the tor. I'll catch up when he's safe on the path back home."

And then he slung his shield over his shoulder and strode off toward the sounds of splashing.

Vola started to protest and then thought better of it. She was supposed to be leading this quest by herself, anyway. That was the whole point. The final test. If she was too scared to let Henri out of her sight, then she wasn't ready to be a paladin at all.

She squared her shoulders. "Right," she said. "Let's get this… guy loaded up and move out."

They each surveyed the swamp…horse…thing and hesitated. No one volunteered to load it up.

Vola had been waiting for a chance to buy a real mount for ages. But this thing was quite a bit different from the picture in her mind.

"What exactly is it?" Lillie asked, her nose scrunched in disgust.

Vola hoped that the smell was only temporary. "It's a mount," she said. "That's all that matters. It will carry our equipment. Or us, if anyone gets injured."

"I'd rather not get that close to it if it's all the same to you," Lillie said.

"Did that salesman seem a little anxious to get rid of it to you guys?" Sorrel asked, hands on hips as she examined the...mount.

"Talon, do you have any ideas?" The ranger had tamed a wolf after all.

"There is no creature I cannot commune with."

"All right, then, commune," Vola said.

The hooded figure stepped up to the swamp creature and bent to look it in the eyes.

"Is anything happening?" Sorrel asked after a moment.

Talon straightened. "There is one creature I can't commune with."

"Maybe it grows on you eventually," Lillie said.

"Like a fungus," Sorrel added.

Vola rolled her eyes at her own hesitance. "We're wasting precious time. Come on, maybe we can still beat Braydon's group to the tor."

She slung the pack over the back of the swamp beast, who narrowed its eyes and hissed at her. "Better you than me," she told it.

She just hoped the damn thing didn't slow them down in getting to the tor. It didn't exactly look fast. She chewed her thumbnail while she examined it. It didn't look fast, but it did look...swampy. With its scales and crest and teeth, it looked like the unfortunate offspring of a mule and a crocodile. Maybe it took after the crocodile half more strongly.

She draped the lead rope over the back of the creature's neck so it wouldn't get immediately tangled and gave it a slap on the rump. "Go on. Find us a way through the swamp."

"What are you doing?" Sorrel asked.

"I think it might know a better way through the swamp than us. No offense, Talon."

"I'm not the one who's been wet this whole time," Talon said with little inflection.

"Why risk ourselves," Vola gestured between them, "when that thing can do the scouting for us? And this way I can take point and Talon can guard our rear."

"Finally, a good plan," Talon said. "I will send Gruff to guard our flanks."

They stood and watched as the creature meandered from tuft of grass to tuft of grass, nibbling some leaves here, turning to glare at them there.

"Aw, the poor thing," Lillie said. "It doesn't know where it's going."

"I don't think it's a poor anything," Sorrel said. "Although you might be right about the second part. I don't think it's going to be a very good guide, Vola."

"Actually," Vola said, watching. "Look. It might not be going in a straight line, but it hasn't fallen into the water yet. Come on. Follow its footsteps. Don't stray from the path it's laid out."

Vola put her words into action and followed the swamp beast, carefully jumping from tuft to tuft. Slower, but much drier, they made their way in the direction of the tor.

# FOURTEEN

Vola followed the swamp beast carefully, easily stepping between the islands of dry land. Behind her, Sorrel swung her arms and hopped, like a gangly frog dressed in a kilted-up shirt. Even Lillie got through the swamp with relatively little splashing. Talon kept their bow ready, hood swinging back and forth in a vigilant arc.

In the distance, the tor actually seemed to be getting closer. Finally.

A short, sharp bark sounded from the right, and Talon's hood jerked up.

"Wait," they said.

Vola ground to a stop and jerked upright, hand on her sword.

"What is it?"

"Ambush," Talon said.

An arrow streaked out of the forest and struck Talon's shoulder. They went down with a cry.

"Shi—crap!" Vola said. She spun, trying to pinpoint the direction of the enemy.

"Talon," Lillie called and threw herself on her knees beside the fallen ranger. She reached out and grasped Talon's shoulder, and a bright light flashed from her hand, washing over the prone figure.

This time, a volley of arrows came from the trees. One bounced off Lillie's shield while another skidded off Vola's armored leg.

Sorrel rushed for the trees at the same time as Vola, but she skidded to a stop and looked back at Lillie and Talon on the ground.

Vola didn't hesitate. She splashed and slipped through slimy mud and shallow puddles crusted with algae and hit the trees running. There, behind the first line of trunks, she found three black-clad figures, masked and armed. All three dropped their bows when they saw her coming and drew their swords.

She hit them with a clash, roaring as she ducked her shoulder and heaved the first one off his feet.

She brought her blade up in a sweeping undercut that caught one of the attackers across the chest. He went down and flickered.

Vola hesitated. That looked just like…

The illusion dropped away, leaving a large man-shaped ball of waxy mud. Just like in town. Except this one didn't fall apart immediately. It shook its lumpy head and rolled to its feet before lurching for Vola again.

"Uh oh." She ducked away. The other two tried closing in on her, wobbling forward with a clumsy sort of relentlessness.

Vola side-stepped, slipped in a puddle, and righted herself to take the mud man's leg off at the hip. It paused and groaned in its weird wordless voice, then toppled to the ground where it tried to crawl across the grass for her.

"Ew." She stepped forward and lopped off the lump she assumed was its head. Finally, it stopped moving, then sagged into a pile of mud.

"All right, easy enough."

Timing her strokes to take advantage of their jerky movement, she hacked at the other two, removing their lumpy heads until nothing remained of the attackers except a squishy pile of mud.

Vola wiped her brow and examined her blade. That hadn't been the worst fight in her life, but instead of blood, dirt covered her sword.

A cry threaded through the trees and her stomach dropped. Sorrel and the others.

Vola lunged back the way she'd come, dodging puddles and tree trunks, praying as she ran the short distance back to where she'd left them. "Please be okay, please be okay."

Between the trees, Lillie knelt beside Talon, shooting little fireballs at one assassin, covering Talon while the ranger rolled to their feet and drew a long knife with their good hand. Their other arm hung limp at their side. Sorrel faced off against two at once while Gruff hung from the arm of another, growling and snarling.

Through the chaos, Vola glimpsed their swamp monster placidly chewing on a long strand of algae, watching the proceedings with a disinterested eye.

Vola sprinted for one of Sorrel's opponents. She leaped and brought her sword down on the enemy's head, cleaving it in two. The lumpy halves fell away from each other with a squelchy thud.

Lillie screamed short and sharp and then gulped. "Oh," she said.

"They're mud, just like the ones in the town. Take their heads off and they melt."

Sorrel nodded, eyes wide, then planted her staff in the soft ground, swung around, and used it to kick the other attacker in the face. Its head snapped back and then snapped off.

The whole figure fell to the ground and slumped into a harmless pile.

"Neat," Sorrel said. Then she pulled her staff from the ground and turned to face the attacker Lillie shot fireballs at. But Talon got there first.

The ranger blocked a blow, ducked, and came up under the attacker's guard. Then swung their knife to lodge firmly in the creation's ear. It lurched to a stop and swayed a moment. Talon planted a foot in its gut and wrenched the knife around, twisting the construct's head right off its shoulders.

Gruff finished his off with a malicious growl while the swamp beast just stood there and chewed.

Vola caught her breath and held a hand out to Lillie. But the wizard knelt in the mud to examine the remains of the constructs.

"This was the same magic that made the illusions in town," she said. "Covering up the same simulacra."

"Almost the same," Sorrel said. "These didn't break apart the moment the illusion was dispelled. They fought on."

"Yes, they are better constructed." Lillie pointed out the sticks that served as primitive bones threading through the mud.

"Great," Vola said. "Now they're stronger. And they're trying to keep us from getting to the to—"

Fire spouted through the trees, a rolling, roaring wave that made them all leap for cover.

"What the…" Sorrel said. "I thought we got rid of them all."

"The spell caster is nearby," Lillie called from the trunk where she'd taken refuge. "The one controlling these golems. I'll bet there's a limit to how far those things can go before they break down."

"Can you pinpoint him?" Vola flinched as another gout of flames hit her tree, making it shudder.

Lillie's lips thinned. "I'll try."

She twisted her hands and mumbled a spell. Bright points of light sprang up, scattered around them, and Vola's breath caught. They were surrounded.

"Don't move," Lillie called. "I don't think those are real."

"What?"

"I think he's using more illusions. The fire blasts are all coming from the other side."

Vola peeked around her tree trunk. Lillie was right. The scorch marks were all on that side. But which of the five points of magic was the bad guy?

"Where is he?"

"I don't know," she said, face pulled in misery. "The spell only detects magic."

"And it's all magic. Great, do you have any more useless spells?"

Another blast hit the ground between them. Lillie screamed and covered her head with her arms.

"Are you all right?" Vola called.

"No!"

"Neither are we," Sorrel called from where she hid with Talon. The ranger slumped against the trunk, arrow still sticking from their shoulder.

Vola rested her forehead against the rough bark of the tree trunk. Rushing across and randomly picking one of the points of light would only get her killed. But staying here would get them all incinerated. She thunked her head against the trunk. She was out of brilliant ideas.

Which meant she had exactly one last option.

"Lady," she said under her breath. "Lady, I need help."

A breeze picked up, shushing through the leaves above them and brushing Vola's cheek.

A voice came out of the wind. "Are you going to keep denying me?"

"Who was that?" Lillie asked.

"I don't deny you," Vola whispered.

"You avoid my name. You hide me from yourself and from everyone else." This time the voice sounded like the sharp ring of metal against metal.

Vola squeezed her eyes closed, her fingers gripping the bark of the tree. It was true.

"Is someone there?" Sorrel called.

Another blast of fire answered her, making her yelp and cover Talon's body with her own.

"It is your choice, Vola. I already made mine."

The third bright spot from the left lit up like a torch in the night, sending out sprays of light.

"That one!" Vola called.

Lillie leaned around her tree, spread her hands, and three hot white flashes flew from her fingers to strike the tree their attacker was using for cover. The enemy ducked back to avoid the sparks.

Taking the opportunity, Vola lunged around her tree and sprinted for the enemy.

Just as she drew up to the trunk, a masked man leaned around as if the shoot off another spell.

Vola roared and swung her blade. He squeaked and dodged right so Vola's sword cut into the tree instead of him. She yanked the blade free and kicked his knee.

He grunted, and she swung one last time to cut him down. He collapsed on the roots.

"Oh, great," Sorrel said behind her. Vola heaved in a breath and turned to see the halfling trying to support the ranger across the intervening space while Lillie followed hands ready with a spell. "We could have kept him alive for questioning."

"I..." Vola started. "I didn't think about that. I'm sorry."

Sorrel shrugged. "I'm not sure I'd know how to go about interrogating someone, anyway."

"Talk incessantly until they give in?" Talon said.

Sorrel glared up at the ranger. "I'm the one holding you up, you know. What happens if I just walk away?"

"Did anyone else hear a voice?" Lillie said. "It was like

someone speaking out of thin air. And I think they lit up the real attacker so we could find him."

The breeze came out of nowhere and touched Vola's cheek, raising goosebumps. The others straightened. Lillie frowned up at the shivering leaves.

Vola sighed. "That would be my lady, Cleavah." Vola noticed the blood dripping from the arrow in Talon's shoulder and stepped forward to examine the wound. "My goddess."

"Oh," Lillie said, mouth round.

"As in Cleavah, goddess of vengeful housewives?" Sorrel said.

"Wasn't that the goddess Becky followed?" Lillie said. "I'll admit I thought she was praying to some kind of kitchen utensil."

"Cleavah," Vola said with a fierce frown. "It's only coincidence that it sounds like cleaver."

"And not because it's the favorite weapon of her followers," Sorrel said, peering around as if waiting for the Lesser Virtue to step out from behind a tree.

Vola gave her a quelling look before turning back to Talon. "Definitely not. And Cleavah is pretty selective about her followers."

"You have to be a housewife," Sorrel said. "And vengeful."

"Or, I have to choose you," the voice said in the rush of the wind.

A hand gripped Vola's shoulder, feeling like strong slender fingers.

Lillie gasped, eyes wide, and Sorrel pulled herself up as if at attention.

Vola didn't bother turning to look. It always felt like her goddess stood at her shoulder, just a breath away. But Vola had never been able to see her. She'd tried but Cleavah never chose to manifest for her.

Vola's shoulders hunched. Might have something to do with the way Vola never chose to talk about her.

"You have work to do, Vola," Cleavah whispered in Vola's ear, then the hand was removed and the breeze died, leaving only still air.

Lillie's hands crept up to cover her mouth. "I've never met a goddess before. Is that usual? My family was never very religious."

"It's pretty unusual for those of us who are, too," Sorrel said. "Maxim's never dropped in for dinner, for example."

"What did she mean, you have work?" Talon said.

"This," Vola said, and touched the arrow shaft. "Healing it will be easier without the hood." The ranger had kept it up through the whole fight. From this distance, Vola would have thought she'd be able to make out some features, but not in the near-dark under the trees.

Talon's good hand flew to the edge of the hood as if to keep Vola from ripping it away. "No," they said, voice going higher than usual.

Gruff whined and padded forward to brace against Talon's legs.

"You know you don't have to hide from us," Vola said, trying to soften her normal growl.

"Like you hid who you work for?"

Heat beat in Vola's cheeks. "That's different."

"I'm not sure it is." Talon hesitated before shaking their head. "It's easier this way. Less questions."

"Will you answer one question?" Lillie said. "Just one?"

"Not if it's about my hood."

Lillie's gaze never wavered. "It's not. Would you prefer to be known as a male or a female?"

Sorrel smacked her forehead, but Vola raised her eyebrows. Lillie might be a klutz but she did not lack for any bravery.

Vola was close enough to Talon to catch the ranger's gasp.

"We didn't want to assume," Lillie said.

Talon hesitated, shadowed eyes glancing between the three of them. "You didn't?"

Sorrel shrugged. "For most people, it's not a question. You pick one or the other and there you go."

"Not all the time," Lillie said. "Some cultures have more than two genders. The Empire in the east has thirty-six different identities to choose from."

"Thirty-six?" Talon said, and Vola got the impression they were a bit dazed. Either by the number or the conversation.

"Maybe we should narrow that down," Vola murmured.

"If neither male nor female are comfortable," Lillie said. "May we call you they? Or them?"

"That…fits better than anything else right now," Talon said.

"Easy enough," Vola said. "Now, hold still. This will hurt."

She snapped the arrow shaft in half, yanked it through as quickly as she could, and slapped her hand over the wound. "Lady bless."

Light flared and Talon's flesh knitted while heat speared through Vola's shoulder. She concentrated on breathing through her nose as the healing wave surged through her body. Through the rent in Talon's cowl, their skin went pink and puckered, but healthy.

"That's…that's all I'm going to be good for for a while," Vola said as the world wavered. "How do you feel?" she asked Talon.

The ranger cautiously flexed their arm and shoulder. They shook their head. "I won't be drawing a bow anymore tonight."

Vola glanced at the others.

Lillie winced. "I won't be much use for anything big."

Sorrel stretched her arms over her head. "I'll be fine with some rest."

Vola nodded decisively. "We'll camp here then. We'll be safe enough now that we've cleared out the assassins."

"Is that what he was?" Lillie asked. "Another assassin?"

Sorrel knelt beside the body. The golems were already sinking into the muck of the swamp. "He's dressed the same as the one that attacked Lord Arthorel. And he used the same magic, didn't he?"

Lillie nodded.

"I think it's safe to say we're getting close enough that the kidnappers don't want us coming any closer," Vola said. "Unless the rest of you are expecting assassins to show up for you someday."

"Anyone coming after me will not bother to hide their identity," Lillie said, indicating the man's mask.

Vola blinked at Lillie, but before she could ask for details, the wizard shook herself.

"Should we…er…loot the body?" Lillie said. "Isn't that a thing people do?"

Vola and Sorrel both gave her a grimacing look.

"Ew, no," Sorrel said. "What sort of books have you been reading?"

Lillie held up her hands in defense. "I just meant, perhaps he has something we can use."

Vola hesitated. "I guess we should see if he has anything to tell us who the kidnappers are. What they're doing here."

Sorrel made another face. "If you say so."

When no one moved, she rolled her eyes. "Oh, you meant me."

"I mean, not specifically," Vola said. "But if you're volunteering…"

"Bleh." Sorrel knelt beside the body and gingerly took his sleeve between two fingers. Her face twisted in several iterations of disgust as she rifled through his clothes. "Ew, ew, ew."

"It's just a dead body," Vola said. "You should be making plenty of these if you're doing your job right."

"That doesn't mean I want to play around with them afterward. And I don't see you doing any looting either."

After a moment of grimacing, Sorrel looked up at them again. "What exactly am I looking for, anyway?"

Lillie and Vola looked at each other.

"Um, gold?" Lillie said.

"Armor, weapons, things we can sell," Vola said. Then after a moment's thought, added, "And written orders. Something that tells us who they are and what they're doing here. That would be very convenient."

"Too convenient," Sorrel said, removing her hand from the dead man's clothes. "Yuck. He's got nothing. Come to think of it, isn't that a little unusual? Shouldn't he have something in his pockets? A firestarter? Or dice? Even some lint?"

"Maybe he didn't want anything to lead back to his leader in case he was caught or killed," Vola said. "Let's just roll him off to the side."

Talon snorted and went to set up the tent.

Lillie and Sorrel gingerly took care of the body while Talon finished pulling the tent cords taut. Vola took charge of the swamp creature since Talon was busy. It stood placidly munching on something that crunched. The fight didn't seem to have bothered it in the least.

Vola reached for the lead rope dangling over the back of its neck, and it lunged, jaw snapping inches from her hand.

"Ah!" She yanked herself back.

The beast eyed her balefully. If she looked closely, Vola could swear she saw two pinpricks of red whirling deep in its black eyes.

"Listen, you. I'm a lot bigger and meaner than you. If you want this to work out, you'd better not bite the hand that feeds you." She glared at it.

It seemed to subside for the moment, and Vola grabbed the

lead rope without a problem. She turned to tie it to one of the tent stakes so it wouldn't wander off in the night.

As she walked away, the beast's narrow head snaked back and then lashed forward, teeth closing on Vola's rear end.

"Ouch!"

She leaped forward clapping her hands to her butt.

The beast munched contentedly, probably eating a piece of her. She rubbed her rear end. Her chain mail didn't quite come down far enough to cover the giant hole in her pants.

"You were definitely not worth it. And we got you for free."

No one had the wherewithal that night to light a fire and cook dinner. Inside the tent, Lillie passed out strips of dried meat and Becky's bread, which was going stale on one side and growing mold on the other.

"I think that swamp thing is secretly evil," Vola said, pulling her chain mail up and twisting around to get a good look at the hole in her trousers.

Talon already snored in the corner.

"What do you mean secretly?" Sorrel said.

Lillie's mouth dropped open. "It can't be that bad," she said. "No creature is inherently evil."

"That one is," Vola said.

"Most creatures just need to be shown a little love and they'll blossom. What if we give it a name?"

"You think that's going to make it not evil?" Sorrel said.

"What about Frank?" Lillie said.

"What about Floppy?"

"What's floppy about it?"

Vola finished piling her armor in the corner and fell into her bedroll. She didn't remember anything after that.

# FIFTEEN

Vola came awake suddenly with the complete and gut-sinking knowledge that she'd forgotten to set a watch.

Sludgy water climbed up her body, and she splashed to a sitting position.

"Holy—" The tent was already half a foot deep in water and it seemed to be rising rapidly.

"Wake up!" She reached across to shake Talon with one hand and Sorrel with the other. Lillie snored and rolled over, her hair floating around her head like some sort of poetic damsel in distress.

"Wake up, we're sinking!"

Talon sat up as swiftly as Vola had and was instantly on their feet.

Sorrel gasped, and in the process, sucked in a mouthful of water. She sputtered and choked, and her flailing woke up Lillie.

"What's happening?" the wizard said, rubbing her eyes. Then she blinked down at her wet hands.

"Get up," Vola yelled while she slapped Sorrel on the back. "Get out, we're sinking."

Lillie scrambled for the tent flap, but it was only as she reached for it that Vola realized that was where most of the water was coming from.

"No, wait!"

Too late, Lillie pulled back the tent flap and cried out as a wave of sludge and mud cascaded into the tent. The water level outside was much higher than in. In the back of her mind, Vola was impressed the cheap tent hadn't just collapsed against the onslaught of the swamp, but the front of her mind was screaming, "we're gonna drown in a tent! I don't wanna drown in a tent!"

"Swim for it," Vola said.

Talon was the first one out. They pushed through the rapidly rising mud and kicked out like a diver. Their booted feet disappeared in the torrent, and Vola could only hope that they'd managed to find clear air.

Vola tried to stand, but the canvas shifted and slid under her feet and she feared she was just pushing them further down.

"Now, Lillie!"

Lillie dove for the flap with a grimace and shoved at the mud. Vola set her shoulder against the wizard's wide rump, giving her a good shove before her feet disappeared, too.

The muddy water reached Vola's waist now, and she turned to see Sorrel clinging halfway up the tent pole to keep her head out of the water.

"I'll give you a boost," she said and grabbed the halfling around the middle.

"I can swim, you know," Sorrel said indignantly.

"Then swim for your life."

She shoved the halfling out of the flap with a squelch.

Then she took a deep breath, closed her eyes, and followed.

She paddled like a dog and kicked her bare feet. The mud pressed into her on all sides, squeezing her chest, making her limbs and movements sluggish.

Two seconds out of the tent, she panicked, forgetting which way was up and which way was down. There was nothing firm beneath her feet, and there were no lights or bubbles to swim for.

She flailed.

Something sharp and strong closed around her wrist and she fought to grab hold of it. A tug yanked her arm free of the mud and hope surged through her, hot and wild. She kicked again, hard, and her head surfaced with a noisy slurp.

She sucked in air as whatever had hold of her pulled on her arm. For a split second she thought maybe the swamp monster had come to save her. But no, it was Gruff with his teeth latched around her wrist as he yanked her from the swamp like a giant chew toy.

She floundered onto dry land and blinked the mud out of her eyes. Sorrel and Lillie coughed from their hands and knees. Sorrel's borrowed shirt hung from her thin frame and Lillie's perfect hair hung in brown, dripping strings.

Talon stood next to them, hands on their hips, staring at the sinkhole they'd just escaped.

Vola concentrated on getting air in and out of her lungs as she stared. In and out. In and out.

A muddy pond, murky and bottomless stood where their campsite had been. Rising out of the very center was the peak of their sad tent.

"Oh my gods," Lillie said. "We almost drowned in a tent."

"It's tides," Talon said. "I'd bet anything. Ground that seems firm in the evening floods and goes all mushy in the middle of the night." They looked over at Vola.

Vola shuddered and tried to push down the feeling that the swamp was trying to eat them.

The swamp beast stood beside a couple of trees, its tether broken. Over head, stars winked at them cheekily.

There was really only one thing for them to do in the middle of the night with their gear buried in mud. They dug. Carefully. They used what was left of the swamp monster's lead rope as a lifeline, and Vola dove through mud and water—mostly mud—to reach the tent. Sorrel volunteered since she was the smallest but Vola overruled her as the strongest.

Lillie stood on the edge of the sinkhole with a brilliant bursting ball of light, illuminating the process. Sorrel took the recovered gear from Vola as she dove over and over into that dark pit. Talon laid the soaked gear out, hoping to dry it out enough to brush the mud off.

In the end, Vola found her chain mail shirt, Sorrel's old clothes, Lillie's spell book, and one and a half pairs of boots. Talon had slept in theirs. So now Vola was stuck with only one boot, and Sorrel had no sandals.

The food was gone. The tent was gone. The bedrolls were gone. Vola refused to give up until she'd found the weapons, but even though she recovered her sword and Sorrel's staff, Talon's bow was waterlogged and the quiver was a lost cause.

They raced against time. As the sun rose, the water stopped flowing into the sinkhole and the ground grew firmer and firmer. Vola finally pulled herself out with the last of her strength as the water turned to mud and the mud turned to ground.

They all sat beside the recovered gear, watching the peak of the tent slowly dry into position as the sun turned the sky pink and orange. Soon enough the ground was firm enough that Sorrel could walk over and kick the peak of the tent.

Then she collapsed on the ground and just sat. Vola, Lillie, and Talon watched.

That was where Henri found them. From the amount of light in the sky, Vola guessed it was nearly midmorning.

He stood between two trees and surveyed the scene, taking in their bedraggled and muddy appearances, the ruined gear lying in rows along the ground, and the top of the tent sticking up out of the mud.

Vola would have felt like a moron if there was room for anything in her besides exhaustion.

The swamp beast made a snuffling squeal and trotted up to Henri, laying its narrow head against his chest. Henri rubbed the foul beast between the ears, and it moaned with pleasure.

Then Henri planted his fists on his hips with a quirky grin that made Vola want to punch him.

"Looks like a lively night. Are we ready to leave yet?"

# SIXTEEN

Just after noon, the five of them—plus one swamp beast—trudged up the side of the tor. The hill itself rose straight up from the swamp like a stick stuck in the mud. Or like the top of their tent from a puddle.

A treacherous trail wound around the tor, leading eventually to the ruins at the peak. Vola led the bedraggled group, her chain mail grating over top of her mud-encrusted shirt. Sorrel wore her tunic again, now stained with sap and algae and mud. Lillie had tied her hair into a muddy knot at the base of her neck, and Talon had slung their bow across their back and now carried their knives.

Henri brought up the rear, whistling through his teeth as the swamp beast trotted happily beside him.

At the top of the path, Vola slowed and waved the others into silence. Big, square-cut boulders and fallen masonry littered the steep incline around them as if the tower or fort on top of the tor had just given in to gravity and finally toppled over.

Vola squeezed behind a boulder. "Quietly. I don't want anyone to know we're here yet." Especially since it looked like they might have beaten Braydon.

Lillie promptly sneezed.

"Shhh," Sorrel said.

"I'm sorry," Lillie whispered and wiped her streaming nose. "I think I'm allergic to whatever is growing on me."

Ahead of them, walls tumbled across the path creating a maze of white stone glinting in the sunlight.

"Is this it?" Sorrel whispered by Vola's shoulder as they crouched behind a block of stone. "The lair of the bad guy?"

Vola's brow drew down in a heavy frown. After days of battling everything from carnivorous flowers to invisible assassins to the swamp itself, Vola was ready to kill this kidnapper and crawl home. Rage clawed its way through the exhaustion, making her fists curl against the rough stone. Normally, the anger that simmered in the orc half of her was something she kept carefully tamed and controlled.

Today, she welcomed it. She'd never get through this fight without it. And it was going to be a good fight, she'd make sure of it.

"Expect more golems," she said. "And spell casters. Maybe illusions. And keep an eye out for the prisoners. Hopefully, this is the end of the line, and we can all go home after this. Talon, Sorrel. How does the approach look? Can you guys go in from the sides to flank them?"

Sorrel poked her head over the boulder and squinted, but Talon shook their head. "Too exposed. We'd lose the element of surprise."

Vola set her mouth in a hard line. "Straight up the middle, then."

"Good," Sorrel said. "Let's end this."

"I'm ready," Lillie said.

Vola eyed her. "Whatever you do, just don't hit us."

Lillie glared.

"Gruff and I will go for the walls," Talon said. "We'll jump them when we hear fighting."

"Henri, fill in as needed," Vola said. "Go."

"Don't you mean charge?" Sorrel asked.

Vola growled and vaulted the stone that hid them, Sorrel a second behind her.

*Yes*, something inside her cried. It was good to be on the attack, finally.

Vola sprinted to the wall, around the end tumbled by weather and time, and fetched up with her back against the masonry. Too many walls, too maze-like. She couldn't see. She had to listen.

Something shuffled on the other side of the wall, sounding like leather on stone. There was the shing of a blade being drawn.

Vola spared a glance at Sorrel to be sure she followed, then pushed herself off the wall.

She rushed around the corner, roaring at the top of her lungs, sword drawn back for a blow.

The battle cry of a war orc had never failed to strike fear into the hearts of the enemy. And it didn't fail now.

The bent figure on the other side of the wall shrieked and grabbed up a glass flask. Then she threw it against the ground where it shattered, sending glass shards skittering across the floor.

A billow of smoke rose from the scattered glass, and Vola charged headfirst into it.

She coughed and staggered, the smoke making her lungs burn and her eyes water. She swept her blade in an arc, trying to find the enemy, but it just swooshed through the air making the smoke eddy.

Somewhere behind her, Sorrel yelled and coughed and gagged, and Vola heard a bright clang as something struck the stone floor.

The black smoke cleared just enough Vola could make out a figure at the other end of the room. She held her breath this time as she charged.

About five feet away, Vola realized she was charging an old woman. She tried to stop and managed to trip over her own feet and run shoulder first into a crooked wall.

"Ouch." She pushed herself upright and faced the woman as the cloud dissipated. "Where are the kidnappers?"

"What kidnappers?" she said, voice pitched to be heard for miles. "There aren't any kidnappers here."

"Then why did you attack us?"

The woman threw her arms in the air, making her patchwork dress swish. "You charged into my home, screaming and waving a sword around. What did you expect me to do?"

Vola dragged in deep breaths of clean air, pushing back the red that crowded her vision. "I'm sorry—"

"You should be sorry," the woman shrieked. "Scaring the crap out of me like that."

She straightened up with a sniff and tugged her dress straight. It was a patchwork of scraps sewn together with meticulous stitches. Blues and greens and browns arranged in an oddly pretty spiral. The woman wore her bright white hair in a long neat braid, a stark contrast to Vola's black braid which had mud and twigs sticking out of it at the moment.

The last of the smoke cleared from the room, and Sorrel appeared, facing the wall, a dented copper basin rolling at her feet.

"How would you like it if I were to try to kill you?" the woman said.

"We're not killing you—"

"Who are we not killing?" Lillie said, appearing around the same corner Vola and Sorrel had charged around a moment before.

"Me," the old woman said. "Astrid, if anyone cares. You're not killing Astrid."

"Where are they?" Vola cried. "The townspeople. The kidnappers. The assassins."

Sorrel gave Vola a quelling look and held out her free hand.

Vola grimaced and swiped her forehead with her sleeve. The rage still pulsed under her skin, tinging her vision red, and she concentrated on pushing it down.

*Not now*, she told it.

*When?*

*I don't know, but you'll be the first to know.*

"Astrid, we're really very sorry," Sorrel was saying. "We're tracking down some missing people."

"You see any townsfolk here? Or kidnappers? No. Now get out of my house."

"Please, if we could just ask you some questions," Sorrel said.

"No! I'm not dressed for company."

Talon poked their head over the wall.

Vola fought the urge to retreat in the face of the woman's hostility. "We've already apologized—"

"You think that half-assed 'sorry' makes it all better? I said get—"

"Is everything all right?" Henri said, stepping into the room.

"I—oh…" Astrid said, staring at Henri. She tucked a bit of hair behind her ear. "Er, hello."

Henri's eyes brightened, and he gave her a little nod. "Ma'am."

Vola paced, letting the nervous energy play itself out. She needed to hit something but there was no one to hit.

Astrid's eyes drifted from Henri to Vola and then to Sorrel. She sighed. "All right, what kidnappers are you all talking about?"

"There have been kidnappings in Water's Edge," Sorrel said. "Lord Arthorel pointed us here."

"And you listened to him?" Astrid made a face. "Pfft, that man has been trying to get me off this land for years. He wants to sell it. He's broke as an old brick layer's back."

Vola stopped pacing. "He lied to us?"

"Guess that depends on what he told you."

"You don't know anything about the kidnappings?"

"Nope."

Then they'd been following the wrong lead the whole time. The stuffed rabbit hung limp and forlorn from Vola's belt.

The kidnappers were still out there. And so were all the victims.

Vola's legs went out from under her, and she collapsed against the wall.

# SEVENTEEN

"You might as well make yourselves at home," Astrid said. "I was just making some tea." She tilted her chin back to study Talon, who sat on top of her wall. "Would you like to come down, too? Or are you comfy up there?"

Talon's hood shifted as if surprised. "I'm comfy."

Astrid shrugged and bustled around the space which, now that Vola took a moment to glance around, was obviously her home.

Cozy rugs covered well-swept flagstones and handmade curtains hung from the crooked walls. The room was open to the sky, but Vola could see the appeal in that, too.

She rubbed her hands down her face. Gods, what were they supposed to do now?

Sorrel stepped across to stand beside her. "You all right?" she asked under her breath.

Vola straightened, the last of the rage-fueled energy draining from her limbs, leaving exhaustion in its wake.

"I'm fine," she said. She had to be. Too many feelings crowded under her skin. She couldn't handle them all at once so she shoved them aside and focused on Sorrel's concerned expression and the domestic noises coming from the old woman.

Astrid reached for the mismatched teacups that lined one of her shelves, and Henri stepped forward to pull them down for her.

She gave him a sweet smile. "Why thank you, sir."

"Henri," Henri said.

"Sir Henri."

He shook his head. "I train knights, I never claimed to be one."

"I like you even better, then," she said quietly.

Henri blushed to the roots of his hair.

Vola raised her eyebrows while Lillie hid a smile behind her hand.

"Sit," Astrid said, indicating the solid table pushed up against the wall.

Vola bit her lip, noting the precisely made bed and well-swept floor. "Thank you for the offer, but I uh, don't think we should." She held out her arm so the mud crusting her shirt was clearly visible.

Astrid frowned at the mess. "That's...surprisingly astute of you."

Vola bristled. "Why? Because I'm an orc?"

Astrid raised her eyebrows. "No, because you're a warrior. They don't tend to care about my furniture. Pick a spot to rest your rump. Everything gets washed down any time it rains anyways." She gestured to the open sky.

Vola sighed and planted herself directly on the floor. Astrid might not care about mud on the furniture, but Vola's mother had raised her better.

"So Arthorel lied to us," Talon said from their perch on the wall. Gruff must be around somewhere, but Vola hadn't seen him since they'd charged in here.

"What exactly did he tell you?" Astrid said, handing a delicate cup to Vola and Sorrel each.

"We're looking for evidence of strange magic. He told us about the lights that appear over the tor at night," Vola said. "And we saw them our first night in the swamp."

"Well, that part's true enough." Astrid settled herself at the edge of her bed. "But the lights are a sign of divine magic. Not mortal. A god's weapon rested here for many years. Long enough for the divine to wear off a bit and stick around."

"Maxim's Warhammer!" Sorrel cried, leaping to her feet and splashing tea everywhere. "It's here."

"Was," Astrid corrected, eyes narrowing on the puddles around Sorrel's feet.

"What do you mean 'was?'" Sorrel said. "Where did it go?"

"Honey, I sold that thing years ago."

Sorrel's mouth dropped open. "You sold it?"

"What use did I have for a big stick that shoots a pretty light show? Although the divine energy hanging around this place does make my potions that much more potent, so I can't say I haven't benefited from it."

"A stick?" Lillie said, then eyed Sorrel. "I thought you said it was a warhammer."

"Half a warhammer." Sorrel subsided back onto her chair. "The head is back at the monastery. The shaft is the part that's missing."

"Not really missing. I have the receipt around somewhere. I think the man was from Brisbene."

Lillie reached across to place a hand on Sorrel's shoulder. "That means we can track it down, Miss Sorrel. You have another clue."

Sorrel nodded, but her gaze remained fixed on her hands, a little crease pulling between her brows.

Vola blew out her breath and rubbed her forehead. At least

Sorrel had a paper trail to follow. They'd struck a dead end here with the kidnappers. Run into it headlong.

Astrid clearly wasn't an illusion. The ones they'd come across so far weren't nearly so human-like.

She took a sip of her tea and a tingle spread through her chest and down her limbs, washing away the aches and the weariness, erasing the entire night of mud diving from her body.

Sorrel's rash had cleared entirely, and now that she was thinking about it, Lillie hadn't sneezed in ages.

Vola glanced down at her teacup and sniffed. The scent of mint filled her with calm, soothing strength.

"Well," Vola said. "You're clearly not our kidnapper, Astrid. You're not an illusionist. But you might be the best damn apothecary I've ever encountered."

A crack of lightning split the sky and struck the flagstones in front of Vola.

"Okay, what is with the freak lightning storms?" Sorrel said, glaring at the sky. "Is it more divine magic?"

"They do seem to be more frequent here," Lillie said, examining the scorch mark.

"Er, sorry." Vola raised her hand. "That's me. Cleavah doesn't really like it when I swear. She's pretty vocal about it."

"Huh," Sorrel said. "I'm starting to like having a god who doesn't care. Maxim's approach is much more hands-off."

"I wonder what she would do to you if you really let loose?" Lillie said with a gleam in her eye.

"We're not experimenting," Vola said.

"I'm ignoring the divine retribution for now," Astrid said. "Because that's freaky as hell. Why did you think I might be an illusionist?"

"The kidnapped people have all been replaced with illusions," Lillie said. "We thought the lights on the tor might have something to do with that magic."

"Huh." Astrid crossed her arms. "No wonder Lord Arthorel sent you out here then. He's the only illusionist in the area."

Vola sucked in a breath. "What?"

Astrid shrugged. "Not many of the locals know it. He likes to keep it quiet, but I know magic well enough when I see it. He's an illusionist."

Vola's jaw worked. "Then, he would have known your lights weren't illusions."

"He sent us in the wrong direction on purpose," Sorrel said.

Lillie bit her lip. "We don't know that for certain. He could… just be covering up the disappearances."

"What? So, he knows it's happening and isn't doing anything about it? I'm not sure how that's better."

The teacup cracked under Vola's grip. "Either way we can't let him get away with it. Shi—crap."

Talon leaned their head on their hand. "We're not getting paid, are we?"

# EIGHTEEN

ASTRID'S RUINS were made up of half a dozen little rooms formed by the maze of collapsed walls. She had a cistern to catch rainwater and they each got to stand under the spigot as she scrubbed them head to toe with what she called her "special mix." Vola wasn't exactly sure what was in it but when she stepped out of the water, she was squeaky clean and smelled like pie.

Another room held piles of clothes, shoes, jackets, vests, and everything else a person could wear except armor.

"People bring me things," Astrid said. "They can't usually pay for their potions with coin, so they bring me what they can afford to give away. And of course, I keep it. You never know when you're going to have to clothe a seven-foot tall orc." She held up a shirt and eyeballed Vola behind it.

"Half-orc," Vola said.

Astrid contemplated the shirt for a moment. "True," she said. "I guess the human half is as important as the orc half if both are the things that make you you."

"Do you mind that we're using your home as an observation post?" Here, they had the high ground. They could regroup and keep an eye on Arthorel's manor in the distance. The missing townspeople had to be somewhere nearby and maybe they could see them from here.

And somewhere out there, Braydon was still making his way to the tor based on Vola's direction.

"I guess company isn't all bad," Astrid said with a sly look at Henri, who was cleaning out her cistern while it was mostly empty.

Sorrel found a pair of sandals that fit in Astrid's hoard, and Vola squeezed her feet into a new pair of boots. Astrid dug out a quiver to replace Talon's lost arrows. And Lillie spent the afternoon drying out her spell book page by page and using a pen to re-ink the spells that were badly stained by mud.

Vola helped Astrid hang their laundry along the walls. She pulled dripping red petals from Lillie's pocket and grimaced.

"Just lay those out on the table," Astrid said. "They'll dry fine."

"Do you know what they are? A shopkeeper in town asked us to bring them in exchange for our gear."

"Did he now?" Astrid's grin wasn't very nice. "I know exactly what they are. I tell people they're my secret ingredient. That way I know when people are trying to undercut my prices."

Lillie glanced up, brow furrowed. "I take it they're not your secret ingredient. Are you sabotaging the competition?"

"Pfft, if someone who actually knows what they're doing comes to town, I would happily share my trade. They would also know better than to put crimson swamp blossoms in anything other than a laxative. This is just to take care of irresponsible shopkeepers who think they can do my job cheaper and faster than me. I suggest you give them to him and see what happens."

"Astrid, you are conniving and wicked and I love you," Lillie said, completely serious. "Will you teach me to make your tea?"

"As long as you promise not to sell my secrets."

Vola left them to it and went to see how Sorrel was doing with the swamp monster. Lillie had started calling the thing Millford, but the name wasn't sticking.

Sorrel led it around to the side of the tor and tied it to one of the fallen blocks. She tilted her head. "Should I try to feed it?"

They both examined the beast as it chewed menacingly on something crunchy. The only thing they'd actually seen it eat so far was a couple of turtles and a cook pot.

"Maybe see if Astrid has any scraps she wouldn't mind getting rid of," Vola said.

She turned back to the ruins, but a yelp made her spin.

Sorrel was rubbing her leg. "It bit me," she said. "Did you see it bite me?"

"Try to stay out of range."

As she stepped away, Sorrel muttered something about having short arms.

The sky was going pink and purple with sunset by the time Vola climbed the heights to join Talon where they sat at the very top of Astrid's ruins.

Vola plopped down on the broken edge of the wall and shaded her eyes with her hand. "Anything yet?"

"Seems normal," Talon said. "Some movement in town. Not much around the manor."

"Great." Waiting and watching were not things Vola's orc half were good at. Or the human half if she was being honest with herself.

Talon sat, still as a tree, Gruff perched beside them. Vola could imagine them hidden in the underbrush, stalking their prey with unending patience. Alone always. One ranger, one wolf.

"You said you knew what it was like to lose someone," Vola said. "And that's why you wanted to help. Who did you lose?"

Talon was quiet for so long, Vola wasn't sure they were ever going to answer. And honestly, that was okay. Silence with Talon didn't feel awkward like they were ignoring her. They could have been silently plotting to kill all of them, but Vola didn't think that would feel this soothing.

"My pack," Talon said, making Vola jump. The darkness thickened between their words. "The wolves who raised me. They were all killed. All except Gruff." They placed a hand on the big wolf's head.

"You…were raised by wolves." Literally?

"After my first family died. I have lost many people."

"I'm sorry. How did they die?"

"A dragon wiped out the forest where the pack lived. I wasn't there. I know they died, they must have died, but I never found them. Never learned what exactly happened."

Vola fell silent. She still had both parents and a host of relatives on the orc side. She hadn't seen them in a while, but that wasn't the same thing at all.

Behind them, she could make out the murmurs of conversation from Sorrel and Lillie. Henri's low chuckle answered Astrid's higher voice.

"I'm glad I had them for as long as I did," Talon said. "Humans aren't meant to be alone any more than wolves are. There should always be pack."

Vola glanced over at them. She would have described Talon as a loner. But really what did she know about them? Was it fair to call someone a loner if they were quiet and competent and just hadn't found their space yet? Were they looking for a new pack? Somewhere to belong?

Vola hadn't really thought of herself as a pack creature before. The paladin academy had been full of people who should have felt like family but never did. She'd always imagined herself riding away from them. Alone. Why did that thought make her sad, now?

A flare of light from the path lit up the distant shrubs and there was a thud that echoed through the tor. A garbled shout echoed up to them.

Vola stood and drew her sword, then cocked her head to listen.

She thought she heard a blade striking rock, and a yell of pain. Then much clearer and closer, she recognized Braydon's voice.

"Assassins!" he shouted. "Strike them down! They won't stop us now. Ahh!" The last bit died off with an alarming gurgle.

Vola growled, but only took a split second to decide what to do.

Talon was already moving.

"Sorrel, Lillie, to arms!" Vola cried. "Down the path. It's an ambush." And then she ran toward the sounds of fighting. It sounded like Braydon's party couldn't afford any delay.

Vola charged down the hill, voicing her war cry. Just past the bend, she found Braydon flat on his back, his hand clutched to his side. A masked assassin stood over top of him.

The assassin raised his blade to finish the job, and Vola leaped the last six feet of trail.

She brought her sword down as she fell, severing the assassin's head from his body just as her feet thudded to the ground.

The assassin flickered and turned to mud before collapsing across the trail.

"An illusion," Braydon gasped at her feet.

Vola stooped and peeled his hand away from the wound. "How bad is it?" she asked.

Braydon grimaced and shoved her away. "Just a scrape. Get off me."

She decided he would live and figured she ought to save her energy for the rest of his party in case they were worse off.

She stood as Lillie and Sorrel stampeded around the corner. "Lillie, guard Braydon in case any more get past us. Do that shield spell thing on him if you have to. Sorrel, with me."

She spun and led the halfling down the hill. Braydon's companions were pinned against the rocks thirty feet down from where Braydon lay.

As Vola ran, she caught sight of Talon who crouched above them. The ranger drew their knives and fell on the assassin closest to them.

Six left. How many of these things could Lord Arthorel make and send against them?

There had to be another spell caster nearby controlling the golems, but Vola didn't see anyone obvious. Just the mud assassins.

By the time it was done, bits of dirt and sticks littered the path, and Braydon's party lay gasping on the ground.

"Th-thank you," Braydon's wizard said, climbing to his feet. "We would not have made it without you."

Sorrel gave Braydon's ranger a hand up. Huron, Vola was pretty sure his name was.

"Is it over?" Lillie asked, coming down the path with Braydon draped over her shoulder. The man clutched his side, blood streaking down his armor.

"I didn't see the spell caster," Vola said. "Did any of you catch him?"

Sorrel and Lillie shook their heads while Braydon's team looked blank.

Braydon stumbled, and Lillie tried to catch them both, but he went down with a clatter.

Vola blew out her breath in a little huff and stepped to his side.

"Get away from me, monster," he said.

"Hey." Lillie grabbed him by the chin and squeezed his cheeks until he squeaked. "Stop saying that. Or I won't let her do what she's planning to do."

Vola pulled his hand away from the wound and replaced it

with her own. She couldn't tell how deep the puncture went. Not yet. It might go further than she'd be able to heal. There was a limit to what she could absorb. But there was only one way to find out for sure.

"You know, full plate doesn't do you any good if you let them poke at its weak spots. Lady bless."

Light seared the space between her hand and his torn flesh, lighting up the night. Braydon cried out in pain and doubled up.

Sweat broke out along Vola's forehead as her side burned and ached. Braydon pushed her away, and this time, Vola let him.

"What did you do that for?" Braydon grated.

Lillie scowled at him and used gentle fingers to lift Vola's chain mail. "She just saved your life. Twice, you ungrateful swine."

Braydon's eyes widened as she revealed the rapidly healing wound just under Vola's ribs. She'd taken as much of it as she could. It left him much better off, but his body would still be responsible for healing the rest on its own.

He ducked his gaze, still frowning, and climbed to his feet. "I thought for sure we'd beat you here."

It was Vola's turn to grimace. "Much good it would do you. The tor was a bust. There's no one up there but an apothecary named Astrid. Turns out, she's nice, but if you're still looking for the missing townsfolk, head back to town."

Braydon scoffed. "You expect me to believe you? You probably just want all the glory to yourself."

"Hey now, Braydon," the woman with the hand axes said. "She just saved our asses."

"You don't believe me?" Vola said, standing abruptly. "Fine. Go see for yourself. Heck, I'll lead the way."

She stomped up the hill, refusing to look back until she got to the crest where Astrid's ruins started. When she glanced over her shoulder, Braydon followed on her heels, scowl fixed in place, while the others trailed behind them.

She poked her head around the wall into Astrid's sleeping chamber, mouth open to say "I told you so."

She froze. The room was empty. Except for the bloodstains.

"Astrid?" she called, racing into the room. "Henri?"

"What is it?" Lillie asked as she and Sorrel came around the corner. Lillie's hands flew to her mouth.

"Well, that's not how we left it," Sorrel said, hands on her hips.

"Check the other rooms," Vola said. But the sick feeling in the pit of her stomach told her the two wouldn't be there. The bloodstains were a big clue.

Sorrel and Lillie scrambled to obey. Where was Talon?

Vola strode for the doorway, but Braydon deliberately stepped up in front of her. "Is this some kind of trick?"

"No, this is serious. They're missing." She made eye contact with the other three warriors in Braydon's group. "Search the tor. At least one assassin must have made it this far, and we never caught the spell caster. Be careful, they know how to be invisible. Who knows what other tricks they have up their sleeves?"

They glanced at each other for only a moment before scattering.

"Hey," Braydon huffed indignantly. "You can't just—"

Vola pushed past him without listening.

She searched the ruins herself. And the surrounding overgrown landscape. She even searched up and down the path that led to the summit.

She couldn't find Henri or Astrid.

Or Talon.

# NINETEEN

VOLA DASHED UP THE PATH, fists clenched hard enough to make her knuckles creak. Was Henri dead? Injured? Or just missing? The tang of blood hit her nose as she passed into Astrid's main room, and she fought for control over a surge of rage. Was the blood Astrid's or Henri's? Which was worse? She couldn't deal with this not knowing.

Braydon's people waited for her at attention while Braydon perched sullenly on the edge of a block.

The woman stepped forward and saluted. Vola blinked and slowly returned the salute.

"No sign of any other assassins, ma'am," she said. "We were as thorough as we could be. Obron has a spell that can detect magic, and there weren't any illusions anywhere on the grounds."

Vola's lips tightened. "Lillie has something similar. They must have escaped. Thank you, anyway."

"We didn't find anything either," Lillie said.

Vola ran a hand over her hair and down her braid. "And I still don't know where Talon is."

"Here," a raspy voice said.

Vola spun and found the ranger in the doorway, bow in hand. "Talon."

"I caught a group of assassins trying to leave the tor. They had Astrid."

"Was she hurt? What happened?"

"I don't know. Henri went after them, but I thought it was important to stay together. Gruff is following them. We can catch up if we hurry."

A little of the tension bled from Vola's shoulders. If Henri was there, nothing bad would happen to Astrid.

Sorrel bounded to her feet, swinging her staff. "Are we going? Come on. They said hurry. Not drag your feet."

Lillie darted to Astrid's shelf. "We should take some tea."

"Tea?" Sorrel cried.

"Astrid's tea, in case she's hurt."

"Sorrel, get the swamp beast, please," Vola said.

"Ugh, only because you asked so nicely." She disappeared around the corner.

Vola turned to Braydon and his party. "You can go back to town or you can follow. I don't care which. But goddess help you if you get in my way." She didn't wait to see what they chose.

Talon led them down the tor, sure-footed even in the black of night. Vola had no idea what sort of trail Gruff had left for them, but Talon followed it without faltering, leading them around the wettest bits of swamp. Braydon and his party followed.

Moonlight lit their path, and in an hour, they reached a line of trees standing in a row along the edge of a murky pool several hundred feet across.

Henri stood silhouetted against the scene. Beyond him floated three flat-bottomed barges crowded with the now familiar golems in their illusory masks and clothes.

Vola skidded to a stop beside Henri, her boots sending up a spray of water. "Henri."

Henri didn't answer. He raised a hand to point at the center barge.

A familiar figure stood with one arm wrapped around Astrid's neck. Captain Wiselyn, Lord Arthorel's guard captain. He raised his square chin to meet Vola's stare.

"Well, if there was any doubt about Arthorel," Talon said as Gruff padded up next to them, "It's gone now."

"They have boats?" Sorrel hissed. "All along there have been boats? Why didn't anyone tell us that?"

Vola slashed her hand through the air, commanding silence.

"What do you want with her?" Vola yelled across the water.

"A hostage," Captain Wiselyn said with a smirk. "For good behavior."

Vola cocked her head. "Ours or hers?"

Astrid chose that moment to sink her strong teeth into his arm.

Wiselyn growled and shook her off. He brought his hand back and hit her across the face. The sound of the blow cracked across the water.

Henri surged forward, splashing into the shallows just as Talon put an arrow through the nearest golem's neck. It fell into the water and the illusion flickered away as the mud dissolved and sank.

Captain Wiselyn grabbed Astrid by the hair and laid his sword across her neck.

Vola grabbed Henri's shoulder to keep him from wading any farther.

"Don't do that," Vola said. "Or you'll lose your bargaining chip."

"What do you want?" Lillie asked, her voice cold and soft but still crisp enough to carry.

"Like I said. Good behavior," Wiselyn said. "You're not demonstrating a lot of self-control right now."

"We're listening," Vola said, signaling to Talon to lower their bow.

"Leave Water's Edge, leave Lord Arthorel's lands, and she lives." They couldn't see any difference in the way he held the sword, but a little trickle of blood ran down the side of Astrid's neck. "Stay, and she dies."

"What assurance do we have that you will honor that?" Henri said.

Wiselyn shrugged. "My lord deals in living bodies. Not dead ones."

Vola felt Henri's shoulder stiffen under his pauldrons.

"Take me, then," Henri said.

Vola's hand spasmed on his shoulder. "What?"

"If you want a hostage, I'm more valuable to them." He jerked his chin over his shoulder at Vola and the others. "They only just met her."

"You must think I'm an idiot."

"No, I think you're a professional. So am I. I know how this works." His mouth tipped in a mirthless smile that pulled at the scar along his cheek. "You take me and you won't get a fight. You can bet I won't bite you."

What the hell was Henri trying to pull here? It had to be a trick, but if it was, Vola couldn't see the end of it. There were fifteen of the golems. Sure, they were trapped on the barges, but fifteen golems would make a mighty fine bridge if Wiselyn decided to push the issue.

Wiselyn's eyes moved between Vola and Henri.

Was she supposed to look more worried for Henri? Or for Astrid? Which one did she want him to take? Neither if she could manage it.

"Fine," Wiselyn said. "I prefer my women willing, anyway. You walk over here slowly. Just you."

Henri waded forward, arms out from his sides, away from his

weapons. When he got close enough to the barge, Wiselyn signaled a golem who knelt and dragged Henri aboard.

Then Wiselyn pushed Astrid into the water.

Vola splashed forward to catch her as she slipped and fell under the surface.

*Now, Henri,* she thought at him, wishing her thoughts were arrows. *Do it now. Whatever* it *is.*

Vola lifted Astrid and as her arms were full and Henri was half in and half out of the water, Wiselyn brought the hilt of his sword down on Henri's head with a crack. Henri went limp across his feet.

Vola cried out, but Wiselyn angled his blade to prick the back of Henri's neck. "Don't move."

Vola stood hip-deep in the water, supporting Astrid while the others stood silent and frozen behind. She glared at Wiselyn, wishing she could spring forward and drag him from the barge. She could hold his head under while he thrashed beneath her.

But there were too many. Too many and Henri lay there helpless at their feet.

"Same deal," Wiselyn said, meeting her eyes. "Leave Lord Arthorel's lands, and we'll let him live. Stay and make trouble, and he'll die."

"What will you do with him?" Vola growled.

"Doesn't matter. All you have to know is he's alive somewhere. Or he's in his grave. Your choice."

He rolled Henri further onto the barge and barked an order at the pole men who pushed them away across the water.

And Vola had to stand there and let them go.

# TWENTY

Vola waded back to firmer ground with Astrid under her arm. She wasn't entirely sure who was holding up who considering her knees threatened to buckle with every step. Astrid clambered up onto the water-logged patch of ground, swearing under her breath while Vola braced herself against a tree root and tried to breathe.

Arthorel had Henri. The local lord hadn't just tricked them into running around in circles. He still had the missing townsfolk, and now he had Henri, too.

She hauled herself out of the water and stood dripping along the edge of the pool.

"What now?" Sorrel asked as Vola's hands clenched and unclenched. "Do we...do we leave to save Henri?"

"Is saving him even an option?" Lillie said. "If we stay, they'll kill him."

"If we go, then we're letting them win," Talon said. They crossed their arms and their hood trained on Vola. "Do we want to let them win?"

"No." Vola snapped her arms out to shake the water from

them and cracked her neck. "No. It doesn't matter what they threatened. I can't leave Henri here. I have to go after him."

It wasn't that he'd been kidnapped on her shield quest. And it wasn't that she'd screwed up badly enough that he'd had to trade himself for Astrid. Those weren't the main reasons her stomach crawled into a knot and burned bad enough to make her stagger.

Henri was her trainer, but the word wasn't enough to encompass everything he'd been to her. When she'd stood in the chapel surrounded by Cleavah's light and all the other knights had turned away in disgust, Henri had chosen her. When she'd wasted time crying over all the paladins who would never accept her, he'd held her. When she hadn't believed in herself, he'd believed for her.

She wasn't leaving him.

She strode to the swamp beast and grabbed the lead rope.

Someone cleared their throat behind her, and she turned to catch Braydon and his party shuffling their feet. She hadn't even remembered they were there.

The woman with the axes looked at her fellows. "We...we can't go up against our lord," she said.

Braydon's ranger nodded. "It would be suicide for us."

Vola opened her mouth to say "but your people are still missing." But she thought better of it. "I understand," she said instead.

They exchanged a glance and the ranger and the wizard turned to start back into the swamp. The woman hesitated. Then she stepped forward to offer Vola her axes. "Just in case you need them."

Vola took them with a solemn nod. "Thank you."

Braydon remained for a moment after the others left, staring at Vola. She expected him to say something, though from his expression she couldn't tell what.

He didn't. Finally, he turned to follow his party in silence.

At least that was an improvement.

Vola braced herself and turned back to Lillie, Talon, and Sorrel. "I don't expect you to come with me—"

"Why?" Talon said, hands on hips.

Vola blinked. "Because this isn't what you signed up for. Lillie needs money and you can bet we won't be getting paid now. And Sorrel knows where to go to find Maxim's Warhammer."

Sorrel rolled her eyes. "Clearly you haven't been paying attention."

"We're coming with you," Talon said. "There are still families who are separated. Children who are missing."

"And kicking ass is so much more fun than my abbot led me to believe," Sorrel said. "Besides, it's Henri. Teacher extraordinaire, friend to kids and dogs. He's like the embodiment of all that's good in the world. The Warhammer can wait."

Vola's chest swelled. Maybe Talon was right. Maybe mortals did need a pack, and this one was theirs.

They all glanced at Lillie.

Lillie bit her lip. "What if Lord Arthorel is unaware of Captain Wiselyn's actions?"

"What?" Sorrel cried.

"He seemed so nice. And he's their lord. It's unthinkable that he would break that sacred trust."

"Lillie, he's the illusionist," Vola said. "He's tried to kill us on multiple occasions."

"The assassin in his manor was aiming for us, not for him," Sorrel said.

Lillie covered her cheeks with her hands. Clearly, she didn't want to believe it.

"You have to choose," Vola said, trying to keep the growl out of her voice. "You have to choose who to believe."

Lillie took a shuddering breath and finally spoke. "If he's kidnapping his people…if he's aware that Captain Wiselyn kidnapped Henri, then he's broken his vows as a noble of Southglen." She pulled her hands from her face. "He deserves neither pity nor mercy. If he won't protect the people under his care, then we must."

She finally met Vola's gaze, her eyes going fierce and bright. "I want to hit something," she told Vola.

Vola grinned. "Great. Follow me, and I'll find you something to set fire to."

"Astrid," Sorrel said. "You want an escort back to town?"

"You'll be safer there," Vola said.

Astrid snorted. "I'd be safer on the tor. But I want to be nearby in case you screw something up. You're going to need more than tea."

# TWENTY-ONE

They moved a lot faster through the swamp now, either because they were more practiced or because they traveled with Astrid, who seemed to know all the pathways and secret trails that didn't plunge you into murky water every five steps.

Vola's mind felt clearer than it had for days now that they had an actual enemy ahead of them. Captain Wiselyn and Lord Arthorel's faces floated in her mind's eye, keeping her moving forward.

She led the way with Astrid while Talon and Gruff followed. Lillie hurried to keep up and Sorrel brought up the rear, keeping an eye out for ambushes.

Of course, it was just a coincidence that being out front meant she was out of reach of the swamp beast's teeth. From Talon's occasional yelps, that was a very good thing.

By mid-afternoon the next day, they walked back into Water's Edge hot, sweaty, and annoyed. But at least they weren't covered in muck. Lillie's sniffles had subsided, and Sorrel's rash hadn't shown back up after a dose of Astrid's tea.

Vola's plan was to slip into town unnoticed so they could get a head start up the hill to surprise Lord Arthorel. Henri's life depended on them being quick and quiet.

So the last thing she wanted to see was a mob waiting for them in front of Becky's Tea and Tap Room. Townspeople crowded around the steps, the dull murmur of their voices echoing against the buildings.

There was something wrong about a mob gathered in full daylight. There should be pitchforks and clubs all lit by flickering torchlight. Not muggy sunlight outside a tea room.

"Er, anyone have the urge to run in the opposite direction?" Sorrel said.

"Cheer up, Miss Sorrel," Lillie said. "These are our friends. They're the ones who asked for our help." Despite her words, her eyes darted left and right as if looking for an escape route.

The crowd rippled as someone near the front caught sight of them. The people parted, and Becky stepped down from the porch, lips pinched and brow furrowed.

"Here they are now. They'll tell us the news." Becky pushed forward. "Paladin Lightbringer. Have you found our people yet?"

"Oh, er…" Shit. Maybe her plan should have been to avoid town altogether until they had more answers.

Sorrel glanced at Vola before stepping forward. "No," she said quietly. "But we have good news. We know where to look now."

"Then it's true. They really don't know what they're doing," another voice said.

The crowd shifted and stepped back from the squirrely looking man with dirty spectacles. The council representative had stood just behind Knight Commander Imralen's shoulder on the day Cleavah had chosen her. He'd whispered in Imralen's ear the day she and Henri had left the academy.

How much whispering had he done while they'd been fumbling through the swamp? Enough to do some damage. The people around them eyed Vola.

"They've been gone nearly a week and they've done nothing so far," he said, his voice barely more than a whine. "Your people are still missing. Your wives and husbands and children are still unaccounted for."

"What have you been doing all this time?" someone else said.

"You were supposed to be helping us."

"They saved my life," Astrid said from just behind Vola's shoulder. "That's a damn sight better than doing nothing."

"But one life for how many others?" The representative pointed at Astrid. "Is she a fair trade for all those missing families?"

"That's not how this works," Vola said as Astrid glared down her nose at the representative's finger. "I didn't decide to save Astrid instead of someone else. I'm on my way to save the others right now." Hopefully.

"But how can we trust you when you've done so little?" The representative shook his head sadly. "Maybe this town needs a different hero. Anyone else."

Vola's fists clenched at her sides. He was just trying to keep her from getting her shield. That was it. He didn't care about these people. He didn't care about Becky's husband, Porter, or the orphans who didn't even have families here, or Henri.

He would hurt all of them just to discredit her.

And there was nothing she could do to fight him. Neither her words nor her actions to this point had convinced the townsfolk to trust her. And punching him in the face would only get her into trouble she couldn't afford.

"This town needs someone else," he repeated and turned theatrically so the gathered crowd turned with him. "One of their own."

Vola's heart sank. Braydon and his party lounged on the bench outside Becky's tea room.

Braydon's eyes locked on Vola, then he casually surveyed the angry crowd. He'd removed his blood-stained breastplate and pauldrons, but he still wore his sword in its sheath. Somehow, he managed to look fresh even after several nights in the swamp.

Vola could feel the dirt and sweat gathered in each of her joints and under her fingernails, and she fought the urge to itch.

"How about it, Braydon?" the representative asked.

"Fuck off," Braydon told him. "You have no idea what you're talking about."

Lillie choked. Vola laughed before she could think better of it.

"Vola and her team saved us. Twice," Braydon said as his party nodded behind him. "She healed me when I was hurt. And she was the one who figured out Lord Arthorel is kidnapping our people."

A cry went up from the crowd.

"Our own lord?" someone said.

"What's he doing with them?"

"What do we do now?"

Braydon raised his hands. "We might not be able to fight him. But she can." He gestured to Vola. "Paladins are supposed to right wrongs. Even if it goes against the nobility. The normal rules don't apply. Not when she answers to the gods themselves." He blew out a big sigh. "We're done playing hero. You might as well trust a real one. She's earned it."

The crowd glanced at each other, murmurs cascading back and forth.

But the representative pulled his lips back in a sneer. "You want to talk about the gods?" he said. "You don't even know who she serves. The Lesser Virtue of bitchiness and mockery. Not a real goddess at—"

Vola stepped up to him and leaned into his face. "Bullshit," she said deliberately.

The lightning bolt streaked down to strike the street, sending out a branch to sting him on the rear end.

The representative yelped and scurried away.

"She really does like her lightning, doesn't she?" Sorrel said to no one in particular.

"Now go home," Braydon told the crowd. "And let the paladin do her work."

Vola half-expected a catch, but Braydon plopped back down on the bench and leaned his head against the wall with his eyes closed.

Becky touched Vola's shoulder as the mob grumbled and glanced fearfully at the sky.

"My lady Cleavah certainly showed them, didn't she?" Becky jerked her head at the tea room. "Come inside. If you're going after Lord Arthorel, you don't want to be on the streets. He'll see you coming. You can have a cup of tea before you go up the hill. And maybe something a little stronger on the house for Miss Sorrel."

"Aw, Becky, you remembered my favorite thing," Sorrel said, trotting up the stairs to the tea room.

"Beer?" Vola said.

Sorrel held up a finger. "Free beer."

Vola let the others file inside first while she waited at the corner of the porch where the swamp monster was tied. When she was alone, she bit her lip.

"Thank you," she told the air. "For defending me."

A whisper of breeze and the pressure of a body made it feel like someone stood right behind her shoulder. But she didn't turn around to look.

"He deserved a lightning bolt up his butt," Cleavah said out of the breeze.

"But I've been acting just like him," Vola said. "Hiding who you are."

"You are not perfect, Vola. But you're a fool if you can't see the differences."

Vola glanced over at Braydon. Maybe, but even now she didn't want anyone else to see exactly who she was talking to. Cleavah was just too hard to explain. Vola didn't even know if she *could* explain the goddess everyone laughed at. Cleavah didn't seem to mind, but Vola did.

"I chose you," the Lesser Virtue said. "I chose you without any caveats. I chose you when you weren't perfect. Nothing you do can change that."

*No*, Vola thought as the pressure behind her fluttered and dissipated and she stood alone on the porch. *But I can do better.*

The swamp beast reached out to take a bite out of her, and she danced back.

Inside the Tea and Tap Room, Becky had left a cup of tea on the bar for Vola. Sorrel was already swigging her way through a mug of beer. Talon didn't have a drink, but Gruff lapped at a bowl of water at their feet.

Vola turned to see where Lillie had gotten to and found her next to the door, speaking with Braydon's wizard. Obron she thought his name was. The older man pressed a book into Lillie's hands before he clasped her on the shoulder and left.

"What'd you get?" Sorrel asked as Lillie joined them at the bar.

"A new book," Lillie said. "Obron said he didn't need it anymore since he was giving up the adventuring life. Too much hanging upside down for his taste."

"What is it?" Sorrel asked, lifting the corner of a page with two fingers.

"A book of spell techniques," Lillie said. "This will help me refine my spell casting."

"Will it keep you from setting fire to your party?" Vola asked and took a swig of tea.

Lillie brightened. "Maybe. Let me see." She started flipping through pages.

"What would you like to drink, Miss Lillie?" Becky asked.

"A glass of port, please. A ten-year ruby," she replied absently.

Becky's brow furrowed. She bent to rummage under the counter for a while and came up with a dusty bottle.

Vola slugged back the rest of her tea and tapped her fingers on the bar. They needed to get going before word reached Arthorel that they were coming for him. But all their food was at the bottom of the swamp. If they were going into battle in the next hour, Vola wanted to do it with a full stomach.

Sorrel leaned forward as Becky poured Lillie's drink. "Is that what she asked for?" Sorrel whispered.

Becky eyed the liquid with a rueful grimace. "Well, it's red. And I'm pretty sure it's been under my counter for ten years. So…yes?"

She slid the glass to Lillie who took a sip without looking up from her book.

Vola heard a cough in the corner and turned on her stool. There was a man in the corner desperately trying to hide under his ragged hat. His clothes were still stained green from algae.

Vola nudged Sorrel and nodded to him. Sorrel took one glance and her expression darkened.

"Him…" she said.

Vola raised an eyebrow.

"Yes," Sorrel hissed as slid off her stool. "Corner him."

Vola strode over to the swamp beast salesman and plopped down at his table so he had to look her in the eye.

Sorrel slipped up beside him and said, "Hi! Glad to see you got out of the swamp alive."

He jumped. "Er, yes. Me, too?"

Vola leaned forward with a smile that deliberately showed off her tusks. "So, about that mount you gave us…"

"Oh, yeah. Splendid specimen, isn't it? Think nothing of it." His eyes darted around the room, looking for an escape.

"Yeah, splendid," Vola said. "Take it back."

"What?" He flinched. "No, no. It was a gift."

"Please?" Sorrel said, rubbing her shoulder where she still had teeth marks.

"No?" he said.

Vola gripped the edge of the table. "That thing isn't a mount. It's a menace. And you knew it. Now take it back."

"Fine, fine," he said, sweat breaking out in tiny beads along his upper lip. "I will relieve you of my gift. For one hundred gold."

"What?" Sorrel said.

"You're expecting us to pay you to take back a faulty gift?"

The salesman began sliding out of his chair, inch by inch. "That's the deal. One hundred gold for the swamp monst—I mean, specimen—and I will take it off your hands."

"Pockets!" Lillie cried from the bar, her nose still buried in the book.

Vola's brow furrowed as she glanced at the wizard.

That was enough of a distraction that the salesman bolted for the door.

Vola could not in good conscience run him down and demand justice. She groaned instead.

Sorrel planted her hands on her hips. "I can't believe he swindled us twice. On something we didn't even pay for."

Vola sighed and stood up. "Maybe we can convince Becky to take it. We'll call it a gift for all her hospitality."

"That's low, Vola," Sorrel said.

"Would you rather take it along with us? We don't even have a tent for it to carry anymore."

"I didn't say that." Sorrel trotted to keep up as Vola strode back to the bar. "Surely someone as nice as Becky will have no trouble loving the swamp beast."

# TWENTY-TWO

WHEN THEY CLIMBED the hill to Lord Arthorel's manor, they kept to the trees at the side of the road. Late afternoon light filtered down through the leaves, making Vola squint in the patchy light.

"So, this is it, right?" Sorrel whispered as they crouched, staring at the manor looming over the end of the road. "We know we're heading into a fight. We're not just going to scare little old ladies this time?"

"Right." Vola tightened the straps of her armor and loosened her sword in its scabbard. "Hit them hard and fast."

"We'll…we'll make sure they're guilty first, right?" Lillie said.

Vola stopped to consider. "Okay, yes. No slaughtering innocent servants. But we have to go quickly and quietly. If Lord Arthorel knows we're coming, he'll kill Henri. Maybe even all the prisoners."

"If they're even in there," Talon muttered.

Vola's lips thinned.

Lillie glanced between them and put a soothing hand on Vola's arm. "If they're not," she said quietly. "Then at least we'll be able to look for clues to find where he took them."

Talon peered through the trees. "Sorrel, want to go climbing?"

Sorrel scoffed. "Does a dragon like fried food?"

They all blinked at her.

"Um, I don't know," Lillie said. "Do they?"

Sorrel threw her hands in the air. "Yes. Duh. Come on. Dragons? Breathe fire? All their food is fried."

"It's a bit of a stretch," Lillie said.

Vola shook her head. "Whatever. Talon take the left wall; Sorrel take the right. You guys flank while Lillie and I go up the middle."

Lillie bit her lip. "It's quite open."

"Are we doing this or not?" Vola snapped.

"You can borrow Gruff." Talon gestured to the big, black wolf before disappearing into the trees around the manor. Sorrel followed.

Vola jerked her head at Lillie and pushed out of the trees to step up to the gate.

The same gangly guard leaned against the wall, shuffling a deck of cards. Vola opened her mouth ready to distract the boy so she could knock him out, but Lillie marched straight up to the gate.

The guard straightened, but before he could say anything, Lillie had reached through the gate, grabbed hold of his breastplate, and hauled the boy against the iron bars.

"You remember who I am, peasant?" Lillie said, voice pleasant like she was ordering tea and biscuits.

"Yesh," the boy said, face mashed against the gate. His eyes rolled between them, the whites showing all around.

"And you remember not to get in my way?"

"Yesh."

"Then open this gate and let us through. We have business with your lord. Pray we don't have business with you as well."

She let the boy go with a little shove, and he landed on his butt in the dirt. Then he scrambled to his feet with a muttered "yes, ma'am" and fumbled for the key at his belt.

Vola glanced at Lillie out of the corner of her eye. "So is there a switch somewhere that you can just turn that on and off?"

Lillie gave her a rueful look. "No. It's built-in."

The boy yanked the gate open with a clang.

Over his shoulder, Vola caught movement. Captain Wiselyn came into the courtyard from the manor.

The last time they'd seen the man, he'd been getting away with an unconscious Henri. And somewhere around here, he was keeping Vola's trainer imprisoned.

Vola rushed forward, smashing the gate guard out of the way.

"Wait—" Lillie started.

But Vola wasn't waiting. If Wiselyn sounded the alarm, Henri was dead.

She charged. Red threatened to bleed into her vision, but she pushed it back. She didn't need rage right now. She needed speed and strength.

Wiselyn saw her coming and smiled.

Vola's heart leaped. She could kill this bastard easily. Strike him down in a moment before he managed to raise the alarm, and then they could just waltz inside and free Henri. Without his bodyguard, Lord Arthorel would be much easier to handle.

Vola drew her sword and swung it down in a perfect arc. In a fair world, it would have beheaded the man in one blow.

In this one, Captain Wiselyn turned his armored shoulder into Vola's gut and spun her until she dropped harmlessly into the dirt.

An arrow whistled past his ear, but since he'd side stepped, it thunked into the column beside him.

Then he reached over to a bell that hung just outside the door and pulled the rope, sending a ringing peal through the air. The carillon tower above the manor took up the alarm.

Shit, shit, *shit*. That did not go the way she'd thought it would.

Vola glanced up to the opposite roof where Talon stood, hands out in a "what was that?" gesture.

Vola rolled to her feet while Captain Wiselyn drew his sword and more guards boiled from the barracks beside the manor.

Talon picked them off while Sorrel jumped down from the other roof.

Guards shouted and pointed at them, spreading out to cover both sides.

So much for the element of surprise.

Vola lunged for the captain. He raised his sword, locking their blades together. Vola's blood beat in her ears as she leaned, using her height and weight against him. His feet slid against the dusty flagstones, but he held his own against her. He finally fetched up against the wall and used it to brace himself so he could fling off Vola's attack.

Sorrel spun, her staff a blur as she fended off three guards. The rest were climbing to Talon's perch while the ranger shot into the courtyard.

Back at the gate, Lillie flung spells, keeping the stray guards from getting too close.

Vola turned back to her opponent and swung. He danced back, but this time, she anticipated him and spun in a counter-strike, catching him by surprise. Her sword bit into the gap between his breastplate and shoulder guard.

He jerked free with a grunt and staggered back, his hand going to his bloody shoulder.

A sizzle and a blast of hot air made Vola leap out of the way as a fire bolt whizzed past her ear.

She turned to glare. "Lillie!"

Lillie danced from foot to foot, her hands covering her mouth. "I'm sorry, but you're in the way."

Vola growled and stood back up, brushing the dust from her knees. Captain Wiselyn staggered upright as well, bits of his armor blackened and his left arm hanging limply at his side as blood dripped from his shoulder.

"Where's Henri?" she said.

He just smiled and shook his head.

Vola roared and charged. She bashed the captain into the wall and tried to kick his feet out from under him, but he shifted his weight and broke free so she had to grab him again.

"Miss Vola, move," Lillie called.

Vola snarled under her breath. She didn't have to move. She had him. He'd be dead in a moment.

A sharp pain broke through her anger, and she glanced down to see he'd dropped his sword and stabbed her with his belt knife, finding one of the many holes in her chain mail.

Lillie screamed.

Vola twisted to glance back and saw the guards advancing on the wizard. Sorrel was still pinned down on one side, and Talon was busy keeping the guards from flinging them off the roof. Lillie faced the enemy alone, fire bolts barely keeping them back. Gruff circled her feet, snarling and snapping at the men who surrounded them.

They were too spread out. Forces spread too thin and over-whelmed.

Vola clenched her jaw till her teeth creaked. Wiselyn squirmed under her grip, out of weapons. If she left him now, he'd regroup or worse, escape.

*Hang on, Lillie. Just a few more seconds.*

Vola growled, then roared. She thrust against Wiselyn, freed an arm just long enough to drive her elbow into his nose.

He reared back.

And Vola used the opportunity to slash her blade across his throat.

The captain fell.

Vola turned with a wince, her side stinging.

Sorrel planted her staff and kicked down her second to last opponent. Then snapped her weapon up to catch the final guard in the gut.

On the roof, Talon drew a knife to stab at the guards trying to pull them to the ground.

With a low snarl, Gruff leaped from Lillie's side, and his teeth closed around the nearest guard's sword hand. The man screamed as he was dragged under the giant wolf.

Lillie's hands twisted, and she reached out to grab an enemy. Waves of lightning flashed through his body as he jerked and fell at her feet.

Vola sprinted for the last guard. Her feet felt like they moved through molasses as he raised his blade.

Lillie screamed and lunged to the side, but not quite quick enough.

Vola's sword bit through the man, cleaving him in two even as Lillie fell to the ground.

# TWENTY-THREE

VOLA ROLLED bodies out of the way so she could get to Lillie. Sorrel skidded to a stop beside them.

They pulled the wizard out from the pile of singed, bloodied enemies. Lillie's face was pasty white, a stark contrast to her normally flushed features, and she bit her lip, hard enough to make it bleed.

"I'm all right," she said, breathlessly. "It's…it's just a scratch."

"Are you saying that because you think you're supposed to?" Sorrel asked.

Talon shoved the last dead attacker off the roof and then slid down a drainpipe. They stepped forward to lean over Sorrel's shoulder. Gruff pressed against their hip.

Vola carefully pulled Lillie's leg straight.

"It's fine, Vola," Lillie said. "I twisted it on the way down. I promise it's fine."

Vola's lips thinned as she gazed at Lillie's face, looking for the truth. She could take care of this right now. But…she could only heal so much in a day. And who knew what shape Henri would be in when they found him?

The leg looked fine. A scratch disappearing back under Lillie's pants. That was it. And Vola wasn't even considering healing her own wound. What was a little knife in the gut, anyway?

"We need to go after Henri," Lillie said. "Don't we?"

Vola nodded, letting out her breath. "Yeah. We haven't exactly been stealthy."

"I could have handled Wiselyn without a sound," Talon said as Sorrel helped Lillie to stand. "If you hadn't rushed in."

Vola's face grew hot. "I saw an opportunity, and I took it. I wanted to get to him before he raised the alarm."

"Great job," Talon said.

"Yeah, thanks," Vola snapped. "I know how bad this is. Believe me. Henri's probably already dead."

Lillie balanced on one leg, her hand resting on Sorrel's shoulder. "Don't say that. Captain Wiselyn implied that Lord Arthorel needed living victims. Henri is probably worth more to him alive."

"Is that better?" Sorrel said, cocking her head. "Seems ominous to me."

"Alive is always better. Then there is the chance for rescue."

Talon's hood remained fixed on Vola, and she could practically feel the censure coming out from under it, but the ranger kept silent.

"Is it over?" a quavering voice called from behind them. The gate guard crawled out from behind the corner where Vola had flung him.

"Yes," Lillie said with a grimace as she tried to put weight on her leg. "It's over. Run home. If you can."

They walked into the manor, and the hall ahead of them twisted like a twig in a flame. What had been a very normal looking hallway the last time they'd been here split into three branching passageways as they watched wide-eyed.

"Uh, I'm not drunk, am I?" Sorrel said. "Did Becky slip me something stronger."

"You're not drunk," Vola said. "Hallways don't normally do that."

"It didn't do that the last time we were here," Talon said.

"No, but Lord Arthorel is an illusionist. He was the one cloaking the assassins and disguising the golems. I'll bet this whole place is full of things that look real but aren't."

Lillie smacked her forehead. "The magic in the parlor. He said it was protection spells, and I believed him. Ugh, I can't believe I fell for it."

"Bleh, it's making me nauseous," Sorrel said. "How do we stop it?"

"Lillie, can you dispel it somehow?" Vola glanced at the wizard.

Lillie looked stricken and leafed through her newest spell book. "Um, no? You have to learn spells, you know. They don't just happen."

Without a word, Talon and Gruff strode forward. As they walked, the hallway shivered and stretched straight again. Although the three new branchings remained.

"Good call, Talon," Sorrel said and trotted after them. She stopped at the corner and glanced down one passage, then another. "This way."

"How do you know?" Vola asked, following. Lillie limped behind her.

"I don't. I just like to go clockwise."

"I suppose that's as good of a reason as any."

Lillie muttered under her breath.

"What are you doing?" Vola asked.

"I'm casting that spell that lets me know when magic is around."

"Oh. Is it working?"

"Um, yes…It's definitely magic."

Vola planted her face in her palm. "Very helpful."

Sorrel came to a door. "Shall we try it?"

Vola glanced up and down the empty hall. So far no one had come to attack them. Maybe all the guards had been in the courtyard. "Henri's probably locked up somewhere. I can't imagine he's sitting nicely in one of these rooms."

"Yes, but we'll never find him if we don't look," Lillie said

"All right, good point."

Vola placed herself on one side of the door, Talon behind her while Lillie and Sorrel stood at the other. Sorrel turned the knob and flung the door open.

Vola darted around the door frame, yelling, and stopped short when her feet sank into deep loam. Trees surrounded her and moonlight filtered down through thick leaves and branches.

"Uh, what?" Vola turned toward the door. Which had disappeared. Of course. "Crap. Sorrel? Talon? Is anyone there?"

"Vola?" Sorrel's voice came through the tree trunks as if she stood just out of sight.

Vola sprinted for the sound of her companions.

But she found no one. "Where are you?" she called.

"We're still in the hallway," Sorrel said, now behind her. "'Cause we didn't go rushing into a strange room in a castle of illusion."

She heard Lillie snort. "This is hardly a castle," the wizard said.

"We can argue about what it's called later," Talon said, in their gravelly voice.

"Yeah, how do I get out of here?" Vola said. At least they could all hear each other.

"Just walk out the door?" Sorrel said.

Vola tipped her head back to sigh at the sky. "There is no door back here. Just endless forest."

"Oh, that's weird. From here it looks like a pit of black. We just figured you were looking for the lights."

"Not helping."

"Well, it's an illusion, right?" Lillie said. "So it's not real. Try… challenging its realness."

"What the hell does that mean? Speak common, not magic, Lillie."

Lillie blew out her breath in exasperation. "Hit something. Is that common enough?"

Vola gladly spun and swung her unsheathed weapon at the nearest tree. It made a satisfying "thunk" when it got stuck.

"These trees might be more real than me," Vola said. "That didn't work."

"Okay, okay," Sorrel said, obviously thinking. "So let's think real things, then. How do you get rid of a forest you don't want?"

"Fire," Talon said.

"Great, Lillie?"

"Wait," Vola called. "Not that—"

There was a whoosh, and Vola ducked to cover her head as a blast of heat seared through the trees. Light flickered behind her eyelids.

"Hey, it worked," Sorrel said.

Vola looked up to see her companions standing in the doorway. The room around her was scorched but looked like a normal library now with blackened books on the shelves and old worn furniture standing on a threadbare carpet. Her sword hung two feet off the ground, lodged in a thick desk.

"Anyone else think this looks a little…I don't know, worn in?" Sorrel asked as Vola planted her foot against the desk and yanked her sword free.

"I wasn't going to say anything," Talon said as Gruff sniffed at a hole in the carpet.

Lillie studied the room, head tilted. "Well, if you're a master illusionist, I guess there isn't a reason to keep things really looking nice. You can just cover it all up with magic when company comes over."

"At least until the company bashes through your illusions," Sorrel said.

Vola stalked from the room into the hallway and turned to continue through the manor.

"Wait," Sorrel said. "We should see if there's anything useful in there."

"No time," Vola said. "We have to find Henri before Lord Arthorel carries out his threat."

"But there are drawers to open. What if there's a chest?" Sorrel said as Talon dragged her down the hall.

"I thought you said monks had no need of worldly goods?" Lillie asked.

"That doesn't mean I don't want to see what's inside. That's the fun part."

"We'll come back after all this is over," Vola said.

"Promise?"

Vola started to promise, but that was when her feet went out from under her.

She had just enough time to suck in a surprised breath and then twist in midair and fling as much of herself backward as she could. Her torso hit the floor, and she caught the edge of a pit under her arms. Her legs kicked in the open air.

"Miss Vola!" Lillie tried to bend and help her climb back up, but her leg collapsed, nearly pitching her into the pit beside Vola.

"Just let Talon and Sorrel do it," Vola gasped.

Although Vola outweighed both of them put together, the ranger and the monk managed to haul her back onto firm ground. She shivered against the floorboards, trying to hide her reaction.

"So, I take it the rug was an illusion."

Lillie put her hands to her cheeks. "I don't know. I told you, everything in here is magic. I can't see individual spells if everything's lit up like a holiday bazaar."

Vola forced herself to breathe and not growl at the wizard. It wasn't her fault Lord Arthorel had turned his manor into a not-so-fun circus.

"I'll go first," Talon said. "To test the terrain."

"We just need to get rid of the illusions," Sorrel said. "Then we could sweep through this place as fast as possible."

"Yeah, except the easiest way to get rid of the illusions is to get rid of the caster. Who is currently hidden by the illusions." Vola's fingers clenched against the floor, her nails leaving gouges in the wood. She stood with a huff. "Lillie, is there any other way to get past the magic?"

Lillie used the wall to climb unsteadily to her feet. "I don't really know. I'd have to study it. Maybe there's some sort of focal point or trigger."

"You work on that while we walk," Vola said. "We'll go room by room for now. I don't want to miss Henri in case he's tucked away somewhere unexpected, but I don't want to trigger any more traps."

Talon took the lead, testing the ground in front of them very carefully before stepping forward. It was slow going, but they didn't find any more traps in the hallway.

The next room Vola opened carefully, and she didn't rush inside this time.

In the middle, stood a large man with bulging muscles and a tiny loincloth. Vola made a face.

He caught sight of them at the doorway and bashed a plain iron sword against his shield with a clang. "Ha, come fight me."

Sorrel shrugged. "Okay." She started forward.

Vola caught her by the arm. "Wait. It's probably just another illusion."

"So? Doesn't mean it wouldn't be a good fight."

"They're just here to slow us down," Vola said. "There's nothing that says we have to fight everything we see. Look, he's not even coming after us."

"Come fight me!" the man roared. But Vola was right, he stood with his feet planted on the carpet.

"The room is probably trapped," Talon said, glancing at the blank walls and bare floorboards. "We go in to fight, then it locks us inside."

"I don't think it's even covering anything interesting," Lillie said, squinting over their shoulders. "Just a storeroom."

"Oh, fine, if you want to be boring about it," Sorrel said.

They started to close the door, and the illusory man's face fell. "Come fiiiight!"

"I'm sorry," Sorrel called to him as she closed the door.

The next door they came to they opened slowly as well. A wave of humid air hit them in the face, smelling like moss and mold, and Lillie immediately started sneezing. Past the doorframe were a bunch of familiar-looking drooping trees, separated by murky puddles covered with green pond scum. Between a couple of trunks, Vola could make out the vibrant crimson of the swamp flowers which tried to eat them a few days ago.

The party looked at each other.

"Nope," Sorrel said for all of them and closed the door.

The next room was almost as dark as the first had been, except for one shaft of light in the center, illuminating a figure in a chair.

"Henri," Vola breathed.

Talon reached out a hand to stop her, but Vola wasn't stupid enough to think it would be this easy.

"I think he's another illusion," Lillie said, her hands combing through the air and her eyes focused on something distant.

"So what?" Sorrel said. "You just want to leave this one, too?"

Vola's heart clenched. She clamped her teeth shut on useless arguments.

"We'll never get through all this if we don't find a way to unravel Lord Arthorel's magic. I need a chance to study it."

The illusory Henri's hands were bound to the arms of the chair, and he looked up at Vola with blood running down his face. His lips moved in the shape of her name.

She spun to Lillie, who studied the room with a delicate frown on her brow.

"Well?" she said.

"I don't have enough to go on, yet. Give me a second."

A deafening roar from the corner of the room made them all jump. Vola drew her sword.

Another roar, and out of the darkness stepped an enormous lion with ridged horns sprouting from its head. Its tail whipped back and forth, a snake's head hissing from the end.

"We don't have another second," Vola said.

Lillie glanced at Sorrel. "You wanted to fight something, right?"

Sorrel's slow grin spread across her face, and she pulled her quarterstaff from her back. "Yes, I did. Haaaaaa!" Sorrel sprang for the horned lion with a yell.

"I thought we weren't fighting the illusions," Vola called, but she followed Sorrel, anyway.

"I need to see it in action," Lillie said. "Just keep it busy."

Vola couldn't roll her eyes while fighting, but she tried really hard. She sprang at the beast with a yell while Sorrel dealt a solid blow to its face, then ducked between its front legs. The beast was tall enough the halfling could run underneath and pop out the other side.

It swung its head around and caught Vola with one of its horns. Clearly, it wanted to fling her across the room, but Vola grabbed hold and held on as the thing tossed its head.

An arrow whizzed by and lodged in the beast's side. It roared again, this time in pain. Vola glanced over to see Talon covering Lillie while she brushed and stroked the air, causing ripples of light to eddy around her.

The beast tried to knock her loose against the wall, but Vola tightened her grip. She let go with her sword hand and slashed across its head, her blade cutting deep.

It reared, and its tail lashed toward her, the snake's head hissing, teeth gleaming.

She leaped out of the way and tumbled from its back. Sorrel sprang in front of her, twisted to avoid the teeth, and brought her staff down on the serpent's head.

There was a sharp crack, and the serpent fell limp.

A whizz and a pop. Then an arrow shaft sprouted from the beast's remaining eye.

It moaned, clawed at its face, then fell with a thud.

"There!" Lillie cried. "Perfect. I know where we're going."

Vola stood on shaking feet and brushed herself off. She deliberately ignored the image of Henri calling to her from the chair.

"All the magic is concentrated at a single point and it gets weaker as it travels out. We're still skirting the edges of the affected area."

"Great," Vola said. "So where is Henri? Where's Arthorel?"

"In the basement." Lillie pointed down and to the left. "At least something is being guarded down there. It's either Henri or the key to the illusions, which should lead us to Henri if we can get rid of them."

"Then what are we waiting for?" Vola said.

# TWENTY-FOUR

It took a few minutes, but they finally found a way down through all the illusions, and they crept down the staircase to the manor's dungeon. Actually, it was a cellar, but Vola didn't really want to think of herself as a noble hero storming a cellar.

With Talon scouting the way, they didn't trigger any more traps, at least not in the hallways. The cellars were a lot darker than the hallways upstairs had been, but Lillie pointed them unerringly to a room lined with casks.

"Why am I not surprised the noble loves his wine?" Vola said.

Lillie cast her a sharp look before turning to examine the room.

"Is this the place?" Sorrel said.

The room itself stood open beside the casks lining the walls and two support columns in the middle. A couple of flickering torches revealed stone walls, stone floors, and a very boring dead end.

Vola glanced at Lillie.

"This is where the magic is most concentrated," she said, with a frown.

"Do you suppose it's all an illusion?" Sorrel said. She glared at the wall. "Reveal your secrets, fiend," she said. And then punched the stone with a shout.

The other three stared at her.

"How'd that feel?" Vola asked.

Sorrel winced and shook her hand. "Not great."

Something shifted in the shadows at the back of the cellar. Vola braced her feet and raised her sword as Sorrel and Talon drew their weapons. Lillie squinted, then she threw up her hands, casting light into the air to hang above their heads, illuminating all the dark corners of the cellar. From the back wall, four figures shuffled forward.

Vola's eyes widened as the first figure stepped into the light and raised its head.

A half-orc, complete with green-gray skin, gold eyes, and a black braid down her back. She wore battered chain mail and a sword sheathed at her hip. She grinned when she saw Vola.

Behind her strode a halfling with curly red-brown hair, dressed in a gray wrap-around tunic with a lovely, blonde wizard beside her. Behind them lurked an androgynous figure in a hood carrying a bow.

"Is there a mirror in here?" Sorrel said.

"It's just an illusion," Lillie whispered. "We know that."

"Yeah, but he stole our images. Is he allowed to do that?"

"He's also stolen people," Talon said. "Do you think he cares about rules?"

"This might actually be the most innocuous thing he's done," Vola said.

The mirror copy of Vola drew her sword, and the other Sorrel followed suit.

"Still creepy," Sorrel said with an involuntary step back.

"This room is the key to all of the illusions on the manor," Lillie said. "If we dispel these illusions, we dispel them all."

"Could one of these be Arthorel?" Vola said as the opposite party shifted into fighting stances.

Lillie hesitated. "Maybe."

Vola grinned and turned her foot to better launch herself and called, "Charge!"

She lunged for the false paladin, who met her blow with a bone jarring parry.

They each took their mirror image, Sorrel closing with the other halfling while Lillie flung spells at the other wizard.

Vola swung again and the other paladin blocked her. She spun and finally managed a hit, but at the exact same time, her enemy's blade scored a strike across her arm. Every blow was blocked or matched, and Vola glanced desperately at the others.

They weren't faring any better. The two Sorrels were locked in furious combat, staffs whirling and cracking together. Talon ducked behind a column and popped their head out long enough to shoot, then had to jerk back again to avoid the other ranger's arrow. The false Talon crouched atop the barrels while Gruff circled underneath, trying to find a way to drag them down.

Lillie was the only one unevenly matched. Her counterpart wasn't limping and could leap out of the way, while the real Lillie looked a bit singed. Vola hadn't even known the illusions could cast spells. Arthorel must have gotten better at them.

This had been a really bad idea.

Vola caught her opponent's blade on her own and grunted with the effort. The other Vola grinned, showing off her tusks, and pressed harder. Vola growled and with a heave, threw off the other Vola's attack. She stepped back for a split second to yell at her party.

"Switch," she called. "Switch targets or this will never work."

Her words caused a break in the fighting, just long enough for everyone to break eye contact with their opponent.

Instead of returning to her duel, Vola lunged away from the

other paladin and tried to find another target. But that was her second mistake. With everyone shuffled, she had no idea who was who. Which Sorrel was the real one? Which Lillie was the one limping? She couldn't tell if they were standing still.

Then an arrow whizzed past Vola's ear, and she spun with a grin. Clearly, the one shooting at her was the wrong Talon.

The other ranger had leaped to the ground, and Vola bore down on them. She dodged an arrow. Another grazed her leg that she ignored. Then she was close enough to swing and the other Talon had to leap back and draw a knife.

They used it to deflect Vola's second blow. But she had enough momentum to swing around and cut through the other's arm.

No sound came from the deep hood, creeping her out more than their perfectly mirrored images. The figure jerked, and the hood fell back.

Vola swallowed a curse. Nothing lay under the hood, just a blank clay blob. Obviously, Lord Arthorel had never seen enough of Talon to imagine a face for them.

Vola shook off her reaction and roared. Then she spun and took the creature's clay head off with a swipe.

It crumpled into a heap of mud.

Beside her, the real Talon wasn't even trying to shoot at the false Sorrel anymore. Even illusory monks were too fast. Talon waited while the false Sorrel darted past the columns and Gruff lunged to catch her. Talon bore down on the struggling monk while Gruff took pieces out of its hide, leaving gaping wounds of fresh clay.

The real Sorrel chased the false Lillie around the cellar, landing blows on her back and legs. The wizard evidently didn't want to close the distance with a melee fighter but couldn't run fast enough to stay ahead of her. Finally, the wizard stopped, turned and reached with lightning coated hands to grab at the monk.

Sorrel ducked, struck out with her staff to sweep the false Lillie's legs out from under her, and aimed the next blow at her pretty head.

Well if the rest of them were all accounted for, that just left the real Lillie facing…Oh no.

Vola spun, ready to leap to Lillie's defense, but a wave of heat made her eyebrows curl and she stopped short.

Lillie stood, feet planted, hands outstretched as flames poured from her palms.

The false Vola stood frozen in the middle of the cellar as if she'd tripped in the middle of a charge, and Vola watched as the figure just melted. The clay of the golem underneath the illusion puddled on the floor and bubbled in the heat.

Lillie stepped back, breathing heavily.

"Holy crap, Lillie," Vola said. "Is that what that spell is supposed to do?"

The wizard pushed the hair out of her eyes. "It is if I can get a clear shot without worrying about anyone."

Vola opened her mouth to say that she was a fighter. She was supposed to fight things. She wasn't supposed to have to worry about what was going on behind her. But if Lillie could stop an orc in full charge like that, maybe Vola could afford to step aside once in a while.

Vola's cheeks burned, and she snapped her mouth shut on her reply.

Lillie dropped her gaze.

Talon and Sorrel stared down at twin piles of mud and clay.

"Where's Henri?" Vola asked. The cellar looked exactly the same as it had before the fight except for the mud on the floor. None of the illusions had hidden Lord Arthorel, and if there were any more down here, they weren't broken as Lillie had said.

Lillie glanced around with a frown. "I don't…"

"I thought you said the illusions would be broken if we beat them?"

Lillie planted her hands on her hips. "I did. They should have been. But…" She closed her eyes and turned her head from side to side. "They weren't. For some reason, they weren't."

Vola growled and gripped her hair. "Then why? Where is he?"

"I don't know!"

"Vola, give her a break," Sorrel said. "She's gotten us this far."

"Which isn't going to do us any good if we can't find Henri."

"We will," Lillie said. "Just give me a moment." She limped further into the cellar with her hands raised. "I was sure that would break the spells. Why didn't it?"

There was a snarl, and a shadow detached itself from the back wall. A duplicate Gruff leaped for Lillie.

Vola yelled as the wizard went down under the wolf's snapping jaws.

# TWENTY-FIVE

Vola and Talon leaped forward to drag the creature off of Lillie. The false Gruff snapped at their hands. Vola was just a second too slow and a line of fire snaked down her hand as she yanked away from his teeth.

Talon didn't even flinch. They grabbed two handfuls of fur and rolled the wolf off his feet, then Vola raised her blade and cut him in half.

As the golem fell to pieces and turned to mud and clay, the casks around them disappeared and the wall at the back of the cellar opened onto a passageway that hadn't been there before.

The last illusion now broken.

Sorrel fell to her knees beside Lillie, pulling her head and shoulders into her small lap.

"Is she all right?" Vola asked, sheathing her blade.

Sorrel glanced up, a frown creasing her forehead. "I doubt it."

Lillie winced, eyes closed against the pain. "My leg," she whispered.

Vola knelt beside the wizard and gently stretched the leg out. The scratch that had marred the back of her knee before now gaped, ripped crosswise by vicious teeth. Now that her pants were torn so far, Vola could see the wound had stretched further up her thigh and deeper in the muscle than they'd noticed before.

The breath in her chest went cold and tight. Lillie had been walking around like this the whole time? Without complaining? Why hadn't she said something? Why hadn't she just insisted they stop?

Something slammed down the passageway. Like a door. Or the fall of an ax.

Vola jumped and glanced into the dark, imagining Henri tied to a chair. Executed because of every mistake Vola had made in the last two days.

When she looked back, Talon and Sorrel were looking at her. She couldn't see Talon's expression under the hood, but Sorrel's lips were thin and white and her eyes darted away from Vola's.

"You still want to go after Henri," Talon said.

Vola swallowed and looked down. Lillie wouldn't be walking anywhere. She shouldn't have been walking on that "scratch" in the first place.

The knot in her gut tightened. Anger and shame mixed and burned in her throat. Anger at herself. Anger at Lillie. They were so close and now the wizard lay bleeding on the floor.

"You did this," Talon said.

Vola sucked in a breath.

"It wasn't her fault," Lillie said faintly.

"Like hell. She pushed us. She rushed in. She doesn't lead, she just runs ahead and expects us to follow and clean up her mess."

"I just wanted to get to Henri."

"And that was worth this?"

"Talon," Lillie said, stopping the ranger's tirade. Lillie reached for Vola's hand, but Vola shifted far enough away she couldn't find it. Lillie let her hand drop. "Go, Vola," she said. "He doesn't have time. I do."

Vola looked up again, but Sorrel didn't meet her eyes.

"Go then," Talon said. "It's what you want."

Vola stood, either to go or to argue. She wasn't sure which yet.

"But don't expect us to follow."

Talon knelt to tend Lillie, but their words seemed more final somehow. Like a sword thrown to the ground in defeat.

"Talon."

"Go." The anger was gone, replaced by weariness. "I thought you were something you're not. That was my mistake, I guess."

Vola couldn't even look at Lillie. If the wizard had just said something…If she'd just made them stop…If she'd stayed out of the way…

Vola swallowed down the taste of bile. How had it all gone sideways so fast? How could she fix it?

Lillie breathed through her teeth on the floor.

"I'll come back," she whispered. "As soon as I fetch Henri. I'll be right back."

"Doesn't matter," Talon said. "We won't be here."

Vola turned, eyes burning, and she sprinted down the dark corridor, trying not to feel like she was running away.

Vola pounded down the passageway, boots beating against the rough flagstones in rhythm with her heartbeat. She hoped to Cleavah she found Henri at the end of this hall. Because if she didn't, all of this would have been for nothing.

And a tiny dark part of her hoped they didn't find him. Because then she wouldn't have to explain to him how she'd let her party split down the middle. She'd let Lillie get hurt. And she'd destroyed the one chance she had to become a paladin because she hadn't acted like a paladin.

The walls sped past her, and suddenly with a burst of clarity,

Vola realized there were dancing shadows in what should have been darkness. A brilliant ball of light followed her overhead. The same ball of light Lillie had conjured in the cellar.

Vola collapsed against the wall as cold washed down her limbs, settling like a weight in her gut. Her fingers curled against the stone wall, and she struck out with her fist.

Her knuckles bled and she grunted in pain, but she did not cry out.

"Now who's hitting walls," Sorrel's voice said behind her.

Vola spun to see the monk standing a few feet back down the passage as if she'd been following. Her normally cheerful face was grave, no sign of the smile or dancing eyes that Vola had come to expect.

Lillie was hurt, Talon was leaving, and Sorrel was sad. Vola had managed to break all of them.

"We all want to save Henri," Sorrel said quietly as Vola pushed herself off the wall. "But you're acting like you don't trust us. Like you have to do this all yourself. He's a grown man, a skilled warrior. He kept us alive in the swamp. If anyone could take care of themselves, it would be Henri. So, why is this so important?"

"Wiselyn said they'd kill him."

"And like Lillie said, Arthorel is kidnapping living people. If he gets away, we'll just track him down. So why is this so important? What's driving you?"

"He's…my teacher."

Sorrel waited for more with her head cocked.

"No one thought I could be a paladin." Vola dropped her gaze to her pock-marked armor. "No one wanted me to be a paladin. My parents taught me to fight, but they didn't really understand. They thought I should be a mercenary. It's…easier work for an orc."

"Half-orc," Sorrel said quietly.

Vola ran her hands over her face. "The other paladins all think we're evil. Only capable of violence because we worship the Obstacles. They said no matter how hard I tried, I'd only ever bring evil to my friends. No one believed I could be anything but vicious. No one but Henri. He's the best trainer there is. And they laughed at him for taking me on. They laughed at him and told him I was a lost cause. I would only be his downfall."

Vola's voice ground to a halt as her throat clogged. She cleared it. Then growled, "I will not prove them right."

She turned and stalked down the hall, drawing her sword, ready for anything to come at them through the dark.

Sorrel's footsteps shushed along the stones behind her. The halfling said nothing, but still, she followed Vola down the hallway that looked more and more like a tunnel.

Vola's heart sped in her chest as the walls grew closer and closer, damper and damper. Lillie's light still blazed, but it wasn't much use when stone closed in around her shoulders.

Finally, she could see something at the end of the hall. The light bounced from straight lines and dark locks, and Vola realized she was looking at a line of cell doors standing open.

She stopped, the silence and emptiness pressing against her until she felt like she couldn't draw breath. Slowly, she slid forward to peer into the cells.

Empty. Bare walls and stone floors stared back at her, yielding no clues about their recent occupants. Who they'd been, where they'd gone.

"No one's here," Sorrel said, padding lightly from door to door.

Vola shook her head, teeth clenched. She walked down the row, counting off cells. There were more than enough to hold the missing townsfolk plus Henri.

At the end, the hall opened into an alcove, and beyond it, a door swung open.

The fresh breeze made Vola's nose twitch, and she grabbed the edge of the open door. Beyond, stretched the night sky, stars staring down, their gaze cold and accusing.

There were no convenient footprints or a road lit by moonlight to tell Vola where the captives had been taken. Nothing but a narrow stretch of grass that led directly to the swamp at the bottom of the hill.

"Vola," Sorrel said behind her, and something in the halfling's voice, some pity or sympathy, made her stiffen and turn.

Sorrel stood in the alcove, which was piled with clothes, armor, and weapons. Half-full travel packs spilled out across the flagstones. The personal effects of all of Lord Arthorel's prisoners.

A round shield stood propped against the wall, its once shining surface gouged and battered. A black burn stretched across it where a swamp blossom's acid had scorched the metal.

Vola stepped closer and knelt. Her fingers reached out to brush down the scarred surface of the shield.

Then she bowed her head so Sorrel couldn't see her face.

# TWENTY-SIX

She'd failed. Just like all the paladins had said she would.

Everyone was worse off now than they'd been before. She hadn't rescued Henri in time. Her party had fallen apart. And she was left standing here empty-handed with no idea how to make things right.

She was so far from earning her shield that she might as well have been in the next country. And the funny thing was that wasn't even what mattered the most in this moment. Getting her shield wouldn't make Sorrel smile again. It wouldn't make Talon stay. And it wouldn't heal Lillie.

It wouldn't make her the leader she needed to be to fix what she'd broken.

With both hands, she grasped Henri's shield and pulled it toward herself. Images flashed through her head, one after another. A cascade of painful memories, their sharp edges searing her as they passed.

Henri kicking a ball with a group of kids. Henri slathering cream on Sorrel's red arms. Henri dodging in front of Lillie, catching a spray of acid on his shield. Henri helping Talon slay swamp blossoms.

More images flashed, too fast to register, too many to count. A flood of feeling as she watched Henri train her, teach her, coach her. His voice wove through it all, always calm never raised. "Keep your shield arm up, and your feet planted." "If you go down, get back up again." "Your strength is not in your arm, it's in your head and your heart." "A Paladin is a light in a dark world."

What would he say if he could see her now? What would he do to fix this?

What had he been doing the entire time? While Vola had been walking out front, leading her party into trouble, he'd been following along behind.

He didn't rush ahead, trying to kill everything that threatened them. He didn't try to solve every problem.

He protected them. He trusted them and their skills and kept them safe so they could do their jobs.

Henri wasn't a good leader. He was a good protector.

"I am a light in the dark," the paladin oath went. "I am courage when others have none. I am strength when others are weak. I am their sword when they are weaponless."

She was supposed to get the job done, yes. But if that meant rushing ahead and leaving others to get hurt, then she was as good as an oathbreaker. Her job wasn't to be the leader. Her job was to protect the ones who needed her sword. The victims she was trying to rescue, but first and foremost, her party, who needed her to keep them safe so they could get the job done.

Vola closed her eyes. *I can do better. I can always do better. Trust the party. Keep them safe. Get the job done.*

Vola took Henri's shield and carried it awkwardly by the rim as she trudged back up the hallway to the cellar. Sorrel trotted along behind her without a word.

Talon knelt beside Lillie, tearing rough strips out of a sheet for a bandage. The ranger must have gone upstairs to find it.

Vola's heart clenched. She'd expected Talon to be gone by now, but no. Of course, they were here, taking care of what was left of their pack.

Vola propped the shield up against the wall.

Lillie's eyes locked on it and her face fell. "Oh, Henri."

Talon's hood tracked Vola's movements as she stepped to their side and knelt.

Vola bent over Lillie's leg and very carefully touched the edges of the bandage. Despite her care, Lillie hissed through her teeth.

Vola sucked in a breath. She knew from the first touch just how deep the wound went. How much damage had been done. And she knew she couldn't heal it entirely. Maybe if she'd tried back when Lillie first fell in the courtyard…

Still, she spread her hands over the wound and whispered, "Lady bless."

Half spell and half prayer, the power poured through her, a gift from Cleavah. But the skill had to come from Vola.

Her leg ached as the wound transferred to herself, but there was still a nasty puckered scar reaching up Lillie's leg. And Vola could tell the damage underneath remained deep.

*Lady,* Vola asked in her head. *Is there anything more I can do?*

*Learn,* the goddess said. *I can only heal through you.*

And the healing would be as faulty as the vessel. Vola bowed her head.

"I'm sorry," she told Lillie.

Lillie put her hand on top of Vola's head. "It wasn't your fault, Vola."

Vola's lips thinned. "No, Talon's right. I should have stopped and made sure you were okay."

"I told you I was. I should have been honest."

"And I should have checked for myself." She took a deep breath and looked up to glance between Talon and Lillie. "I've made a lot of mistakes in the last couple of days."

Her eyes settled on Talon. Talon, who'd been searching for a new family to belong to. Vola and the others could have been that family if she hadn't screwed it up.

"I'm sorry I left." Vola swallowed. No one liked admitting they were wrong, but adding on talking about why she'd been wrong made her want to crawl in a hole. "I thought I was supposed to lead you. I thought I was supposed to be the best so we could rescue everyone. But I just got you guys hurt. I should have been protecting you so you could do the things you're good at. 'Cause you're good at so many things that I'm not. Sorrel was right. I screwed up by not trusting you and now I'm worried that you won't trust me."

Lillie bit her lip and looked down. Vola glanced at Sorrel, who always had something to say, but the halfling leaned against the wall, staring at her sandals.

It was Talon who cleared their throat.

Then the ranger reached for the edge of their hood. Gloved fingers gripped the fabric and pulled it back.

Vola stared. Talon wasn't that mysterious after all. They were human with light blue eyes and pale skin that didn't get a lot of sun. Sandy colored hair had been cropped unevenly around their round ears and a patchy beard wandered over their chin.

There was nothing shocking for Talon to hide, but they'd worn the hood anyway, keeping themselves apart. And Vola decided to take this moment for what it was. A gift, and a measure of trust.

Vola met Talon's eyes. "Is it too late to trust my pack?"

Talon grimaced. "It just sounds stupid when you say it."

"What? Pack? Because I wasn't raised by wolves?"

"Yeah." Talon heaved a sigh and crossed their arms. "All right, let's do this."

"Do what? Give me another chance?"

Talon jerked their head at Gruff, who came to sit at their side. "We'll stick around for a bit. See if you're worth following now that you're paying attention to the right things."

"So how do we fix this?" Sorrel said. "We're pretty deep in the hole."

"Not exactly," Lillie said. "We have Lord Arthorel on the run. We took away his manor and his captain of the guard. All he has left is his magic and his prisoners. If we can catch up to him…"

"We'll be in a much stronger position than when we ran in here," Vola finished. She tapped her teeth. "Talon, there's a bunch of cells at the end of the passageway. And a door out to the swamp. I think that's where Lord Arthorel escaped with his prisoners. Can you and Gruff track him, figure out where he's going? I couldn't see anything obvious."

Talon nodded once, decisively. "We'll look for the less than obvious." The two of them disappeared down the tunnel together.

"Sorrel," Vola said, and the halfling straightened up off the wall. "You were really good at talking to people in town. Getting them to trust you. Will you talk to them now? See if you can convince them to rise up against Arthorel. It'll take some work, but we have his manor now. We'll have enough evidence by the end of the night to bring him up against the nobles court and try him for…" Vola waved her hand vaguely.

"Neglecting his duty, abuse of his tenets and properties, and treason," Lillie supplied. "Plus whatever it is he's actually doing to his victims."

"Magical experiments?" Sorrel said. "Slavery? I can probably use that to get the townsfolk angry enough to revolt."

"Do it."

Sorrel jerked her chin up and gave Vola a mock salute. "Whatever you say, boss." She trotted up the stairs toward the manor proper.

Vola watched her go. Sorrel had been a pretty good second so far. It was time Vola recognized that and used it.

"What about me?" Lillie said quietly.

Vola hid a wince. By sending the others off, she'd left herself alone with the person she'd let down the most. The urge to run made her feet itch. She could do it. Make up some excuse. Tell Lillie she was too hurt and send her off to town to recuperate. Vola would never have to look at her again.

She shook her head roughly and slung Lillie's arm over her shoulder. "You are going to look for clues about what Lord Arthorel is planning," Vola said. "You're a spell caster. I figure if anyone can tell us what he's up to, it's you."

"And what will you be doing?"

"I'm going to be your crutch," Vola said without rancor. "It's the best place I can be right now."

She wasn't supposed to be out front leading the charge. Her place was here, beside her people. Meeting their needs.

# TWENTY-SEVEN

VOLA HELPED Lillie limp all the way up the stairs to the top floor of the manor. No one bothered them. They must have taken care of all the armsmen in the courtyard and the other servants had seen what was good for them and fled. If there'd been any.

Their boots scuffed an old worn carpet, and Vola's toe caught a hole, making her stagger into the wall with Lillie.

The wizard clenched her teeth but made no sound until they were upright again.

"This place is a mess," she said, finally. "Arthorel's finances must be even worse than we thought."

"And he was covering it all up with magic. Illusions to make himself look rich and prosperous. Damn nobles, appearances are so important," Vola said.

Lillie concentrated on her feet. "Not all nobles are like this."

Vola opened her mouth and then thought better of what she was about to say. When Lillie had turned on the charm with the gate guard and Lord Arthorel, she'd talked about playing a part. Vola had thought that meant literally. But maybe it didn't. Vola acted like a paladin because she was supposed to be one. Because it helped her feel real. Maybe Lillie meant something similar. Maybe nobility was a piece of her she could put on and off. A piece she wasn't necessarily proud of.

But what was a noble like Lillie doing in a place like Water's Edge looking for a job? Unless, she was running from something.

"We need to find an office," Lillie said, interrupting Vola's train of thought. "Or a study. Somewhere Arthorel keeps his paperwork."

They poked their heads through a couple of doors, finding spare bedrooms with furniture covered in dust covers. Finally, toward the end of the hall, they opened a door on a room lined with bookshelves and a huge mahogany desk standing in front of a wide window.

"Jackpot," Vola said and put her shoulder under Lillie's arm to help her inside. She had to bend nearly in half to make it work.

Vola helped Lillie plop in the chair behind the desk and searched for something to prop her injured leg on. It didn't go very well.

Vola expected sumptuous chairs, end tables, little knick-knacks. Things that would make a study feel lived in and homey. Instead, the room was nearly empty except for the desk and a single bare chair behind it. The bookshelves stood silent and devoid of books and knick-knacks.

It was almost creepy how sparse it was.

"You want to poke through the drawers?" Vola said. "I'll go find a footstool. And when I get back, I can fetch and carry for you. Anything you need, I'll bring to you so you don't have to get up."

Lillie's brow furrowed, and Vola escaped through the door before the other woman could ask what was wrong. She felt like a coward every time she turned her back on Lillie, but it was so hard meeting those green-blue eyes knowing what she'd done wrong in the past twenty-four hours.

The next room held a huge four-poster bed with no canopy and a single blanket tossed carelessly over the end. The vanity sported a couple of tins of old cosmetics and empty bottles of cologne. Vola stole the stool from the vanity and carried it back to Lillie.

Lillie had lit the gas lamps along the walls, and now she poured over a stack of loose paper with a book open beside her.

"Here," Vola said and knelt to place Lillie's foot on the stool. While she was there, she went ahead and checked the wound.

No seeping. But Lillie's movements were stiff, indicating a lot more damage underneath the scarring.

A stillness above made Vola look up, and she found Lillie staring at her.

Heat beat in Vola's cheeks.

"Why do you hate me?" Lillie said quietly, the flickering glow of the lamps reflecting in her bright hair.

Vola jerked and snatched her hands away from Lillie's leg. "I don't hate you," she said quickly.

Lillie tilted her head. "Maybe not now, but I think you did. Otherwise, you wouldn't be trying to make up for it so much."

Vola glanced away, chest tight. How to explain something she wasn't even sure she understood herself? She'd fallen into step with Sorrel and Talon without missing a beat, but somehow, every time Vola had looked at Lillie, she'd tripped, mentally. Like finding a stone in her boot.

"Sorrel told me you three have been standing watch most nights." Lillie brushed her hair over her shoulder. "No one ever woke me to take a turn."

Vola blinked. Truth was she'd never even thought of waking Lillie to stand watch. The other two were warriors. And that was the problem. Vola looked at Talon and Sorrel and saw fighters. Vola looked at Lillie and saw something else. Something from a long time ago that had no place in her current life. She looked at Lillie and saw a memory.

Vola wanted to stand. It would make her tower over the seated wizard, give her a position of unconscious power.

But she ignored the impulse and stayed where she was, kneeling beside Lillie, their heights flip-flopped for the moment.

"I've disregarded you this whole time," Vola said. "Disregarded and underestimated and maybe hated you. Just a little bit."

"Why?" Lillie said. "I mean, I know I'm not very good in the wilderness." She flushed and glanced at her hands. "I'm pretty terrible at it. But I didn't think I'd done anything to make you hate me."

"You didn't," Vola said, and Lillie glanced up, catching the emphasis Vola had put on the word "you."

"Then who?" Lillie said.

Vola sighed. Why did everyone always want words? Blades were so much easier. They didn't get wrapped up and twisted around until you couldn't point them straight. It would be better if she could pace, walk the nerves out while she found the words, but she was too afraid she'd take the opportunity to walk right out the door, avoiding the question.

"I grew up in a little town a lot like Water's Edge, but a lot further east," Vola said. Might as well start at the beginning.

Lillie waited patiently. Maybe her parents had told her stories growing up, and this ritual was familiar.

"A human village. Mostly. But our clan had settled down right next door. The humans were fine with us, as long as we kept to our side of the street and didn't make trouble. We served as a buffer, a protection against the wilds and the bandits that raided occasionally. Maybe it would have been fine if I'd been a full orc. Or a full human. I would have fit in somewhere. But my parents wanted me to go to school with the other kids in town. The local priest taught them all how to read. He, uh, didn't think it was worth it for me."

Lillie watched with a small frown of concentration.

Vola swallowed and stared resolutely out the window. She'd rather tell the story about how she'd beaten a full knight to earn her place at the paladin academy. Or about the way she'd saved the human kids when the school had burned down. The racist priest, too. He'd made her life miserable, and she'd repaid him by saving his life.

But those stories didn't explain what was going on. They didn't tell Lillie what ate at Vola from the inside.

"The girls in the village. They were all perfect and beautiful. Skinny and blonde and blue-eyed. And I was…I was half an orc. All green skin and black hair."

"And they were mean to you," Lillie said. Evidently, she'd heard this story before.

Vola nodded and then shook her head. "Of course. They made fun of my skin, my teeth, my height. They called me monster. But that's not the worst part. I could handle that. It didn't even make me cry anymore. The part that hurt, the part that still stings, is that I wanted to be them. I wanted to look like those girls, all perfect skin and hair. Delicate and pretty. And I hated myself for it."

Lillie sank back into the chair, her mouth open. "Oh."

Vola rubbed her hands over her face. She'd never put the story into words before. She hadn't thought she'd ever have to. It was a part of her that she'd left behind in that little town. She'd walked away and shed the skin of that hurting, hate-filled Vola and put on a tougher more-accepting skin. But talking about it made it feel like she hadn't really gotten rid of it at all. All that pain was still buried somewhere inside her. Was it something she'd carry with her always? Or would there ever be a time when she could breathe free?

"I think I understand," Lillie said. "You want to like who you are. You want to be comfortable in your skin, but it's hard when the world is telling you that skin should look a certain way. It takes a certain strength to ignore the world. And you hate yourself when you don't have that strength."

Vola glanced at Lillie out of the corner of her eye. "That's… well, yeah. That's it. How'd you know?"

"It's easier to see other people's hang ups than our own, I've always thought. But I don't see why you hated me."

Vola raised an eyebrow. "Because you remind me of my weakness. You're the spitting image of those perfect girls I so wanted to be."

Lillie snorted. "Yes, because fat and clumsy is so very attractive."

Vola opened her mouth to say, "No, curvy and golden is beautiful," but found her voice dying in her throat. Maybe that was one of Lillie's hang ups. The one she couldn't see because she was too close to it.

"At least you're not green," Vola said and she managed it without any bitterness. "So, are you a noble?"

Lillie's face fell, and she turned back to the desk. "Not anymore."

Definitely running from something. Maybe a fiancé. Maybe a husband. Noble women were always running away to escape marriage. At least that's what they did in all those bad adventure novels.

Vola almost asked. It seemed only fair to get some answers, but if Lillie really had run away from her family and her way of life, then she'd lost something important. Something integral to who she was. Recently.

"I'm sorry," Vola said.

Lillie glanced at her out of the corner of her eye. "You don't even know what happened."

Vola shrugged. "I'm still sorry. And I'm sorry for lumping you in with my personal ghosts. You're nothing like those girls, and I should have given you time to prove it." Vola took a deep breath. "And I'm sorry I disregarded you for so long. I didn't treat you like a friend. Or even like a full member of the party. I put you in a corner. I didn't let you do your job. I rushed us, and I didn't take the time to make sure you were okay before pushing ahead."

She clenched her fists and met Lillie's eyes. "I don't know if you'll ever walk the same again."

Lillie's gaze was steady. "I know."

Vola swallowed. "You're not…not mad at me?" The others had all been mad. But Lillie was the one whose life would change.

"I'm mad," Lillie said. "But I can't work with you if I don't forgive you. So, I forgive you."

Vola jerked. Was she joking?

"Just like that?" she asked, harshness slipping into her voice. "Don't you need time to forgive?"

"We don't have time." Lillie gestured around them. "Isn't that what you've been saying since we left the tor?" She hesitated, fingers playing with the edge of a page. "Forgiveness is a choice. Not a feeling. I choose to forgive you."

Vola heard the rest even if Lillie didn't say it. She chose to forgive Vola even if Vola didn't deserve it.

Vola bowed her head. She rubbed her thumb over her knuckles, over and over again. "I'll try to do better from now on," she said, voice quiet. It was the only thing she could do. To make up for the mistakes she made. Try not to make them again.

"I know that, too," Lillie said, and Vola looked up when she heard a smile in her voice. "That's the only reason I can make that choice."

# TWENTY-EIGHT

L ESS THAN AN HOUR LATER, Vola caught sight of Talon in the doorway, hood still around their shoulders. She straightened up off the corner of the desk where she'd been waiting for Lillie to need something.

"You found us," she said.

"All the illusions are gone, and this is the only room that's lit." They indicated the light flickering along the walls.

"Did you see Sorrel out there?"

"Right behind me."

"Great, what do you have for us?"

"Gruff and I found Lord Arthorel's trail. He travels with a dozen prisoners who are dragging their feet and making life difficult for him."

"Ha, serves him right," Sorrel said, coming through the door. "Hey all, are we speaking to each other again?"

"We're quite well set," Lillie said from the table without looking up from the papers. "Now that we understand one another better."

"You want to be in on this discussion?" Vola said when the

wizard made no move to leave the desk. "Planning, meeting thing."

Lillie waved a distracted hand. "Keep going. I'll hear you. I would never have made it through university if I couldn't read and listen at the same time."

Vola shrugged. "I don't even like to read and read at the same time, but if you say so, I believe you. Talon?"

"We tracked him to the edge of the swamp. Gruff is keeping an eye on him, but I came back to guide you. He heads southeast, straight along the only road out of town."

"Where is he going?"

"I don't know. What lies at the other end of the swamp?"

"Harbor," Lillie said. Without looking up, she held out a map and Vola took it.

Sure enough, the rough sketch showed Water's Edge right on the outskirts of the swamp. One trail skirted the edges of the mire and came out the other side at the small Ghost Creek Harbor.

"It might be tiny," Lillie said. "But it's strategically significant for the area. The only way to get goods this side of the river."

"So, he's moving the prisoners," Sorrel said. "Getting the heck out of…well, here. But why?"

Lillie finally looked up and straightened the pages she'd been reading. "He's selling them."

"What?" Sorrel said.

"Slavery is illegal in all fifteen principalities," Vola said.

"I don't know if they're going to be slaves," Lillie said with a frown. "I'm not sure he knew what was going to happen to them after they made it to the buyer. He just needed the money." Her lips went white and thin. "The bastard was broke. So, he started kidnapping people and selling them. At first, he stuck to criminals and bandits that nobody would miss."

Sorrel nodded thoughtfully. "That explains the low crime rate."

"But when he ran out of those, he started stealing his own people to sell." Lillie's voice rose and her knuckles went white on the edge of the desk. "He completely ignored his duties as a noble and preyed upon his own people. How anyone could betray their duties so-so…" She stopped herself and focused on Vola once more. "Sorry. Go on."

Vola raised an eyebrow. "Who was he selling them to?"

Lillie sat back with a grumble. "This doesn't say. I expect the best way to find out would be to run the bastard to the ground and make him tell us. Painfully if at all possible."

Vola raised an eyebrow. "You get feisty when you're angry, don't you?"

Lillie flushed. "Maybe a little."

"Then it's a good thing we can follow him," Sorrel said, giving the three of them a grin.

"Sounds like you have good news on that front." Vola tilted her head.

"We have horses," Sorrel said. "And Braydon. And the small army of townsfolk that Braydon plans on leading."

"Holy crap. Well done, Sorrel," Vola said.

"He said to tell you not to worry about your backside. He'll watch it for you."

"Aw, that's nice of him," Lillie said.

"Yeah. Unless he meant butt."

Vola shook her head. "What?"

"Maybe he meant he'd watch your butt." Sorrel tapped her lip. "That's not as helpful. And kind of creepy."

"I think he meant back," Talon said. "He seemed stubborn. Not lecherous."

"You're probably right. I know very little about butts and watching them."

"Which is funny given your height," Talon muttered.

"I know, right? I just don't see the appeal."

"You do an excellent job of kicking them, though," Lillie said.

"Which we're gonna go do," Vola said, raising her voice. "Now. We've got to get to the harbor. Stop Lord Arthorel before he sends Henri and the others to…wherever he's sending them. If we're too late…"

"We won't know where to go next." Sorrel finished for her.

Vola nodded. "Lillie? Think you can sit a horse?"

Lillie levered herself to her feet. "Try to stop me."

# TWENTY-NINE

Vola stepped into the courtyard and blinked in the sudden flickering torchlight. She held up her arm to shield her eyes and sucked in a breath.

Braydon waited at the foot of the manor steps, his sword in one hand and a torch in the other. Dozens and dozens of angry townspeople were arrayed behind him, armed and armored with leather aprons, pots and pans, and pitchforks. Too many torches splashed light up the walls of the manor making the night beyond seem that much darker.

Holy crap, they were going to get themselves killed outfitted like that, but from the set mouths and hard eyes, they knew what they were doing and Vola wasn't going to be the one to disappoint them.

"Ready when you are, boss," Braydon said with a grin that looked entirely unnatural on a face that had only ever scowled at her before.

"Uh, right," she said, pushing down her discomfort. She cleared her throat. "I trust you to call the shots for the townsfolk."

She leaned in toward him to whisper. "Keep them alive, would you?"

He rolled his eyes. "Don't worry. I'll point them in the right direction." Braydon gestured to the crowd, which parted to reveal their mounts. "You four go on ahead. Catch Lord Arthorel before he can escape with our people. We'll be right behind you ready to mop up and reinforce you if you need it."

Vola couldn't respond because she was too busy groaning at the horses. Well, three horses and one swamp beast.

"You've got to be kidding me," Talon muttered.

"I would really like to swear right about now," Vola said.

"One of us could do it for you," Talon said.

Vola considered it for a split second, but…"I feel like that would defeat the purpose."

Sorrel danced from foot to foot. "I'm sorry. This was all they had."

"Millford!" Lillie limped toward the swamp beast. Who promptly reached out and bit her on the shoulder.

"Ow!" Lillie stumbled back and glared at the creature with a mixture of pain and betrayal.

Vola sighed. "I'll take it. Everyone else mount up."

Braydon gave Lillie a leg up while Vola approached the swamp beast from the side with her hands out. It lunged one way, but Vola was ready and lunged the other way, then swung her leg over the makeshift saddle. Someone had gotten close enough to the thing to tie a blanket around its middle.

Vola was tall enough that her feet dragged unless she held them off the ground. This was just going to be so much fun.

It didn't have a flowing mane or tail. And its teeth were more like fangs but at least it was too mean to be afraid of her. That actually made a pleasant change.

She glanced over to see Lillie and Talon mounted. Talon had drawn their hood up as soon as they'd stepped outside and seen all the people. Lillie was taking the books Braydon handed up to her and stashing them in the satchel she'd acquired somewhere between the study and the front door.

"Are those multiplying by themselves?" Vola said. "Or are you collecting?"

Lillie gave her a hurt look. "We might need them."

Sorrel scrambled up the side of a surprised looking horse as if it were a tree. She perched on top of the animal, legs swinging, stirrups a million miles below her feet. The monk didn't seem to care.

Sorrel grabbed her reins and shouted "Yee haw!"

Her horse stood there, looking nonplussed.

Sorrel tipped her head. "That's how you get them to go, right?"

Talon shook their head and kicked their horse into a trot.

Sorrel's followed amiably while the monk's eyes went round. "Oh," she said.

Lillie followed her, and Vola urged the swamp beast into motion so she could guard her party's rear.

The crowd parted as they cantered through the gate, and when she cast a glance over her shoulder at the bottom of the hill, the torches were streaming out after them, ready to follow them to the harbor.

She set her face into the wind, keeping an eye on her people ahead. Riding behind the others should have made her anxious, but her spine relaxed a bit. From back here, she could see them and guard them and it felt like a missing brick fitting back into a wall.

She resigned herself to the fact that she'd be staring at a lot of butts in the future.

Talon led them at a gallop along the road, the only solid path through the mire of the swamp. Talon rode as if they were one with the horse, and Vola suspected the ranger of secretly communicating with the creature.

Sorrel clearly had no idea what she was doing, but she clung to the saddle, sticking to the back of the horse even as it followed Talon's headlong pace.

Lillie rode stiffly, like someone who knew the right way to sit a horse but couldn't quite manage it at the moment and felt like they were cheating by not pushing themselves.

The swamp beast ran like a belligerent crocodile, all sinuous motion and malevolent intent. Vola was pretty sure the only reason it ran was to catch and eat the things fleeing in front of it. That didn't bode well for when they finally stopped.

Just as dawn lit the sky with streaks of burning orange and pink, the trees gave way around them, stretching away on either side where the sea met the land in a series of muddy little islands. Buildings rose ahead, gray with weather and the salt air. Nets and strings of buoys hung between them. The mildewed sock scent of the swamp faded, replaced by a fishy pall.

Three docks jutted out into the harbor, and Vola's heart sank as she realized there wasn't a single ship tied up there.

A sharp bark and a growl heralded Gruff's appearance. He peeled away from the last of the drooping trees and fell in beside them. Talon leaned over the side of their horse as they raced toward the harbor buildings.

"He's on a ship," they called back. "There! He's leaving."

Talon pointed, and Vola stood in her stirrups to see the masts that rose against the horizon out in the middle of the harbor.

"Shi—crap!" she said. "Can we catch him?"

They clattered onto the boardwalk between the buildings, and Sorrel threw up a hand. "There's a ferry!"

The flat-bottomed barge was already pulling away from the docks, but vines sprouted from the pier and snaked around the edge of the ferry, sinking thorns into it and holding it in place.

"Thanks, Talon," Vola called.

Sorrel kicked her horse, which pulled ahead. She threw herself from its back, leaping the gap between the dock and the ferry. She hit the edge of the raft, rolled, and popped to her feet as her horse skidded to a stop and milled about at the end of the pier.

"Beware, citizens," she said to the two ferrymen. "We are commandeering your vessel."

"You can't just do that," one of the men protested, pushing a floppy hat up so he could glare at them.

"Watch us," Lillie snapped, pulling her horse up. She clambered down from the saddle, and Talon helped her across the gap.

"Look out," Vola called. She tried to pull the swamp beast to a halt, but it lowered its head with a wet snuffle and plowed for the ferry. Vola lunged forward and wrapped her arms around its neck just as it jumped the distance.

The ferrymen screamed and plunged into the water on either side of the boat.

The swamp monster's claws scrabbled across the wet wood of the ferry's deck, not slowing its momentum in the least.

Vola flung herself from its back and rolled across the deck as the swamp monster disappeared over the side with a squeal and a splash.

Sorrel peered at the ripples it left. "Can that thing swim?"

Frothy bubbles broke the surface for a moment and then trailed away toward the docks where the ferrymen were climbing out of the water.

One screamed and scrabbled at the pier. The other swarmed out of the water and reached to help his buddy.

"Something's in the water!" he yelled.

"Time to go," Talon said under their breath, and the vines released the ferry from the dock.

"Hang onto something," Lillie said, then whispered a spell.

A huge gust of wind slammed into the side of the ferry, and

they shot out into the harbor. Vola grabbed hold of the edge and clung for dear life. Sorrel turned her face to the wind and laughed.

Spits of swampy land surrounded the harbor on both sides, leaving a narrow passage of deeper water just ahead. That's where Lord Arthorel's ship was headed.

The wind pushed the ferry so hard it shoved the back end into the water and waves sprayed over the front. Vola shifted her weight to keep the thing from capsizing and watched Arthorel's ship grow closer and closer.

The wind died off, and the ferry settled back into the water, coasting the rest of the way toward the ship.

Sailors and several black-clad figures Vola recognized as golems covered in illusions yelled and pointed as they drew up beside the ship.

Vola grabbed at the slippery ladder that trailed down the side of the ship and steadied the ferry.

"First priority is to keep him from escaping with the prisoners. Sorrel, Talon, clear the way on deck. Lillie, I'll toss you up and guard the rear."

Sorrel didn't wait for anything further. She swarmed up the side of the vessel, yelling, "For Henri! For Maxim!"

Talon followed.

"You didn't mean *toss* toss, did you—"

Lillie's voice cut out as Vola scooped her up and heaved her clear to the top of the ladder. All she had to do was stop squealing and climb aboard.

Vola climbed up after and popped her head onto a deck full of chaos.

Sailors rushed back and forth, calling orders as a row of golems advanced on them. Talon's knives flashed out, keeping them at bay.

Vola glanced around. Sorrel was up on the next deck, taking swings at the captain who defended the wheel.

Lord Arthorel pressed against the railing, screaming orders down at the golems.

Vola swung Henri's shield off her back and settled it on her arm, then drew her sword. She spun to face a couple of sailors who crept forward with rusty cutlasses.

Vola raised an eyebrow. "Really?"

They glanced at each other. "You're boarding our ship. That's piracy."

"We don't want to hurt you. We just want him." She jerked her chin up at Lord Arthorel.

One of the sailors bit his lip. "Yeah, but…he's the one who's paying us. So…"

They attacked.

Vola caught the first swing on Henri's shield, thrust it away, and returned with a swing of her own.

One sailor stepped forward and swiped for her feet. Vola had to dodge back a step with a wince.

She wasn't exactly worried about them maiming or dismembering her. She was more worried that they'd give her some sort of disease with their rusty blades.

Vola roared to throw them off balance and pressed forward. But the older sailor clearly had fought off pirates before. He held his ground and feinted well enough to trick her into meeting his blow. He used the advantage and punched her square in the jaw.

She went down to one knee.

A streak of light and sizzle of heat made Vola's skin tighten. Uh oh. Lillie.

She hit the deck and threw her shield over her head.

The sailors screamed, but Vola felt nothing except a pleasant draft.

She peeked over her shield. The sailors beat at the flames, but Vola lay in a clear patch of deck, the fire bending around her.

She blinked at Lillie.

Lillie beamed. "Pockets!" she cried.

Vola didn't stop to question whatever the hell that meant. She surged upward and caught one of the smoldering sailors under the breastbone with Henri's shield. She heaved and popped him over the railing.

He disappeared with a splash.

Vola expected him to surface—she hadn't hit him that hard— but there were just some frothy bubbles. The other sailor hung over the railing, waiting for a sign of his friend.

"There's something in the water!" a sailor called from across the deck.

Vola met her last opponent's eyes. "Whatever he's paying you isn't worth this," she told him amiably. "He's broke."

Something below them went bloop and the trail of bubbles streaked away, around the other side of the ship.

"Yeah, okay," the sailor said. "You do whatever you have to do, lady."

He stuck two fingers between his teeth and gave a sharp whistle. The sailors remaining on the deck all scrambled into the rigging, leaving Lillie, Talon, and Vola with the last of Arthorel's golems.

Above them, Sorrel swept the captain's feet out from under him and lunged for the ship's wheel. She leaped for a spoke above her and hauled with all her weight.

The ship began a ponderous turn.

Arthorel screamed and grabbed at the sides of his head. "You can't do this to me."

He threw himself at Sorrel.

"Lillie," Vola said calmly.

Lillie muttered a spell, and Lord Arthorel's feet stuck to the deck as though glued. Talon notched an arrow and let fly. It cracked against Arthorel's chest, and a flash of light washed over him.

"He has a shield," Lillie said.

"What'll take it down?"

"Enough blunt force. Sorrel's staff or…" Lillie glanced at Henri's shield hanging on Vola's arm.

Sorrel was still hauling on the ship's wheel, turning the vessel from the harbor's opening.

"All right, Talon, you've got the golems," Vola called. "Lillie, cover them."

Vola braced herself for a charge, but suddenly the breeze died and fog sprang up around the ship, obscuring her view.

"What the—"

Thick tendrils of fog curled up her legs and waist, reaching for her mouth. She coughed and threw her arm up over her face. The fog reached down her throat, stealing the breath from her lungs.

"It's just an illusion," Lillie called.

"That won't matter if he convinces our bodies they're dying," Talon said between coughs.

"Hit him," Vola said. "If you can see him, hit him. It'll distract him."

Somewhere in the fog, Sorrel cried out. In triumph or pain, Vola couldn't tell.

Vola lunged for the sound. She tried to hold her breath to keep the coughing to a minimum.

There, ahead of her, the fog curled around a blurred shape. A smaller figure whipped around it, and the sound of wood on flesh rang out.

Vola paused, and as soon as the smaller figure dodged away, she swung with her shield.

Lord Arthorel fell like a rock, and the fog dissolved into the morning sunlight.

Vola turned to check the others and caught the flash of trees looming directly in front of them. "Aw crap, brace yourselves!"

The ship struck one of the little muddy islands that made up the shore, the bowsprit plowing through the trees ahead.

The impact made them stagger, and most of the golems plunged over the side into the waist-high water at the edge of the swamp. It wasn't deep enough to dissolve the clay figures apparently because they lurched to their feet.

A roar echoed between the trees and the townsfolk of Water's Edge poured out of the swamp to swarm the golems.

"Hey," Sorrel said with a laugh. "Reinforcements."

"You can definitely forget about being paid, now," Lord Arthorel said from behind them.

Vola spun in time to catch Arthorel's kick smack in her chest. She fell backward, down the stairs to the main deck.

Sorrel leaped forward, staff swinging. Arthorel disappeared into the air.

"He's invisible," Sorrel called into the empty air. "Gods dammit. More illusions."

Arthorel flickered back into existence beside Vola.

She swiped at him, but she didn't have her feet under her yet and he avoided it easily.

"You've betrayed your people," Lillie called. Talon stood beside her, bow in hand. "You've broken a sacred trust. Are you prepared to face justice, Lord Arthorel?"

"Who are you to demand justice in my own lands?" He flickered away again.

Lillie clenched her fists and squealed in frustration. She shot an arc of fire to cover the entire deck, flames bending around the rest of them.

There was a grunt from beside them, and Arthorel appeared beside the railing. Talon took aim against him, but he rushed the ranger, trailing bits of flame and smoke, and knocked the bow from their hands, sending an arrow zinging uselessly into the water.

As Talon staggered, Arthorel raised both hands and aimed at Lillie and Talon.

Vola could charge him, knock him over the side or knock his head clean off. But she'd never do it before he got that spell off.

She lunged the other direction and slid on her knees in front of Lillie and Talon. She flung Henri's shield up just as a wash of gray light fell over them.

The light hit her shield with a clang, and a brilliant flash pushed back Lord Arthorel's spell, keeping it from touching any of them.

A breeze touched Vola's cheek and a chuckle sang in her ear.

"Thank you, Lady," she gasped.

"Never say I'm stingy with my gifts."

Vola thrust the shield out, and the gray light rebounded, flashing back against Lord Arthorel.

He staggered.

And Sorrel leaped at him from the upper deck, flying toward him feet first. She kicked him across the face. Sorrel landed on one leg, spun around, and kicked him in the groin, sending Lord Arthorel to one knee. Then she planted one foot behind her for balance, took a split second to line up, and her tiny fist shot forward into Lord Arthorel's chest, which was now the perfect height.

The blow cracked across the water, and Arthorel fell, slumping against the rough planks of the deck.

Vola stared, breathing hard. Was this just another trick? An illusion to make them think he was down while really he was escaping around the back?

She sidled closer.

"Is he dead?" Lillie called.

Sorrel shook her head and prodded him with her foot. "Just stunned," she said. "I kind of wanted him to go to jail."

"That's a good thing," Lillie said. "We can deliver him to the proper authorities, and they can carry out the law."

Shouting caught their attention from over the side of the beached ship. The deck listed, and they all staggered to the railing.

"The proper authorities might not be on our side right now," Talon said.

The harbormaster and his assistant had run the entire way around the edge of the swamp to get to them. They skirted Braydon and the townsfolk, who were mopping up the last of the golems below, and stood below the edge of the ship.

"What do you think you're doing? We hang pirates around here, you know."

Gruff circled them, hackles up. Talon stepped across to tie up Lord Arthorel.

"We're going to need some proof that we're not just pirates," Lillie said, biting her lip.

"A cargo hold full of the illegal slaves he was transporting should do it," Sorrel said. She grinned at Vola. "You want to do the honors?"

Henri.

Vola blew out her breath. "Gladly."

# THIRTY

VOLA SLUNG Henri's shield over her back again and sprinted for the hatch fastened with big metal bands. She pulled a belaying pin from the rail and used it to wedge open the fastenings. Then, she threw the hatch open and stared at the narrow ladder that descended into the dark.

She swung her legs over and started down. The shield stuck halfway and Vola shimmied until she could slide down and duck under the low ceiling.

So much for the mighty hero.

A couple of carefully placed lamps lit the cramped space. It stretched from one side of the ship to the other, but Vola still had to bend almost double to walk under the beams of the upper deck. She blinked, letting her eyes adjust.

Bars marched on either side of her, set into the planks in a hasty attempt at a cage. Clearly, this wasn't normally a slave ship. Frightened eyes stared out at her from behind the bars. Dozens of dirty faces waited, barely breathing.

What had it been like down here? Had they heard the fighting? Had they sat here wondering what the winner would do to them? Had they felt the impact when the ship ran aground?

All that and then the first one they saw was Vola in her patched chain mail with swamp mud on her boots.

The nearest faces to hers were young. Children dressed in plain pinafores and grubby shorts.

The kids from the orphanage.

Vola stepped forward to the big lock set into the side of the cage. She drew her sword and brought the hilt down with a clang. Once. Twice. Until the lock broke free and she could swing the door open.

"It's all right," she said as gently as she could. "You're safe now. Lord Arthorel is captured. You can all go home."

They blinked at her, and she got the impression that they would be quick enough to move if she wasn't standing in the doorway armed to her very large teeth.

She spun to break the lock from the other side as well and flung the door wide.

Finally, the prisoners shifted. Just a flutter of movement at first, then they were tumbling, clattering towards the doors, their voices rising as they laughed and called out and greeted each other.

Townsfolk poured from the cages, sweeping up the orphans in their enthusiasm. A few grubby figures in the back were probably outlaws. The bandits Lord Arthorel had captured before he'd moved on to his own people. They stood back, watching with wary eyes.

People pressed against her, shoving their way toward the ladder and the sunlight and fresh air above.

"Henri!" Vola called over the hum. She tried to straighten to see over them but knocked her head on a beam. "Henri!"

"Vola!"

She pushed through the freed prisoners, parting them like water as they streamed around her until, finally, she found him.

At the back. Making sure everyone had gotten out okay.

She hit him with an awkward clang, her arms going around him, armor and all. She had to duck so far she'd never be able to uncrick her neck, but it was worth it.

Henri clapped her on the back, letting her hold on to him as long as she wanted before he finally pulled her along with him, up the ladder and back into the morning sunshine.

The rescued prisoners poured out over the deck and down the sides of the ship to the swampy ground. Some helped each other down the ladder, and some just jumped into the arms of their loved ones waiting below.

Henri walked to the bow and stared over the railing. His hair was damp and tangled, his face dirty and the scar that cut across his cheek and jaw stood out stark white against his grizzled stubble. He looked like the worst sort of mess.

And he managed to look like the best thing ever at the same time.

He stared out over the townsfolk milling in the waist-deep water with a little grin on his lips. Astrid moved between them all, checking for injuries.

The sailors argued on the other side of the ship, and Lillie and Sorrel stood speaking with the harbormaster who had Lord Arthorel tied at his feet.

Vola handed Henri's shield to him and opened her mouth to say something, to confess it all. To tell him the academy had been right, and he'd been wrong about her.

"Well done, knight," he said quietly.

Vola winced. "Don't say that." Her hands trembled, she forced herself to meet Henri's wise blue eyes. He gazed at her, and in his gaze, she saw all her failures, from her mistreatment of Lillie to letting him get captured to the way her party had fallen apart around her.

"I screwed it all up. The moment you were gone, it all fell apart. They didn't want me to lead them, and I didn't blame them. I forgot everything you taught me, and my actions got them hurt."

"And then?" Henri scanned the celebration below. Everyone was moving back toward the docks now. Everyone except the sailors.

"What?"

"That's not the end of the story."

"No, but it could have been."

Henri chuckled. "Vola, every failure feels like an end. But it's only the end if you let it be." He speared her with a glance. "Clearly you didn't leave it there. They followed you here."

He gestured to the distance where they could see Lillie's round figure and Sorrel's short one. Two dark figures ranged alongside them, one tall and slim, one low and sleek.

"I apologized. They gave me a second chance I didn't deserve."

He shrugged one shoulder. "So, you failed first before you succeeded. You're a fool if you think any success comes without failure. The only way to win for good is to figure out all the ways to lose first." He turned to face her, forcing her to meet his eyes. "Do you trust me?"

Her brow furrowed. "Of course. But what—"

"I'm your trainer. I decide your fate. You agreed to that when you accepted my mentorship. The academy accepted that when they made me a trainer."

He held out his shield to her.

She shook her head.

"What does a paladin do, Vola?"

"I am a light in the dark," Vola whispered. "I am courage

when others have none. I am strength when others are weak. I am their sword when they are weaponless."

The oath. Her oath.

"I don't believe you've broken that," he said. "And I don't think you do, either. Take your shield, Vola. I couldn't ask for anyone better to carry it for me."

Vola swallowed and let him settle it on her arm.

"Am I ready?"

"There is no magical ready or not ready. There're only those who keep trying over and over to do the right thing. To do better."

He stepped back and away from her and went to climb down the ladder.

She traced her fingers over the rough edges of the shield. In her mind, she'd always seen herself dressed in gold, riding a white charger, carrying a shining shield perfectly cast and polished.

But the image bothered her now. That shield was too perfect. Too clean. It had never protected anyone.

She flattened her hand against the burn mark and the ridges of cuts and gouges. And smiled.

Vola felt a tug at her waist. She glanced down to see a little girl in a plain pinafore. One of the orphans. The only one left on deck.

"'Scuse me, that's my bunny," she said.

Vola's hand went to the stuffed rabbit she'd carried in her belt since the first day.

"So it is," she said and pulled it free. She handed it to the little girl, who beamed up at her and then scampered down the ladder to the swamp.

Vola followed at a more sedate pace.

Henri and Astrid walked ahead of her, arm in arm through the muck as the other townsfolk made their way back to the docks and the buildings that crowded around the harbor.

A squirrely man with dirty spectacles and prominent front teeth waited on the edge of the boardwalk, tapping his foot. He opened his mouth when he saw Henri. Then he saw Vola's shield.

The council representative turned a shade of crimson that looked better on a swamp blossom.

"You gave her a shield?" he shrieked. "Do you even know what's been going on while you were away?"

"If the council didn't trust my judgment, they wouldn't have made me a trainer of knights," Henri said mildly as he gave Astrid a hand up out of the muck. "But they did. And there's nothing they can do to gainsay my decision now."

"You'll hear about this when you get back to the academy," the representative said, spittle flying. "Mark my words."

"I'm not going back to the academy," Henri said.

"What?" Vola paused in the act of climbing up onto the boardwalk.

"What?" the representative said.

"They've spent the last few years undermining my protegé. Obviously, they don't trust her or me. Therefore, I won't be training anymore knights for them. I'll be training paladins on my own."

"You can't do that. Paladins must be vetted by the highest authorities. It's a sacred tradition. Only the right people get to take the oath."

The representative waved his hands in the air, tangling them in a net that hung from the nearest building. The net fell and caught the edge of a rake which smacked Henri across the face.

Henri touched the red mark on his cheek. "You can tell the council I won't be returning. I'll be finding a new place of residence."

"Mine's free," Astrid said.

"Seems like a good place to start," he told her.

The representative scrambled out of the way and disappeared between the buildings.

Vola raised her hand to the spreading bruise on Henri's cheekbone. "Want me to get that for you?"

"Nah," Henri said, and as she watched, the bruise flared and faded away. Just like when she healed someone.

"Wait. How did you —"

"You didn't think you were the only one with a connection to the gods, did you?" Henri gave her a wink and turned to walk away with Astrid on his arm.

"Wait. Henri! Did Cleavah send you in the first place? Henri!"

Henri didn't answer. Cleavah remained silent as well, though Vola did think the sky seemed smug about something.

# THIRTY-ONE

Vola surveyed the docks, trying to find her team. Since Henri was abandoning her for Astrid, apparently.

Over by one of the more official-looking buildings, Lillie leaned in to hear something the harbormaster was telling her, a frown creasing her brow.

Talon stood at the edge of the water, hands on hips, watching a suspicious trail of bubbles glide around the harbor.

Vola didn't see Sorrel at all.

"Is Henri all right?" Lillie asked, limping up to her.

"He's great. Told the council representative to stuff it, and I think he and Astrid are going to try to find someplace quiet."

Someone screamed, and Vola whipped around, hand on her hilt.

Talon still stood at the edge of the water, but now they had the slimy end of a lead rope. Gruff lay at the other end of the dock, glaring at the trail of bubbles that fountained into a scaly head with a filmy crest.

"I was really hoping it had drowned," Vola said. "I should have known we wouldn't be so lucky."

"Millford survived?" Lillie said, twisting around to see. "Oh, drat."

The swamp beast snorted a stream of watery snot that narrowly missed their boots.

"Why'd you fish it out, Talon?" Vola asked as the ranger dragged the swamp monster toward them.

"It was eating all the turtles," Talon said with a glare at the creature. "And the fishermen asked me to. Said it was going to scare the fish away."

"Paladin Lightbringer," a voice said.

Vola turned to see Becky with her arm around one of the rescued prisoners. Vola recognized her husband Porter, though technically she'd only met his copy.

"Becky," Vola said.

"You saved them all, just like you said you would."

Vola couldn't help noticing that Porter's gaze kept flickering toward her tusks. She made sure to grin wider.

"You don't have to worry about Lord Arthorel stealing any more of your people," Vola said. "He's been…permanently deposed."

"Do you know what he was going to do to them? Porter just said he was kept in the dark for three weeks, then loaded on a cart to come here. The lord never spoke to them at all."

"He was selling them for some extra money," Lillie said. "That's all we know for sure." Vola couldn't help but notice the way the wizard dropped her gaze. Like she was hiding something.

"Thank you," Becky said. "I know you have to help anyone who asks. I know it's part of your oaths, but we wanted you to have something, anyway. I bashed a couple heads in town to scrape something together. Braydon helped."

She handed Vola a bag that jingled, and her hopes rose just a little.

"Oh my gods, did we just get paid?" Talon muttered.

Vola kicked them. "Thanks, Becky. That means a lot. Hey, have you seen Sorrel?"

Becky rolled her eyes. "I told the barkeep here you were owed a round of drinks. So I think you can guess."

"I think that means we should hurry before she drinks our share," Lillie said, hiding a smile.

Becky steered Porter back towards Water's Edge while Vola squinted at the buildings and tried to decide which of the gray, peeling facades led to the local bar.

She couldn't tell and figured a random guess was as good as any.

She got it right on the first try and found Sorrel perched on the edge of the bar. Astrid and Henri snuggled in a booth in the back corner.

"There they are." Sorrel turned back to the barkeep. "I told you I wasn't making them up."

She jumped down and ran to drag them forward. "Sit, sit. I've got drinks for everyone."

Sure enough, a line of drinks waited for them on the bar. A couple mugs for Sorrel and Vola. Something tall and fruity looking for Lillie. And something dark and mysterious for Talon.

"Henri didn't want his shield back?" Sorrel asked as they settled themselves.

Vola touched the edge with a little smile. "He, uh, gave it to me."

"Oh." Sorrel's eyes went wide. "Oh, that's a big deal, isn't it?"

"It means she's a full knight," Lillie said. "Correct?"

"Well, then that means you can finally have that drink, right?" Sorrel pushed the second mug toward Vola. "To victory!"

Sorrel watched her carefully. Vola bit her lip and spun the mug around without taking a drink. "Actually…"

"What do you mean 'actually?' We beat Arthorel. We saved

Water's Edge. We're supposed to trudge off victoriously into the sunset."

"Trudge?" Talon said.

"Yes," Vola said, dragging it out. "But Lord Arthorel was selling those people to someone. And I have a feeling Lillie knows who."

Lillie's mouth dropped open. "How'd you know I—? I was hoping to surprise you."

"Spit it out, spell fingers," Vola said.

"Lord Arthorel never wrote down who he was selling people to, but I checked the shipping manifests filed with the harbormaster."

Sorrel straightened up. "And?"

"And I know where the ship was headed. The port of Brisbene in Southglen."

Vola caught her breath. It wasn't exactly a name and address. But it was something. A lead. A clue. They could go there, ask questions. They could track this slaver down. They could...

They could do it together.

Vola rubbed the back of her neck and the other three stilled, all turning toward her like they could feel the words gathering behind her tusks.

"I know I haven't been perfect," she said. "I screwed up a lot of things. But...the truth is I actually like you guys. And shield or not, I don't think I'd be very good at all this helping people on my own. So—"

"So we're going to Brisbene," Sorrel shouted. "Woo hoo!"

"She hasn't even asked yet," Lillie said with a mild glare.

"Oh, sorry. Go ahead." Sorrel disappeared behind the edge of her mug again.

Vola rolled her eyes. "So, do you want to help me catch a slaver?"

"Uh, duh," Sorrel said.

"What about Maxim's Warhammer?"

"Astrid said she sold it to someone in Brisbene. If that's not providence, I don't know what is. Besides, I've never been on a boat. That's gotta be exciting, right?"

Vola glanced at Talon. The ranger sipped at the dark beer Sorrel had ordered them, hood up and face unreadable.

"Why are you looking at me?" they said.

"I wanted to know if you and Gruff are coming."

The hood turned, creasing the edge so Vola glimpsed a light blue eye and stubbly jaw. "Of course we're coming. I can't protect my pack if I'm not there."

Vola smiled. "You know, you'd make a great paladin."

Talon snorted and went back to their beer. "No thanks. We have one of those already."

Lillie bit her lip and stared down at her drink.

Vola cleared her throat. "You don't have to come," she said, hiding the way the words felt like a punch to the gut. "You can go forget about me if you want."

Lillie's blue-green gaze flashed. "Don't put words in my mouth. We did all of that already, remember?"

"Then what's wrong?" Sorrel leaned over on her stool to stare at Lillie.

"I want to come," she said. "It's just that…I'm from that area of Southglen."

And going back would mean returning to everything she'd left behind and facing all that she'd run away from.

"We can protect you," Vola blurted before she knew she was going to. "From whatever it is you're afraid of."

"Ooh," Sorrel said. "What is it? Bad debts? Mean family?"

"Ex-lovers?" Talon said.

"Yeah, I'd run from those, too," Sorrel said.

"Do you have any?"

"Thank Maxim, no. Celibate monk, thank you."

Vola met Lillie's wide eyes with a grin. "Have they gotten close yet?

Lillie dropped her gaze. "Something like that, I suppose. Yes."

"Right, so we keep Lillie safe from debts/family/lovers etcetera, and then she's free to join us, right?" Sorrel said, looking at Vola.

"We could definitely use your fire," Vola told Lillie. "Especially if you can bend it around other people, now."

Finally, Lillie smiled. "As long as I get to blast some slavers."

A surge of warmth swept through Vola as she looked at her companions, humbled by their loyalty and friendship.

"We'll need a name," Sorrel said. "Every famous adventuring party has a name."

"Vola and the heroes," Vola said.

"Oh gods, no," Sorrel said.

"Vola and the slightly better-than-average people she conned into joining her," Talon suggested.

That earned a chorus of nos.

"I didn't con anyone into anything," Vola said. "Paladin, remember?"

"We'll have plenty of time on the way to Brisbene to come up with something much more fitting," Lillie said.

Sorrel swung around on her stool to point out the window at the beached ship. "I can't help but notice there is a vessel right here that's already heading for Brisbene," she said. "Though I can't imagine they'll be that excited to see us again."

Vola hefted the bag Becky had given her. "Shall we see if we can persuade them?"

Thank you so much for reading!

The misadventures continue in *Death and Devotion* where Vola and the team find out full time questing doesn't always pay the bills, especially when monks from Sorrel's past stick their self-righteous noses in.

Ever wondered what happened to Vola, Talon, Lillie, and Sorrel before they met? Sign up here to get the Mishap's Heroes prequel, Creation and Calamity, and read their origin stories!

And finally, if you loved spending time with Vola, Lillie, Sorrel and Talon, consider leaving a review so other readers can find more stories about heroes who don't look like heroes but save the day anyway.

Keep reading for a preview of the next book, *Death and Devotion*!

# ONE

A thick fishy pall hung over Brisbene harbor, like a wet blanket that had lain in a corner too long. But after a week cooped up on a transport ship, Vola was willing to breathe anything if it meant standing on dry land again. She stood at the railing and her chest swelled. Then her lungs seized, and she bent over coughing.

A delicate hand tapped her back as if that would help anything. "Oh, dear," the lyrical voice said. "Take a deep breath. Oh wait, don't. That might be the problem."

Vola hacked once more, then straightened. She cast a rueful glance at the woman beside her. Lillie stood only a little taller than Vola's elbow, with plump curves in all the right places, even after a week at sea with nothing but dried rations to eat. The sky was overcast and gray, but of course, a single shaft of light broke through the clouds to glint off her red-gold hair. Vola was pretty sure there was a law of the universe somewhere that said blonde hair and sunlight always went together, no matter the weather.

Vola tossed her own black braid over her shoulder and squinted up at the sky. But no sun shafts sought her out.

"It's noisy," another voice said, this one gravelly with mystery and disuse. Talon hadn't said much during the voyage. They'd conveyed everything they'd needed to with grunts and gestures. Of course, it was all things like, "get out of the way," and "don't wake me up before noon."

A decent breeze made the sails snap overhead but Talon's hood remained firmly in place, concealing their face. The dark edges ruffled against the rough planks beneath their boots.

"Why is it so noisy?" they said.

Vola glared out at the city stretched before them. Buildings with real slate and tile roofs marched all the way to the water's edge where docks jutted into the harbor. Houses, warehouses, shops, and taverns crowded each other, spreading from one end of the world to the other as far as Vola could see. A low buzz crept across the water and Vola could just make out the rumble of carts, the hum of conversation and shouting.

The spires of temples and cathedrals dedicated to the Virtues poked out of the masses here and there, and off to the right, up a cliff, lurked a wide squat fortress of black stone.

"I suppose I'd better go fetch Miss Sorrel," Lillie said. "If we're going to dock soon —"

"Is that fresh air I smell?" another voice said. This one didn't even reach Vola's elbow. More like her hip.

A pale halfling with dark circles under her eyes and curly hair matted with sweat scampered to the railing and climbed up to take a huge sniff. Then she sagged against the wood, arms dangling over the side.

"Are you going to vomit again?" Lillie said.

"Ugh, don't say that word," Vola said.

"Which word? Vomit?"

"Can't you just say barf like the rest of us? Barf at least doesn't make me want to barf."

"And vomit makes you want to vomit?"

"Please stop talking now," Sorrel said, voice thin. "I'm not going to barf. No," Sorrel said toward the sea rolling beneath them. "Y—no." She gulped. "Not this time."

She sucked air in noisily through her nose and let it out through her teeth.

The swell of the waves pushed them closer to shore. The noise got louder.

Talon drew back farther into their hood, which Vola hadn't thought possible. As if trying to escape without moving their feet. A huge black wolf padded up to their side, and the ranger buried their hand in his thick ruff.

"I didn't expect it to be so big," Vola finally admitted.

"What? A city?" Lillie said. "Brisbene is actually the smallest port in Southglen." Though she didn't sound too happy about it.

Vola shifted from foot to foot. "I haven't been in many cities."

"How are we supposed to find Lord Arthorel's slaver in that mess?" Talon said.

Vola rolled her lip between her tusks. It looked like a big maze, but it had to be better than that. Otherwise, people wouldn't flock to live in cities. Would they? Maybe humans were really herd animals, and they just hadn't noticed yet.

"The same way we tracked down Lord Arthorel," she said. She opened her mouth to continue, but Lillie beat her to it.

"By accidentally getting him to hire us and then letting him kidnap one of our friends so we could swear vengeance on him and get lost in his castle of illusions before letting him escape again and then running him to ground in the harbor?"

Vola shut her mouth with a snap as Lillie tilted her head in thought.

"That's pretty much what happened, isn't it?" Sorrel said with her head draped over the railing.

"I really don't think that will work a second time, do you?" Lillie said, finally.

"I meant methodically," Vola said with a low growl in her

voice. "That's all I was getting at. One step at a time. We know Lord Arthorel was selling the people he captured to someone in Brisbene, and we know where the captain was supposed to drop them off. We can go from there."

They stared out at the bustling mass of humanity and non-human species as the ship slid up to the dock and the sailors threw lines to those waiting ashore.

"You make that sound so easy," Talon said.

Vola blew out her breath. It wasn't that bad, she thought to herself. They at least knew where to start, and that was a whole lot better than last time. Vola's palms itched for her sword. She'd always thought of that impatience as the orc side of her. But like Henri had told her, a paladin had to answer a call for help. But a real paladin *wanted* to answer a call for help. So she took it as a good sign.

The captain of the ship sidled up next to them, eying Talon and the wolf warily. Vola grinned, baring her tusks. It was a good day when she wasn't the scariest thing around.

"We'll be parting ways here, sir," she said.

"Good." His hand crept up to clutch his wild gray hair. "Oh, wait. I mean, so soon? You didn't want to ride with us to Gerricksbane?"

He glanced at Sorrel as she groaned.

"No, our quarry is here," Vola said. "We just have to find him."

"Oh, darn," the captain said, snapping his fingers.

"Pretty sure that's sarcasm," Talon said. The wolf stood.

The captain raised his hands. "Your monster will be waiting for you on the dock in thirty minutes. I've got a tide to catch, and if you need a ride back to Water's Edge, please, please find some other ship."

He spun on his heel and stalked across the deck to yell at some deckhands.

"That wasn't very nice," Lillie said. The party turned toward the hatch.

"Well, we did get his employer arrested and free his cargo," Vola said.

Talon crossed their arms. "And I'm pretty sure holding his crimes over his head to get a discounted ride is called blackmail. I don't think he likes us very much."

Lillie jerked back as if affronted, making her long, bright hair sway. "He was going to be transporting slaves. People bought as property. We saved him from not being arrested himself. The least he could do is give us a ride."

"Not sure he sees it that way," Vola said. "Come on. Let's get off this tub."

"Wait," Sorrel said behind them.

They glanced back at her.

Her knuckles went white against the railing, and then she heaved her guts into the sea. Vola and Lillie winced.

Sorrel wiped the back of her mouth. "Last one," she said and followed.

It didn't take them long to collect their things. None of them had much. Just a change of clothes each and their weapons.

In less than twenty minutes, Talon stood on the dock, bow and quiver secured to their back. Lillie had already cracked open a book to pass the time, and Sorrel leaned on her quarterstaff as if it was the only thing holding her up.

Vola slung a round shield—scarred and gouged by battle— over her shoulder and carried her sword and sword belt in her other hand. She'd stopped wearing it on the ship when she kept getting stuck in the narrow corridors, but she fastened her blade and shield to her back as soon as she got out into the open air.

As Vola drew even with her friends, a scrabbling and a squeal drew their gazes down to the other end of the dock. A second gangplank spanned the gap between the ship and the pier where the sailors unloaded their meager cargo. Three sailors had hold of the end of a ragged lead rope and they pulled and heaved, their feet slipping along the gangplank.

At the other end of the rope strained a…creature. Like a cross between a donkey and an angry crocodile. It raised its filmy crest in anger and bared its yellow teeth at the sailors as they dragged it to shore. One more sailor brought up the rear, putting his shoulder to the creature's tail.

The creature's claws flexed and left gouges down the gangplank as the sailors yelled and prodded and pulled.

Vola grimaced.

"I really wish we'd found someone to buy it back at Water's Edge," Sorrel said.

"Maybe here…" Vola glanced back at the city. Surely someone here in this vast gathering of humanity would have use for an ornery swamp monster that ate just about everything and everyone.

Lillie glanced at the altercation down the dock and her brow screwed up in thought. Then she twisted her fingers and whispered a spell, and a very surprised looking turtle popped into existence on the dock at their feet.

"Here you go, Millford," Lillie called. "A nice tasty turtle. Come on, boy."

The swamp beast's eyes narrowed. Its scaly nostrils flared as it snorted. Then it squealed and barreled past the sailors, knocking two of them into the water.

It slid and skidded to a halt beside them and chomped on the turtle.

Then it looked up in consternation and tried again.

"It's only an illusion," Lillie said as the swamp beast's teeth closed on air over and over again. "I didn't have a turtle handy."

"Can we just go?" Sorrel asked, leaning heavy on her staff. "Before I barf again. I don't have anything left to barf up and that's even worse than if you have a whole meal to barf up. It makes your throat burn and your stomach hurt and—"

"Yes, fine," Vola said. "We're leaving. It's not like the dock is moving, though. This is almost as good as dry land."

"I'd rather put as much distance between myself and the ocean as possible, thank you—Ahh!"

Vola spun to see the swamp beast hoist Sorrel into the air by the back of her tunic. It chewed maliciously, its eyes narrowed as if daring them to do something.

Vola rolled her eyes as Lillie and Talon lunged forward.

"Millford, put her down this instant. I thought we were past this. You can't eat party members."

Talon took a more direct approach and bashed the creature on its nose. It dropped Sorrel with a squeal and backed up a step.

Sorrel darted forward and tugged her tunic straight, breathing heavily. "Watch it." She wagged her finger at the creature. "Or we'll see if anyone in this town likes fried fish."

Lillie's brow furrowed. "Is that even a good threat? I'm pretty sure it's part reptile, not fish."

Sorrel threw her arms in the air. "And part horse, so we'll find a glue factory, okay?"

Vola glanced around to find the captain and make sure they were square, but the sailors had all disappeared except for the one fishing himself out of the water, and when she looked toward the ship, all she saw was six pairs of wary eyes watching them from over the railing. They ducked when they realized she was looking at them.

Vola shrugged.

"Let's go." She took hold of the swamp beast's lead rope and gave it a glare. "If you bite me, I'll muzzle you. Lillie, you've got the address, right?"

No time like the present to get their investigation started. They all had a personal stake in this one. Lord Arthorel had tried to kidnap a bunch of orphans and unlucky townsfolk to ship off to this slaver, and then he'd done his best to kill them when they'd tried to stop him. Vola's nature wouldn't let her leave without tracking down this slaver, but she'd discovered in the last few weeks paladins weren't the only ones with a sense of honor and a heart for rescuing people.

Lillie nodded and stepped away with a pronounced limp. A shaft of guilt zinged down Vola's spine. She'd hoped the wizard's wound would have healed more in the week of rest they'd had on the ship. But from the deep lines at the edges of Lillie's frown, the long slice still pained her.

Vola opened her mouth to insist Lillie ride the swamp beast, but the thing was likely to take a chunk out of the wizard if she tried. And if Lillie insisted she didn't need help, Vola didn't dare suggest otherwise.

Lillie led them off the docks, onto a cobbled street lined with open market stalls. Vendors shouted from either side of the lane, hawking spices, fruit, and cloth. A fish as big as Sorrel flew past them and landed with a wet thunk on a bed of ice.

Vola's head came up, and she sniffed. Somewhere someone was barbecuing wargle, just like her Aunt Urag, and Vola's mouth watered.

Unfortunately, Lillie headed in the opposite direction, taking them along the wharf where the water slapped the stained stone.

"Where was the captain supposed to deliver the slaves?" Vola said. "Surely not in the middle of the city?"

"He told me it was a warehouse," Lillie said, checking the weathered signs on the buildings lining their route. "Here." She stopped in front of one that had been red once before the salt air had had its way. The big sliding doors where cargo could be loaded in and out were shut and padlocked, but the little door for human traffic stood open to the breeze.

"Was it really that easy?" Sorrel's face was still a pale green, and she breathed through her mouth, but her eyes surveyed the open door.

Vola frowned. She was right. This was too straightforward.

She left the swamp beast tied outside and led the way through the door. A desk stood across the space just a few feet in, occupied by a pair of feet propped on the surface. Whoever owned the feet remained hidden behind a broad newspaper.

Through a door to their left, Vola could see the rest of the warehouse proper. Rows and rows of cages and crates lined the space, each labeled with a number. Some held animals, pacing behind their bars. Some held boxes and bundles of indeterminate origin and contents. There weren't any people out there. At least none that she could see.

"What is this place?" she whispered.

"Looks like some sort of storage depot," Talon said. "A drop-off for goods and cargo."

Vola stepped up to the desk and tapped her finger against the surface. "Excuse me."

Her only answer was a grunt.

"Do you run this place?"

The newspaper never lowered, but finally, a voice drifted past the headlines. "I sit here," it said. "I make sure nothing goes in or out that's not authorized. And I take payment for new contracts."

"So, you're in charge. You would be able to tell us who's been here."

The voice snorted. "Each box is rented separately and there're over a hundred. I'm not that observant."

"But surely you have records," Lillie said, stepping up beside Vola. Usually, her looks and lyrical voice could charm whoever she was talking to, but that wouldn't work if the voice never bothered looking.

The newspaper rattled in annoyance. "Every box is rented to

an anonymous account number. This is the kind of place where people don't want their names written down."

"What about box number 57?" Lillie asked.

"Also anonymous."

"So, you don't care that illegal dealings are happening out of your depot?" Lillie asked, drawing herself up.

"Nope."

"Well, at least that's straightforward," Talon said.

Vola rubbed her forehead. "I take it waving my sword around won't do any good?"

"Lady, I have no loyalty to any of these people. I also have no details on any of them. Threats won't get you anything, 'cause I've got nothing to give."

"We could go to the authorities."

"Go ahead. My bribes are paid up."

"What about records of anything else that's been stored in box 57?" Talon said.

Vola pursed her lips. That wasn't a bad idea. Track him down from the other side.

The paper rustled. "We don't document what comes in and out longer than a week. Just enough to make sure nobody's taking things out that they didn't put in. All records are burned after that. It's that sort of business."

Vola tapped the rough edge of the desk. "What if we bought the box?"

Lillie raised an eyebrow.

"Then we could check it out ourselves," Vola whispered.

"Box 57 is already paid up for the month. Won't be renting it out again any time soon."

Sorrel blew out her breath in a sigh.

"Means he's probably still expecting a shipment," Talon said.

"Probably the one we just set free," Vola mumbled. To the invisible clerk, she said, "Could we offer you something in exchange for, say, sending word if anything else gets stored in box 57?"

"Probably not," the voice said.

"What self-respecting criminal won't take a bribe?" Sorrel cried.

"Oh, I'd take the bribe. I just wouldn't bother with the whole telling you anything part."

Vola threw up her hands. "Fine." She herded the rest of them out the door.

Lillie paused at the threshold to say, "Thank you."

"What are you thanking him for?" Talon said. "He literally gave us nothing."

"No, but he was very honest about giving us nothing."

# ACKNOWLEDGMENTS

I started out thinking I was writing something fun and light and hopefully hilarious. But it turns out I can't just write fluff. Meaning creeps in from the sides and makes its home between the lines. And then someone likes it, and I have to write more, and more meaning forces its way in, and suddenly it's a whole "thing." I blame these people:

First, the Kickstarter backers, for making all this possible. And for believing in the series before I'd ever sold a copy.

Mom and Dad, for reading every book ever. And always asking where the next one is.

Arielle, Betsy, and Alison, for being the first inspiration for a group of inept heroes who have no idea what they're doing and manage to save the day anyway.

Miranda and Lacey, for sisterhood which looks a lot like party dynamics sometimes.

Kevin and Andrew, for inviting me to play this little game called Dungeons & Dragons.

Kyle, Mary, Amy, Clark, Tim, Greg, Lauren, and Dave, and a host of other party members, for providing endless opportunities for inspiration. These books are all your fault.

Lucy Lin, for all the amazing cover art. I don't think anyone else could have brought Vola and the others to life the same way you did.

Fiona McLaren, for copy edits and flexibility. And for

enjoying my humorous fantasy as much as my slightly more serious stuff.

And Josh and Abby, for endless support. Especially when I decided to launch a series the same month I was supposed to have a baby.

# ABOUT THE AUTHOR

Jared Hagan 2018

Books have been Kendra's escape for as long as she can remember. She used to hide fantasy novels behind her government textbook in high school, and she wrote most of her first novel during a semester of college algebra.

Kendra writes familiar stories from unfamiliar points of view, highlighting heroes with disabilities. Her own experience with partial paraplegia has shown her you don't have to be able to swing a sword to save the day.

When she's not writing she's reading, and when she's not reading she's playing video games.

She lives in Denver with her very tall husband, their book loving progeny, and a lazy black monster masquerading as a service dog.

Visit Kendra at
www.kendramerritt.com

facebook.com/kendramerrittauthor
goodreads.com/kendramerritt
instagram.com/kendramerrittauthor
tiktok.com/@kendramerrittauthor